MW00571324

The Woman who loved Newfoundland

Audrey McClellan

A Scottish Island Novel

4 square books

First published in 2010 as an ebook by www.ebooksforpleasure
an imprint of Ebooks LLC.

This paper edition published 2011 by 4 Square Books an imprint of Ebooks LLC.

Copyright © Audrey McClellan, 2010 and 2011

The moral right of the author has been asserted

All rights reserved.

Without limiting the rights under copyright reserved above, no part of this pub-
lication may be reproduced, stored in or introduced into a retrieval system, or
transmitted, in any form or by any means (electronic, mechanical, photocopying,
recording or otherwise), without the prior written permission of both the copyright owner and the above publisher of this book.

ISBN 978-1-61766-029-0 (ebook)
ISBN 978-1-61766-188-4 (paper)

To order, visit www.ScottishIslandNovels.com or Amazon.com
E-books are available through ebooksforpleasure.com or Amazon.com

Dedicated to the people of the
Province of Newfoundland and Labrador
We love thee, smiling land.

"Ode to Newfoundland," Sir Cavendish Boyle

The Rock
awaits you!
best wishes,
Audrey McClellan

Chapter One

The flowers that bloom in the spring,
Tra-la,
Bring promise of merry sunshine–
As we merrily dance and we sing,
Tra-la,
We welcome the hope that they bring,
Tra-la,
Of a summer of roses and wine.

The Mikado, Gilbert and Sullivan

Cleo English fell in love with Newfoundland when she was eleven years old. Before that she'd been in love with queens and had read everything in her local library about them: her namesake Cleopatra, Anne Boleyn, Elizabeth of England, Marie Antoinette. She'd also been in love with collies, and she had a best friend who was in love with horses.

She first heard of Newfoundland from her fifth-grade geography teacher, Miss Johnson, who pronounced it "new-FUN-land." She pointed to it on the large classroom map so quickly that Cleo didn't have time to figure out where it was, but she was immediately intrigued. What sort of a place could that be? What was the "new fun" that was so wonderful that a whole country was named after it?

Miss Johnson explained patiently that it was not a country. It was the Canadian province of Newfoundland and Labrador, consisting of a large island nicknamed "The Rock" and a stretch of wilderness across the Strait of Belle Isle called Labrador.

The Rock became Cleo's private place of imagination. Whenever she was upset, bored or lonely, she retreated in her mind to New-fun-land, and thought about what sort of people lived there, and what their life was like, and what kind of fun they might be having. She imagined that the sun would always be shining on fields of wildflowers and sparkling brooks fringed by gnarled old trees full of nuts and squirrels and swings. Fried chicken, chocolate cake, pecans and brownies would be the local foods, and all girls would wear lace mantillas draped over their heads, pink or turquoise dresses with flowing skirts trimmed with silver ruffles, and Mary Jane shoes with diamond buckles.

It didn't matter what the boys wore because they would all go to a special school at one end of the island, and not be allowed out until they were old enough to behave themselves, which might be never, judging by the boys she knew.

After a frightening brush with a car when she was riding her bike to the library, she decided that no cars would be allowed on her island. Everyone would ride bikes or (here she was influenced by her horse-loving friend) they would drive little carts pulled by ponies wearing bright-colored feathers on their sparkling jeweled halters.

In the sixth grade Cleo had to write a geography paper for social studies class, and the subject she picked was New-fun-land. When she began her research she discovered that the name was spelled "Newfoundland." She decided that the new name was even better. New Found Land meshed nicely with the stories of explorers her class had been studying, and evoked images of ships sailing around the world and a sailor in the crow's nest with his spyglass, suddenly shouting, "Ahoy! A New Found Land lies dead ahead!" Her island was no longer just a place for fun; it was a place for exciting discoveries. Someday she would visit there. She put herself to sleep at night with her fantasies.

She got an "A" on her paper, and chanted "new-found-land" under her breath as she skipped all the way home from school.

Perhaps she'd go live there forever. Her house would be like a castle, three stories tall with towers, a swimming pool, a beach for collecting shells and making sandcastles, and an ocean for wading in. She would have a pack of collies, a pony cart pulled by two ponies, one black and one white, a library of books about queens, and all the time in the world to read them because she would never have any homework.

As she grew older, she thought about Newfoundland less and less, but it always remained in the back of her mind as a special place of imagination and happiness.

Cleo grew up and married her college sweetheart, and after six years of marriage he died in her arms after a short, terrible illness. Nearly three years after his death, she dreamed her childish dream of Newfoundland one night, and woke up resolved to go there, at last. She was a high school English teacher and she had the whole summer off. This year she wouldn't be a camp counselor, take classes, or work in the local garden store. She would spend this summer vacation on her ideal island.

Ideal or not, getting to her island was a nightmare unenlivened by food, drink or interesting seatmates, a long dull flight from Minneapolis to Newark to Halifax, Nova Scotia, to Gander Airport in the center of Newfoundland. Exhausted, she staggered off the plane and picked up her rental car. She dined on flavorless pizza at a nondescript pizza joint and stayed overnight in the smallest, plainest hotel room she had ever seen, no more than a window, a bed, a toilet, and a cupboard. The "continental breakfast" the next morning consisted of generic shredded wheat, plain white toast, margarine, and something called crowberry jam, which was produced in a place called Dark Tickle.

Pizza with no Italian seasoning? Margarine instead of butter? A hotel room the size of the closet in her apartment in Minneapolis? It was not a promising start. Would eight weeks in Newfoundland prove to be a nightmare instead of a dream? Dubious, but holding fast to her hopes, she hit the Trans-Canada Highway and started the drive to the cottage she'd rented on Last Man Ashore Cove, on the north central coast of the Rock.

The road stretched before her, two lanes in each direction nearly devoid of traffic, except for juggernaut trucks overtaking and sailing majestically past her little rental car. Occasionally an exit road would beckon travelers to towns with names like Tickle Cove, Heart's Delight and Middle Arm. Leading Tickle flashed by before she could do more than giggle. Fleur de Lys promised a hint of French culture. She pulled off at Coffee Cove, hopeful of encountering a Starbuck's, but found only houses, a church, and a wharf lined with decrepit boats draped with fishing gear. No coffee shops. Not even a café.

After two hours of driving, she spotted a sign promising Last Man Ashore Cove in five miles, and five miles further on another sign invited her to turn into a winding gravel road that led to Last Man Ashore B and B. She negotiated it with care, distracted by glimpses of the sea on her right and a mass of bramble roses in vivid bloom on her left. At last she reached a clearing, and pulled into a parking space in front of an elderly rambling Victorian mansion.

It was much more elaborate than those in the towns she'd passed, and it was painted an improbable shade of deep lavender, trimmed with old gold and maroon. Delicate gingerbread adorned the porch that wrapped around the front and side of the house. Flowerbeds in need of weeding and deadheading edged the front walk, and she could glimpse a large flourishing garden around towards the back.

Over the large front double doors she discovered a sign that said "Office." The desk next to the oak staircase was labeled "Reception," but there was no one there to greet her, and no bell to ring for service. Hungry, tired, and needing a bathroom, she went exploring, peeking first into an old-fashioned parlor on her left. It was heavily Victorian in style, furnished with armchairs and sofas upholstered in lush brocades, their dark maple frames ornamented with richly detailed flower and leaf carvings.

Small marble-topped tables laden with framed photographs and vases of flowers and crystal lamps with fringed shades were scattered about. Through an arch she could see a dining room with a china cabinet stuffed with dishes, a breakfront, and numerous small tables set for a meal. At its far end was a door with an attached sign that said "Kitchen–Private." She ignored the sign and pushed the swinging door open.

Across the room a man knelt on all fours, poking a broom behind a refrigerator and muttering curses under his breath.

"Excuse me," Cleo said.

He jumped, banging his elbow sharply against the fridge, and whirled around, his face flushed with annoyance and his mind working furiously. How long had she been there? Had she seen the mouse that had streaked across the floor five minutes ago? It was not a good idea to let B and B guests know that there were mice in the Big House. They tended to get excited and whine a lot, pretend they'd found mouse droppings in the porridge, and ask for a discount on their accommodation rentals, if not an outright refund.

Who the hell was she, anyway? He'd signed in half-a-dozen guests today and he didn't remember this one. And he would have remembered her, because he always took note of the pretty ones, and this one had a shape that would have made him lick his lips if he hadn't been so preoccupied with the mouse.

Whoever she was, she had to learn to stay out of his kitchen. "Private" meant private, and the kitchen was strictly off limits to B and B guests; they always got underfoot, babbled nonsense, and demanded answers to unanswerable questions while he was immersed in culinary pursuits. He gave her an intimidating stare and said nothing.

"Hi. I'm looking for the manager. I'd like to check in," said Cleo, furnishing her face with a bright Minnesota-girl smile. "I have a reservation for Squashberry Cottage."

He rose. He was very tall and his hair was black, liberally dusted with gray, and vaguely curly. He looked as though he should be wearing a wool fisherman's hat, pulled down over his forehead so that only a few curls escaped, and a thick wool turtleneck under a sou'wester. He was, in fact, wearing a tee shirt and jeans, both stretched snugly over a lean and muscular body. Cleo eyed him with interest.

So she was new, he thought crossly. Why hadn't she rung the doorbell and waited by the registration desk as guests were supposed to do? He hated people breaking his rules. B and Bs without rules quickly dissolved into a state of anarchy, resulting in his refrigerator being raided in the middle of the night, people tramping all over his prized vegetable garden, and boom boxes playing loud discordant music at all hours. He'd have to get this one sorted promptly. "I'm the owner. Name?" he snapped.

Cleo was tired, extremely hungry, and her need to use the bathroom was becoming urgent. Grouchiness was not the welcome she expected, and she did not feel the least bit conciliatory. She snapped back, "Don't you know who's rented the cottage?"

It was the wrong thing to say, and she regretted it even before he frowned menacingly and advanced toward her. He was quite a bit larger than she was and the tight tee shirt made his shoulders seem the width of a small truck. She stiffened her spine, stuck out her chin, and held her ground with a mighty effort.

He brushed past her. "Come along to the reception desk. That's where you were supposed to wait for me. I don't allow guests to prowl around the Big House before they're signed in."

"I wasn't prowling, and you weren't there to sign me in," she sputtered to his retreating, uncaring back. She followed him to the front hall and found him flipping impatiently through a reservation book.

"Squashberry Cottage. It's rented to a Cleo English."

"That's me."

"From Minnesota," he said, his tone disdainful.

This was ridiculous. Everyone else she'd encountered so far in Newfoundland had been kind and friendly. Why was this man so hostile? "Yes. What's wrong with that?" she retorted, jutting out her chin even farther and sticking her nose in the air.

"I don't know. You're from there, you tell me." He folded his arms and leaned back against the wall, staring at her.

Cleo had had enough. "You are the rudest man I've ever met."

"You ain't seen nothing yet," he said, and smirked, wondering all the while what had taken possession of him. His B and B owner's conscience told him this was getting out of hand and he should quit now, but he hadn't had a woman to bandy words with in ages, and he was quite enjoying it. She was some cute when she was angry; sparks were shooting from her eyes in a way that would fell a lesser man.

Cleo glared, on the brink of telling him what he could do with his Squashberry Cottage reservation. Then she remembered she'd paid a deposit of half the rental, a considerable sum. Even if she could find another place now at the height of the tourist season, she couldn't throw all that money away; it would mean a two-week vacation rather than an eight-week one. She'd anticipated this holiday for months, no, for years, and she wasn't going to give it up. Once she got settled in her cottage, she could stay out of the way of this arrogant bully.

On the other hand...for a brief, horrible, intense period after her husband's death, Cleo had become a man hunter, adept at stalking and catching any male she wanted, until she'd decided she didn't want any of them. Now she looked at him like a lioness contemplating a tethered lamb. His eyes were a pale icy blue, set in a strong-featured face dominated by high cheekbones and an aggressive nose, and his mouth was wide and stubborn. Very tasty, she thought, if you don't count the sour apple disposition.

He blinked in surprise under her scrutiny, and gave her back stare for stare, taking particular notice of the curvy bosom nicely displayed by a snug sweater and the length of the legs beneath her short skirt. A hint of lightning curled around them and a wisp of sulphurous smoke. Then Cleo's stomach growled, and she was suddenly aware that she was hungry, desperate for a pee, and that she'd given up sex sixteen months ago. "Look, I've had a long drive and I'm tired. Can you show me to my cottage without any more screwing around?" She wasn't going to mention her need to use the bathroom; that was none of his business.

"Sign here." He pushed the book towards her. "You are Number Nine."

"I am not a number, I am a person!" said Cleo foolishly.

He scowled and said with elaborate patience, "Number Nine is Squashberry Cottage. Sign here."

She scrawled her name and he whisked the book away. "Outside. Follow me. You drive. I'll lead."

Mumbling, Cleo stumbled after him. He was already yards ahead of her, striding along impatiently on long legs. She started the car and followed, resisting the temptation to step on the gas and flatten him like a pancake.

He stopped in front of a cottage perched on a ledge overlooking the ocean, a railing-enclosed porch running across the front. It was sagging with age and painted a faded purple with gold and maroon trim that matched the exterior of the Big House.

Oh, God, it's a dump, she thought, and her heart plummeted into her shoes. She'd found it on the Internet, and despite her hours of careful research, it was going to be a fiasco full of mildew and depression, and she'd be stuck there for eight weeks. She had a sudden, intense desire to turn the car around and zoom down the lane to the highway, and be damned to her deposit.

He turned. "Suitcase?"

Cleo sighed and gave up any idea of escape. She'd have to take the cottage mildew and all, but she'd be out of there in two days if it were as bad as it looked on the outside. A couple of days would give her time to prepare her arguments for demanding a refund. "In the trunk." She fumbled for the release button in the unfamiliar rental car while he stood, arms crossed over his chest, impatiently tapping his foot.

He pulled her luggage out, bore it up the cottage steps, groaning ostentatiously under its weight, and deposited it on the porch. He opened the door, beckoned her in and said grimly, "Welcome to Squashberry Cottage."

Cleo went up the steps and through the tiny entrance hall with trepidation, expecting a shambles. But the cottage, though old-fashioned and not in the least fancy, possessed a gentle, welcoming interior. The pine-paneled living room held large overstuffed chairs, an afghan-covered sofa, several lamps, and a fireplace on one wall with a pile of wood stacked beside it. And there was a television set and bookcases full of books, magazines and board games. Why, it's not so bad after all, she thought; it's . . . cozy. Her heart slowly warmed to the place. She was a sucker for cozy.

"Kitchen's through here," he announced, walking through a doorway on the far side of the room.

The kitchen was a total surprise: completely modern, with a new stove and a full-sized refrigerator, a cooking island, and a maple table and two chairs set under a large window with a dazzlingly beautiful view of Last Man Ashore Cove, just down the hill. "Wow," she said. "This is great." Then her glance fell to the floor, violently patterned in eye-aching swirls of red, purple and yellow, and she added, "Except for the linoleum."

"What's wrong with the linoleum?" he growled.

"It's hideous."

"Yeah, well, I remodeled the cottage last winter, and I didn't get the floor done." He grinned suddenly. "It's some ugly, isn't it?"

"It could take the Olympic gold medal for ugly." Encouraged by the grin, which completely transformed his face, she blurted, "Is there any food here?"

The grin was replaced by a forbidding frown. "Groceries aren't provided. Guests are supposed to bring their own food."

"I know, but the grocery stores in Gander were closed by the time I got to them last night, and I forgot to shop this morning." The truth was that she'd been too excited to care about groceries, thrilled by her first glimpses of Newfoundland.

"There's eggs, milk and juice in the fridge. Bread's in the box on the counter." Then he relented. "You can have dinner at the Big House tonight. I have several guests who've booked an evening meal. I'm serving lasagna with garlic bread and one of my special desserts." All my desserts are special, he thought smugly, but tonight's crowberry crumble was going to be spectacular. He'd dreamed up a new variation with diced walnuts and a hint of almond in the whipped cream topping.

"Thank you." They stared at each other; then her defenses crumbled. "Look, I think we got off on the wrong foot. Can we start again? I don't even know your name."

"Max Avalon. I've been rude, too. Sorry." He unbent enough to give her a hint of a smile and a quick once-over top to toe. She had brown hair pulled back in a loose knot slowly sliding out of control at the nape of her neck, big hazel eyes and a body that was definitely beginning to appeal to his baser instincts. Some cute, he thought, and under other circumstances he might be interested, but he'd just remembered that he had a mouse to murder. Got to have the corpse out of sight and the pools of blood scrubbed up before his diners arrived with their bibs around their necks. "Come to the Big House for dinner in two hours."

"Thanks. I'll look forward to meeting your wife," she said as he turned to leave.

He stopped abruptly. "Wife? What makes you think I'm married?"

Flustered, she said stupidly, "Guys don't usually run B and Bs."

He arched a sardonic eyebrow. "Why not?"

She couldn't think of a reason and countered with, "I got answers to my e-mails about renting the cottage from someone named Evelyn."

"She's my rental agent in St. John's. Not my wife."

"Oh." She felt silly. He thought she'd been trying to find out if he was married so she could decide whether or not to make a play for him. Conceited swine, like all good-looking men. And he hadn't answered the marriage question.

"Dinner at seven." He turned and left in a hurry, mind on the mouse.

Cleo sniffed, nose in the air, and summed him up in three words: abrupt, arrogant and cranky. But tasty, assuming a woman liked the Tarzan type. She preferred poets, herself.

Chapter Two

With cat-like tread upon our prey we steal,
In silence dread our cautious way we feel!
No sound is heard, we never speak a word;
A fly's footfall would be distinctly heard!

The Pirates of Penzance, Gilbert and Sullivan

Max Avalon was even crankier when Cleo arrived at the Big House for dinner. The mouse had eluded capture once again; the traps remained unsprung and he'd had no use for the broom. But it had reappeared suddenly, darting across the floor just as he was pulling a hot vat of lasagna from the oven, and he'd almost dropped the pan.

Curses flew, and Maria, his Spanish housekeeper/maid/ kitchen help and all around general tormentor, was shocked. "Is not right you talk like that around me. I a lady," she snapped, black eyes flashing with indignation.

"I don't pay you to be a lady. Why can't you help me catch that mouse?"

"You don' pay me enough. I don' like nasty smelly *rata*. Why you don' get *un gato*?"

That was a good idea. Max hovered over the lasagna, thinking. A cat, hmmm. He liked cats and he'd heard that petting one

18

helped to cure stress. Considering the amount of stress he was under as a B and B owner, a cat would be good value. It would probably work for table scraps, too. Cheap help, and he needed all the help he could get.

He'd had a dog once at the B and B, a huge black Newfoundland with a fuzzy head and webbed feet, named Bear, that he'd loved. But her enormous size had alarmed some guests, even though she was as gentle as a lamb and adored children.

Reluctantly, he'd farmed her out to a friend.

He'd gone to visit her once a week until his friend had moved to Labrador, across the Strait of Belle Isle. Bear always came to him, put her giant head on his knee and stared up at him, her brown eyes soft with sadness and reproach. When he left, she'd sit in the driveway and watch his car as it disappeared down the road. His friend said she'd sit there for hours, silent as a sphinx, hoping for his return.

An unhappy experience for both him and Bear, one that reminded him what a slave he was to the B and B. If he got a cat, he'd get attached to it, and then probably some guest would complain about being allergic to cat dander and he'd have to get rid of the kitty and fumigate the joint. Why would he want to go through all that heartache again?

He threw off his apron and rushed into the dining room to seat his guests as they wandered in. The sight of Cleo made him think even more seriously about cats. She was sleek and feline in a short-sleeved sweater and jeans, her nut-brown hair curled in a tidy knot at the base of a slender, sexy neck. Her hazel eyes were even slanted upwards at the sides like a Siamese cat's.

Max eyed her, and wondered what petting her would do to his stress level.

Cleo was uneasily aware of his scrutiny and turned her pointed nose up in hauteur as he seated her at a table for two. Lots of sex appeal, still a jerk, she thought, and wondered if he was gearing up to make a pass at her. She was wickedly glad she'd worn the tight sweater and her new jeans that fit as though they'd been painted on. After nine months of dressing like a schoolteacher, she liked to loosen up during vacation. She didn't think any of the subtler details of her outfit had been lost on him.

But nothing could have been further from his mind than sex as he sliced the lasagna and dished it up for Maria to serve along with his homemade garlic bread. The accompanying Chianti was a robust little Italian honey, and he rewarded himself with a glass of it, after all the guests had their meals in front of them. He leaned against the doorway and sipped, enjoying the murmurs of appreciation that rose as the lasagna released its pungent aroma to appreciative noses. He was a damned fine cook and he knew it, and all the guests he'd ever had knew it, too, by the end of their stay.

Cleo noticed his lean body lounging against the doorway just as she picked up her glass of wine. Their eyes met. He grinned seductively and lifted his glass to her. She raised her glass and saluted him in return, then gave him her best "not with me you don't, buddy," stare.

Max sighed. Why was life never easy, and women always difficult?

Just to prove she was immune to his charms and his orders, Cleo ignored the "Private" sign once again, and wandered back into the kitchen to compliment him on the meal after the other guests had left the dining room. She planned to say a gracious word or two, then drift elegantly out.

Just as she swung open the kitchen door, the mouse made another daring foray across the floor and skidded behind the refrigerator. Max yelped in shock, and dropped the plate he was rinsing. It shattered noisily on the floor.

Maria shrieked. Seizing any excuse to get off work early, she headed for the back door, shouting "*Madre de Dios, una rata grande! Buenas noches,* Boss!"

Cleo stared dumbly, too astonished to scream. A mouse in his kitchen? Yuck.

A woman who didn't scream at a mouse earned big brownie points from Max. He gave her a calculating, sideways glance and said gruffly, "It's not a rat."

"Well, I know that. A rat is the size of a Volkswagen and its tail would stretch from here to Gander. What you've got there is a common garden-variety mouse." She added primly, "It's unsanitary to have a mouse in the kitchen. Why don't you catch it?"

"What do you think I've been trying to do?"

"Whatever you're doing, you're not doing it very well. The mouse looks like it's in great shape and it's turning your kitchen into the Indy 500."

"I'm open to suggestions," he growled, adding mentally *Little Miss Smart Ass.*

"Peanut butter," Cleo stated in an authoritative tone. "Are your traps baited with peanut butter?"

"I've been using cheese."

"A common misconception. Your average mouse prefers peanut butter."

Torn between irritation and admiration, Max stared at her, then gave up his hostility. "You think?"

"I know. My husband and I had a dingy little apartment seething with mice when we were in college. We'd catch a dozen a week with peanut butter. They were fools for the crunchy kind."

"I'll give it a whirl, then."

"If that doesn't work, get a cat."

"Yeah." This woman had possibilities, he thought. A nonscreamer who knew all about catching mice and who filled out a sweater to perfection. Her hair was easing its way out of the knot at the nape of her neck and curling enticingly towards her pointed chin, a stray curl beckoning him like a signpost. He was out of practice in chatting up toothsome females, and, suddenly anxious to know her availability, committed a huge indiscretion. "So how come your husband isn't here with you?"

"He's dead." Cleo turned her head away, amazed as always at

the sudden burst of moisture that invaded her eyes at the thought of Charlie, pale and wan in his hospice bed.

"Hell. Damn, I'm sorry. I'm really sorry if I've upset you. That was a nervy question." You've put your foot in your mouth, b'y, he chastised himself.

She blinked the tears under control. "It's all right. He died three years ago."

Max estimated her to be in her late twenties, maybe thirty at the most. Her husband had died when she was very young. Touching, that she still had tears for him. He couldn't stop himself from asking, "Was it a car accident?"

"Leukemia. It killed him in five months."

"That must have been terrible," Max said, appalled.

"He died in my arms," Cleo whispered, horrified to find herself confiding her most painful secret to a total stranger. The tears trembled again on her eyelids and began a slow journey down her cheeks.

"Oh, God, I'm so sorry." He moved rapidly to her and for one astonishing moment they both thought they'd end up in each other's arms. Then he stopped and fished a crumpled tissue from his pocket. He handed it to her and patted her awkwardly on the shoulder. "There, there," he said.

His concern was genuine and touching, and Cleo revised her earlier opinion of him. She sniffled and wiped her eyes. "Thanks. I'm okay now."

Max said, "Come on, I'll walk you back to Squashberry Cottage."

"You don't need to do that."

"I want to." In an effort to lighten the mood he added, "To thank you for suggesting the peanut butter."

"Okay."

They walked in silence back to the cottage and said a quiet good night at the door. Cleo went in, resigning herself to a depressingly tearful evening. She'd pull herself out of it eventually by reminding herself that Charlie would not have wanted her to mope. She'd have a little weep and then she'd be okay.

That was how it usually worked out for her.

Chapter Three

Alone, and yet alive! Oh, sepulchre!
My soul is still my body's prisoner!
Remote the peace that Death alone can give—
My doom, to wait! My punishment to live!

The Mikado, Gilbert and Sullivan

Cleo strolled down to the Big House the next morning, feeling much more charitable towards her host. He'd shown a softer side last night, had been kind and had dropped the sarcastic tone. Maybe now they could get on a friendly footing. She had no theoretical objections to a flirtation with an attractive guy, and even more than flirtation should circumstances warrant it. It had been ages since she'd met a guy who interested her, and she might as well take advantage of that attraction to bring herself back to the living. Lately she'd been thinking that she'd better start looking around for a new man if she didn't want to be alone for the rest of her life, and Max Avalon might be good practice for that endeavor.

She'd use the excuse of asking for advice on local sightseeing jaunts to ease her way into his confidence. Besides, she was curious to know whether he'd gotten it together enough to try out the peanut butter on the mouse.

Unfortunately, she arrived at eleven, check-out time, and her occasionally genial host was preoccupied with processing bills for four sets of guests, one of whom was demanding a detailed receipt so he could claim a tax deduction for his trip. Max wondered what sort of excuse for a tax deduction a man who owned a pastry shop would use for a vacation trip to Canada. Professional research, maybe; the guy had spent considerable time trying to worm Max's recipe for crowberry crumble out of him.

He'd been unsuccessful in persuasion and seemed to be getting desperate, though not desperate enough to offer money. Max had begun taking the precaution of carrying his recipe box into his apartment with him each night.

Cleo hung around, pretending to examine the ancient collection of loaner books on shelves in the small sunny alcove next to the checkout desk. When the last guest left, she made her move. "Hi. I wondered if you had any good suggestions for day trips. I'm thinking of taking a little drive today."

Max was fresh out of suggestions, having restrained himself from making a couple of rude ones to the pastry shop owner. He was also hassled by the need to get four rooms ready for the three o'clock influx of new victims, half of whom had not booked dinner but would be sure to ask for it, and whine if it was denied. He prayed nightly for gentle, accommodating, smiling guests who made no demands and were pleased by everything, and his prayers were usually ignored by the merciless God of B and B owners.

Now he had a cute, highly nibble-able female looking at him all wide-eyed and wet-lipped, and she too was making demands. Even though the demands were made in a soft and sexy voice, they still were taking up time he didn't have.

He stared at her, letting his thoughts roam in an unusually undisciplined manner to the pleasure of escorting her on a sight-seeing trip. Maybe a picnic on a beautiful deserted beach and a long hot cuddle on the picnic blanket. It had been too damn long since he'd had a long hot cuddle anywhere.

Cleo read his thoughts in his eyes and her own eyes widened in anticipation.

She was doomed to disappointment.

Max gave himself a mental shake, took himself by the virtual scruff of his virtual neck and told himself, get back to work, b'y. "Right there on the window seat."

"What?"

"Sightseeing brochures, courtesy of the Newfie tourist people. And a flyer I made up with mileage and driving times from here to the major tourist sights. Lists of recommended restaurants and gift shops. Directions to Sobie's, the nearest grocery store. Help yourself. I've got to go buy peanut butter. Have a nice day." He turned on his heel and left temptation behind.

Temptation fumed. She'd been so sure he was interested and now she'd exposed herself to a hearty snub and her most hated expression, "Have a nice day." She grabbed a grubby paperback from the bookcase in frustration. It had a glossy cover featuring a longhaired tart and a muscular warrior with even longer hair, and they were just this side of *in flagrante delicto*.

If she wasn't going to get any heat, she could at least read about it.

She didn't need sex, anyway. She'd had plenty of it starting a year after Charlie died. She'd tried all kinds of ways to deaden the pain of her loss. She'd smoked up the last of the marijuana that had eased his final days, and it had made her cry, remembering how she'd smoked and giggled with him while he was in his last month. Then she'd tried booze but it depressed her into a state beyond crying, brought her close to the edge. Though she'd wanted to die, she couldn't face the thought of suicide. It would have a terrible effect on her students, and teenagers were lured enough towards suicide without her example to follow.

The sex thing had surfaced at a teachers' convention in Duluth. She was sitting in the hotel bar morosely downing martinis, hoping to get loaded enough to be able to sleep. That day too many people, all unknowing, had asked her why Charlie wasn't with her. Each had been shocked at the sad news and had offered condolences ranging from awkward pats on the shoulder to tears. Everyone had said what a nice guy he'd been and how sorry they were, and everyone had asked if there was anything they could do to help.

Not a damn thing, she'd thought, completely wrung out by the sympathy. *There's no help for me, now or ever.* Tears of self-pity were gathering in her eyes, ready to fall, by the time she was halfway through the third martini.

"Hi, Cleo! All by yourself?" A man slipped onto a barstool beside her. "Where's Charlie?"

"Dead," she blurted. A tear dripped down her cheek.

"What? God, Cleo, I hadn't heard. When? What happened?"

She recognized him now through her tears and the alcoholic mist. It was George Chambers, a math teacher from International Falls. She'd served on a committee with him last year and after they'd presented their report to the conference she and Charlie had gone out to dinner with him and had a lot of laughs.

She said, "Leukemia, seven months ago." *And nine days,* mentally calculating as she always did when she thought about Charlie's death.

George put an arm around her shoulder. "Oh, hell, that's terrible. I'm so sorry. He was a wonderful guy."

"Yes, he was." She gulped the rest of her martini and choked on a sob.

Awkwardly, he put an arm around her shoulders. "Do you want to talk, Cleo? We can go sit at a table where you'll be more comfortable."

She shook her head. "I've had to talk about it all day. I can't take any more."

"Of course not. Poor Cleo." He rubbed her back while she wept silently. "Listen, I think you should go up to your room and lie down. Come on, let me help you."

Too wrecked to say he shouldn't bother, she let him lead her from the bar and into the elevator. She gave him her key because she was crying too hard to find the keyhole. He walked her to the bed, arm around her shoulders. He pulled back the covers and said, "Do you want me to help you out of your clothes?"

He had no evil intentions. He'd meant only to remove her blouse and skirt, then tuck her into bed, but suddenly her arms were around his neck and she was clinging to him as though he were a rock and she was drowning. Slowly, relentlessly their mouths neared, touched, clung. And then they were in bed and he made love to her and for a few brief moments she forgot about Charlie and his sad demise.

George left, awkwardly apologizing and saying he hadn't meant to take advantage of her despair. He pulled the covers up around her carefully and gave her a farewell kiss on her cheek, and she fell deeply asleep.

The next morning she awoke, having slept without the nightmares that had tormented her since Charlie's death, and thought she'd found the answer: sex.

That began the next months of her mourning period. She had a reckless affair with a fellow teacher, then a stolid, earthy one with the owner of the hardware store where Charlie had loved to buy boards and nails for a building project he always had underway. They'd got to talking about him and laughing over his futile attempts at carpentry, and it had ended up in dinner and bed.

The third had been with an electronics salesman whom she'd met while shopping for a new computer. She'd broken off each affair abruptly, abandoning her lovers when their comforting sex had begun to fail her and memories had surfaced again. She didn't care about their feelings; she was utterly wrapped up in her own emotional disarray.

The last affair had been with Harry, a lawyer she'd encountered at the sushi counter in a grocery store. That one had been wild and desperate, full of mutual cruelties. One night she'd stood him up and he'd been furious. In retaliation he hadn't shown up for their next date and she'd been furious. There had been angry telephone calls, mutual recriminations.

And she'd realized she didn't care. By then she'd healed, a little, and begun to understand what she was doing to herself. She'd shuddered, thinking how lucky she had been not to have gotten a sexual disease, been raped or beaten up, become pregnant, or behaved so scandalously that she'd set a bad example for her students and shocked their parents into getting her fired. She wasn't ashamed of her behavior, but she'd had enough.

She called Harry and told him she was breaking off their relationship. He'd been disbelieving, then angry, and she'd finally had to hang up on him. He'd called several more times before he'd accepted his dismissal, and ended his last call by telling her viciously that she was an unfeeling bitch and that he was glad to be rid of her.

She was glad, too, and ready to move on. She didn't renew her teaching contract in Owatonna that year. She moved to Minneapolis and got a job in that school system. She threw out possessions ruthlessly and took only the bare essentials to a small apartment in the city, ready for a new start in life, hoping to leave her memories behind.

She visited Charlie's grave before she left Owatonna. She hadn't wanted to bury him and Charlie hadn't wanted to be buried. They'd talked about it and decided on cremation. It had been a relief that she wouldn't have to think about him moldering away in the cold ground, flesh shrinking, falling off the bone until only a rotting skeleton was left.

But Charlie's mother had been appalled at the idea of cremation. She insisted on a proper burial in the family plot. Cleo, exhausted after the long ordeal of accompanying Charlie to his death, hadn't the heart or will to resist her. It would turn out to be one of the biggest regrets of her life. She should have stuck to her guns, and for her cowardice she was rewarded with terrible

Fall of the House of Usher dreams. Charlie, in his grave, opening his eyes, pounding helplessly against the coffin lid. She'd almost gone mad thinking about it. She kept her sanity by refusing to visit the grave and thus denied herself the closure that seeing the gravestone would have brought.

Now she was visiting him for the first and the last time. She put a bunch of white roses on the grave, said a few words of goodbye to Charlie, and left Owatonna forever.

And now here she was, a modern day Alice in Wonderland, in the New-fun-land that she'd dreamed about when she was a kid. She was on vacation and she was determined to put mourning behind her at last and have some fun. She had a good-looking, challenging guy that she might take the trouble to inveigle into a relationship, just to remind herself that her body was alive and well.

Plus, he was a great cook and could make her enjoy eating again. Cooking for herself alone hadn't been worth the trouble, and she'd let herself lose too much weight by skipping lunch and eating only peanut butter and crackers for dinner. Skin and bones weren't attractive in anyone and a woman ought to have luscious curves. Otherwise she'd never get another guy, and it was time she started looking for one if she didn't want to end up as a lonely old lady living with cats in an attic. It was a morose, totally fantastic idea that nevertheless haunted her.

So she had a full itinerary for her eight weeks of vacation from school. Relax, eat lots of desserts, and practice her womanly charms on Max Avalon, boy B and B owner. Could be a worse way to spend the summer.

Chapter Four

Let us fly to a far-off land.
Where peace and plenty dwell–
Where the sigh of the silver strand
Is echoed in every shell.
To the joy that land will give . . .

The Sorcerer, Gilbert and Sullivan

Cleo went up to breakfast at the Big House the next morning. To her utter astonishment, it had snowed lightly and melting crystals sparkled in the sunlight. She had only a sweater to pull on against the nip in the air and only a pair of strappy sandals to protect her feet from the crisp wet grass.

When Max greeted her, she said, "Snow in June! Is this typical Newfoundland weather?"

"Nah, today is kind of weird. In summer we might get freezing rain, sleet maybe, but usually not snow. Be glad you're not in Labrador; they got four inches. Come sit by the fire and warm up." He'd built a roaring blaze in the fireplace, knowing that guests would appreciate it.

He brought her a cup of coffee right away and after breakfast he came and sat down by her. He eyed the sexy sandals. "Aren't your feet cold in those shoes?"

"They sure are, but they're all I brought with me."

"Want to borrow a pair of my boots? They're waterproof and insulated."

She looked at his size-thirteen feet and giggled. "They might be a trifle large."

"So how are you going to keep your toes warm?"

"I'll wrap them in a towel when I get back to the cottage. Or put on three pair of socks. Or maybe I'll take a hot shower. I hope there's enough hot water."

"Let me know if there isn't."

"What will you do about it?"

"I'll come down and heat pots of water on the stove and bring them into the shower for you."

When she blinked in surprise at the idea and turned a little pink, his grin grew wider. "We are a full-service B and B, you know," he said, and the grin edged to just this side of a leer.

"I'll do fine on my own," she said, recovering, and got to her feet. "Thanks anyway." She sashayed out, trying to maintain her dignity and still be sexy.

Max watched her leave, noting her neat little backside with appreciation, and mentally chastising himself. Big mistake, b'y; got to remember not to come on to the guests, he thought. He was usually pretty cautious about that, but she was some cute and he'd been turned on by the thought of slipping off those sexy little sandals, wrapping his large hands around her slender feet, and warming up her cold toes. Must have been the red nail polish. He was a sucker for scarlet toenails.

What a smart mouth the guy had, Cleo thought to herself as she slipped and slid her way back to the cottage over the crusty ground. Offering to help warm up her shower certainly qualified as a pass. She wondered if he was all talk or if she should expect some follow-up. That would give her an interesting afternoon. Putting on extra pairs of socks, watching the snow melt, finishing the hot romance novel, and deciding whether to take evasive action or to engage in combat with Max Avalon.

A full day, and she hadn't taken a sightseeing trip or gone to the grocery store.

New-fun-land was starting to live up to her expectations.

Chapter Five

A wand'ring minstrel I,
A thing of shreds and patches,
Of ballads, songs and snatches,
And dreamy lullaby!

The Mikado, Gilbert and Sullivan

Max was startled by a tap on the door of his apartment the following afternoon. The door swung open, revealing the American couple who'd arrived the night before last. Brimming with Yankee cheer, the male half of the pair said, "Good morning!"

Max looked at them, shocked. Guests never trespassed beyond the kitchen into his private living quarters. It was the absolute, unwritten rule of B and B-dom. The owner's space was strictly off limits.

That subtlety was lost on these people. "Sorry to bust in on you but Betsy's had a super idea," said the man.

Max wondered what her super idea would have been if they'd swanned in a few minutes earlier, when he'd walked into the kitchen fresh from his shower and naked except for a towel wrapped around his slim hips. The towel had fallen off while he was making himself a cup of tea. His lips curled in appreciation at the thought.

Betsy burbled, "We wondered if you'd mind if we used your parlor for a sing-a-long tonight."

Max stared dumbly. "A what?"

"A hootenanny, they called it in the good old days. Karaoke without the karaoke machine."

"Bruce brought his guitar," Betsy added brightly.

"We've been singing our way across Canada," said Bruce.

"The other guests . . ." Max began, repressing a shudder at the idea of wandering American minstrels invading his unsuspecting, innocent, native country.

"Oh, I've talked to the Joneses and they're all for it. They're from Wales; those guys love to sing. The MacShannocks are going out for dinner so they won't be around anyway. And the Betancourts think it's a swell idea. Anything to get those three kids of theirs away from their electronic game whatchamacallits."

Outflanked, Max could only nod in assent, no excuse springing up in his usually agile brain.

"Great! We'll see you in the parlor at eight."

"Me? I don't sing." That was an out and out lie; he had a very good voice, practically professional in quality. Around the Big House he only sang in the shower or occasionally in the kitchen if a meal was going especially well.

"Sure! Gotta have the host." And they were gone.

He tried to hide in the kitchen after dinner, but Betsy invaded his space yet again, cornered him, whisked the dishtowel out of his hands, and gave him a not-so-gentle push towards the parlor. Trapped, he strolled in, sat down in one of the uncomfortable Victorian chairs, and tried to look nonchalant, wishing desperately that the phone would ring, preferably with a complicated reservation that would take an hour to sort out.

Cleo was there too. Now primed to tease and bent on seduction, she'd decided to make herself available in case there was going to be any follow-up to yesterday's toe talk. She'd been roped into the hootenanny when she'd slunk up on the porch a few minutes ago, hoping for a few minutes of verbal dueling with Max. They exchanged embattled glances.

Bruce wasn't bad on the guitar, unfortunately. Had he been terrible, the session would have petered out in a hurry. It was his choice of material that damned him in Max and Cleo's eyes, all hoary old chestnuts with beards a yard long. "Michael, row the boat ashore, hahl-ay-loo-yah," he bellowed. "Everybody sing! Come on, folks, let's hear you shout it out!"

He moved on without a break to "I've Been Working on the Railroad" and "My Darling Clementine," his voice growing louder with each superannuated favorite. Finally he said, "Wow, I'm getting hoarse. Somebody else's turn to lead the singing. Dafydd?" He turned to one of the Welsh Joneses, who blushed and shook his head shyly.

"Gotta be Max, then," Bruce said, turning his large innocent eyes on his startled host. "Whatta like to sing, Maxie?"

Ah, the truth of that old saying, if looks could kill, thought Cleo happily, watching fury and embarrassment struggle for dominance in Max's face.

But he covered it with a bland look. "Hmmm. Give me a minute to think. You know any *lieder*, Bruce? French art songs? No? How about this?" And Max, the pride of the Three Peninsulas Very Light Opera Company's annual Gilbert and Sullivan productions, launched into a rapid rendition of his favorite patter song from *The Pirates of Penzance*.

I am the very model of a modern major-general,
I've information vegetable, animal and mineral.
I know the kings of England and I quote the fights historical
From Marathon to Waterloo in order categorical.

Bruce tried desperately to chord along.
Max's mellow tenor rolled out:

I'm very well acquainted too with matters mathematical,
I understand equations, both the simple and quadratical,
About binomial theorems I'm teeming with a lot of news
With many cheerful facts about the square of the hypoteneuse.
With many cheerful facts about the square of the
    hy-pot-a-pot-teneuse.

Max stopped. "Sorry, am I going too fast for you, Brucie?"

Bruce muttered something incomprehensible and glared down at his guitar.

Max finished with a flourish:

I'm very good at integral and differential calculus,
I know the scientific names of beings animalculous;
In short, in matters vegetable or animal or mineral,
I am the very model of a modern major-general!

He stopped. "God, I love Gilbert and Sullivan," he announced cheerfully. "Sorry, the old breath control's not what it used to be, or I'd sing the next set of verses." That too was a lie, for he could have sung for hours, with a Martyn Green-like recall of all the words to all the patter song of the roles he'd played with the Three Peninsulas Very Light Opera Company over the last six years.

The assembled company quivered with relief.

Max gazed on his hapless victims, catching and acknowledging Cleo's grin without missing a beat. "I know some great college drinking songs, too. Of course, some of them get a little bawdy," he admitted, smiling cruelly at Mama Betancourt and the three surly children gathered around her like mushrooms around a mother toadstool, all of the kids hoping for an excuse to retreat to their electronic whatzits. Betancourts *père* and *mère* shuddered at the idea of naughty drinking songs.

Ah, he's on a roll now, thought Cleo in admiration.

But Bruce had made a valiant recovery. "Say, I've just thought of a good one," he announced in desperation. "How about 'On Top of Old Smoky?'"

"One of my favorites," lied Max smoothly, rising to his feet. "Ms English, there you are. Didn't you say you have a dripping faucet in the cottage?"

"Ah ... I do, indeed. In the bathroom. The shower, in fact. Wasting hot water and keeping me awake at night." She gave him a conspiratorial smile.

"I'll take a look at it right now. Sorry, folks, duty calls. It's been fun, though. Carry on as long as you like; don't bother waiting for me. Leaky faucets can take quite a while to fix," he said, leering at Cleo.

All eyes turned to her, and she went bright red. Damn the man, she thought savagely, as he oiled his way across the floor and eased her out of the room with a finger in her back.

"You are evil personified," she snarled at him as she walked down the front steps, propelled by his firm hand on her elbow.

"What? You don't like Gilbert and Sullivan? Musically illiterate female. How about a slightly naughty French song?" He warbled *"Auprés de Ma Blonde"* suggestively all the way to her cottage.

"Well, good night," she said awkwardly, in front of her porch.

"Hang on a sec. Look at the stars."

They were awesome, a sparkling carpet spread out across a navy velvet sky, and she hadn't noticed them earlier, preoccupied by Max's perfidy. "Oh, wow," breathed Cleo, and leaned back against him for balance as she craned her neck to look upwards.

"More stars in Newfoundland than any place on earth," he said, his breath hot against her ear. His arm slipped around her waist and his hand inched upwards towards her breast. "Plump and luscious and sparkling, like grapes."

"Grapes don't sparkle," said Cleo, suddenly realizing her peril.

"No, I guess you're right," he said, swooping her around to face him, as his mouth descended on hers.

Cleo heard a clap of thunder echo in her ears, then realized it wasn't an approaching storm; it was her jazzed-up heartbeat. It was Max. He bent her slightly backwards while he devoured her lips. Their mouths blended and melted together perfectly.

God, the man could kiss, she thought. So could she. She returned his salute with equal passion and had the satisfaction of feeling him shiver against her. She wrapped her arms around his neck and pulled his hair teasingly. So who's seducing whom, big fellow, she thought.

Max growled against her mouth, slipped his tongue between her lips and pressed his nether regions against hers, all in one smooth operation.

She forced herself to disengage. "Night, Max," she said, backing away towards the cottage steps.

"How about that faucet?" he said. "Thought you wanted it fixed."

"It's not really dripping."

"I could come in and loosen a few nuts so it would drip. Then I could fix it. And anything else you'd like fixed." He put his foot on the steps and leaned forward.

Moving fast, she thought. Better make him wait a little longer. Playing games and anticipation made the ultimate surrender all the sweeter. "Maybe another time," she said, smiling seductively.

Oh, well, he had sticky buns to bake for breakfast. "G'night, Cleo." He turned and headed for the Big House. When he was out of sight of the cottage he paused and adjusted his jeans, which had grown too tight. He licked his lips, savoring the after-taste of her mouth. Going to have her sooner or later, he thought, and the sooner the better.

It was going to be sooner, if Cleo had anything to say about it. She needed help, and she needed it soon. She'd had horrible nightmares in the months following Charlie's death, and she was beginning to sense their return, curling like mist around the edge of her sleeping mind.

The first few nights in the cottage had been remarkably peaceful and quiet, with no outside noises at all except the crash of the ocean waves against the rocks at the bottom of the hill. She'd slept well and had no dreams. That was beginning to change; she was waking up in the morning with a vague sense of unease, of dread, as though something threatening were lurking in the back of her mind. That was the way a series of nightmares always began.

When she'd first started having the nightmares, she'd been frightened enough by their content to seek the help of a psychiatrist, fearing that she was going mad. He'd reassured her on that point, after listening to her describe desperate dreams of loneliness and abandonment.

Although he thought what she was undergoing was normal, he insisted on nipping it in the bud before it became firmly established as a routine of her sleep, and prescribed an anti-depressant and sleeping pills to help her rest more soundly. The combination had worked, most of the time, but had left her feeling flat and logy during the day. She abandoned her prescriptions when she discovered that sex worked even better.

Now here she was in Newfoundland and she'd not brought any medications to stave off the dreams, thinking they'd gone forever. She'd even left behind Charlie's old tee shirt that she'd been sleeping with since his death. She'd been determined to give up emotional props and re-invent herself as a woman who'd lived through a tragedy, survived, and was moving on from it. She'd assumed that her childhood fantasyland would provide enough distraction to help her put herself back together again, once and for all.

That had been a major miscalculation. The leisurely, undemanding pace of her stay at Squashberry Cottage meant she had plenty of time to think, and sleep. And dream.

Sex had saved her before, and distraction during the day would keep the naps and the nightmares at bay. Which left her with two projects, both worthwhile: get up off her duff and go sightseeing, and seduce Max Avalon.

Chapter Six

How could you be so cruel as
To part me from my love?
Her tender heart beats in her breast as constant as a dove.
Oh, Venus was no fairer,
Nor the lovely month of May,
May Heaven above shower down its love
On the Star of Logy Bay.

"The Star of Logy Bay"
Newfoundland folk song

Cleo took her guidebook up to the Big House the next morning, carefully avoiding the crush of checkout time. Max was nowhere around the reception desk or the parlor, so she took a calculated risk on his good humor by easing open the kitchen door and poking her head in.

He was sitting at the kitchen table, consulting a large book, chewing on a pen and muttering to himself.

Not sure whether or not she'd get snapped at, she ventured cautiously, "Hi."

He looked up. A warm smile, turning seductive at the edges, grew slowly on his face as he looked her up and down, taking in every detail of her snug, sleeveless, lilac-colored tee shirt and the pleated lavender skirt that ended well above her knees, Cleo's tribute to the day's warmer weather. A vision in purple, he thought happily; it was his favorite color. He rose slowly to his feet. "Good day," he said.

"Hi. Hope I'm not disturbing you." Relieved that her welcome had been a grin rather than a growl, Cleo returned his smile, putting a little come-hither pizzazz in it.

"You are disturbing me, but in the nicest possible way and in the nicest possible places," he purred.

She giggled. "What are you doing?"

He sank back into his chair. "Recipe calculations. Have a seat and give me a hand. You know anything about math?"

She shook her head. "I'm a high school English teacher. Math isn't my strong point."

"Mine neither, but I always have to re-calculate the amount of ingredients in each recipe because I have a different number of guests every night and make a different meal for them each time. I have notes on most of my recipes, but this one's new so I haven't worked out all the figures yet."

"What is it?"

"Breast of chicken poached in white wine and marmalade. For eight people, unless you're joining us tonight, which would make nine."

"I would love to join you. Eight people? How many rooms do you have here?"

"Real or imaginary?"

"Huh?"

Max grinned. "Officially, eight in the Big House. But Number One is my apartment, and Number Seven is a broom closet."

"Why does a broom closet have a number?"

"Makes the Big House seem bigger. Guests walk by it and wonder why nobody ever goes in or comes out. If anybody asks, I tell them it's the honeymoon suite. Or sometimes I tell them that a very strange couple rented it and they never come out in the daylight. That usually puts an end to questions. How much is one-eighth and one-sixth?"

What a weird sense of humor, the guy has, thought Cleo, and then realized that he'd asked her a question. "Uh ... hmmm ... seven twenty-fourths. Call it one-third."

He shook his head. "Can't. It's saffron, costs the earth and a small portion of the sky. Have to measure it very carefully." He was quiet for several moments, writing furiously in a notebook. Then he pushed it away and smiled genially. "What can I do for you today, Ms English?"

"Why so formal? Can't we just be Cleo and Max?"

"We can be anything you want us to be, teacher."

Ah, a nibble, signaling the opening of combat. "Do you have any interesting ideas?"

"My ideas are always interesting."

"I was thinking of sightseeing tips," she responded primly.

"There's a lots of things to see in Newfoundland. And do. Some of them are even close to home."

"How close?" she blurted, then realized she'd stepped right into his trap.

"How close do you want them to be?" The familiar leer curled around the edges of his mouth.

It was a very nice mouth, she thought, remembering what a good kisser he was. Yes, he was definitely coming on to her. Cooking and running a B and B might be the primary thoughts in his head, but there was clearly room in there for other ideas. "Oh, within walking distance, maybe. I feel like getting some exercise today."

"There's a great beach down the hill in front of your cottage. Have you been there yet?"

"No."

"Did you bring your bikini?"

"No."

"Good, because swimming in the ocean can be dangerous unless you're really good. I advise wading instead."

"Hmmm. That sounds like fun. Would be more fun with company, though." She looked down at her feet, feigning shyness.

Max considered the possibilities of volunteering himself as her escort to the beach. Too bad about the bikini, but if she'd brought shorts and a skimpy little top for sunbathing, that would be almost as nice. He followed her gaze down to her scarlet painted toenails, clearly visible in the little strappy sandals. How was it possible for a woman's feet to be so sexy? He usually found it easy to control wayward thoughts of lust around his guests, but there was something both tempting and tantalizing about Cleo that made her damned near irresistible.

He dragged his eyes back up to her face, which wore a hopeful expression. "Tell you what . . . I don't have anyone checking in this afternoon. Maybe we could take a little walk along the beach together later. Maybe around two o'clock?"

Cleo smiled, dazzling Max. "I'd love that."

Ah, yes, he thought. He hadn't misread the signals; they were on the same page of a very intriguing book. "I'll come by the cottage and pick you up."

Cleo tripped back to Number Nine, feeling happy. There was nothing like a flirtation with a good-looking, responsive, slightly dangerous man to keep depression at bay. All she needed to fend off the nightmares was a little distraction, and Max seemed as though he'd be quite distracting, now that they'd exchanged signs of mutual interest.

That afternoon they scrambled down the hill to the beach hand in hand, Max reaching for her with a protective gesture, indicating that the climb was steep. Halfway down he paused briefly, said, "Your fingers are cold," and squeezed her hand.

"Cold hand, warm heart," Cleo replied.

"Sure hope so," he said, with another little squeeze, then slipped that arm around her waist to help her over what he described as an especially slippery batch of rocks.

Enjoying her warmth, he was reluctant to remove his arm when they reached the beach, and Cleo had to detach herself gently. She was still following a "go-slow" policy.

The beach was glorious, all pebbles and large rocks stretching out forever, washed by the vigorous waves of the Atlantic. Cleo stared, feeling peace fill her, and made a mental resolution to come down here every time she felt blue during her stay.

They strolled along the beach, saying little. No words were necessary: the ocean said it all. Afterwards, when they'd climbed back up the hill and were standing in front of Squashberry Cottage, Max turned to her and put his hands on her shoulders. "Nice walk, Cleo. Thanks for the company."

"It was my pleasure." She looked at him expectantly, and he took the hint. He bent down and brushed his mouth across hers.

"You don't mind?" he whispered against her lips.

"No. I was looking forward to it," she said, and put her hand on his neck, burrowing under the black curls.

He kissed her with a surprising tenderness, given the kiss of a few nights ago. "You taste good," he said softly.

Cleo, shivering with pleasure from the feathery touch of his mouth, said, "So do you," and wrapped her arm around his neck to coax him to her again.

The next kiss showed signs of developing into passion. He dragged her body close to his, with predictable results. They clung together for a long moment, then he managed to pull himself away. "Gotta go . . . dinner to cook," he said and for almost the first time in his career as a B and B owner felt that cooking was a real drag. If it weren't for dinner, he could ease her up the cottage steps and maybe even further. Maybe into her bedroom. "Ah, Cleo. Wish I could stay with you longer."

"I wish you could too."

They gave each other a long, wistful look and then he turned and loped up the hill to the Big House, suddenly conscious of the time and the dinner preparations that hadn't even been started. Cleo watched him leave, sighing. "See you at dinner," she called after him and received a wave in reply.

She walked up the steps and sank into the swing, and sat, swaying gently, staring down at the cerulean blue water at the foot of the hill. So far, so good, she thought in satisfaction. The fish was definitely nibbling at the hook, and what a prize he was going to turn out to be. And "catch and release" was not part of her plan.

Chapter Seven

I'se the b'y that builds the boat,
And I'se the b'y that sails her!
I'se the b'y that catches the fish
And takes 'em home to Lizer.

"I'se the B'y"
Newfoundland folk song

Where the three hearty, good-looking, middle-aged men came from and what they were doing in his province and his B and B, Max had no idea. And he didn't know why they raised his hackles and put him very much on his guard, but they did.

They said they were on a golfing trip. But if Newfoundland had more than three golf courses and if any of them were up to smart Yankee businessmen's requirements, he'd be a Jiggs dinner. More than likely they were here on some devious mission of the Toronto-New York-Houston axis, planning to buy up half of the countryside and fill it with dark satanic mills belching lung-destroying smoke, for the purpose of manufacturing plastic dohickeys for useless Yankee loodle-laddle.

Or maybe they were planning on cornering the crab fishery, consolidating it into one enormous corporation that would ruin individual fishermen, the way unrestrained competition from foreign boats had ruined the cod fishing industry.

Or maybe he was just paranoid.

Max watched the men and brooded and thought dark satanic thoughts, all covered by the bland smile of the professional host, while he fetched drinks, made polite conversation, and grinned until he felt like a performing monkey.

It didn't matter that the three were unfailingly polite and respectful to him, called Maria the housekeeper "ma'am," and loudly praised the B and B grub. Or that they were dressed casually in golf shirts and shorts, had only one suitcase each, and drove an unostentatious rental minivan instead of a gigantic Hummer.

They were mainlander businessmen, and he was suspicious. Suspicion turned to horror when Cleo appeared at the front porch next evening when the three were gathered, relaxing in a drink after a hard day of doing nothing, at least as far as Max could tell.

He was coming out of the house with a tray of drinks, which he nearly dropped when he caught sight of her in her trademark tee-shirt, tiny skirt and strappy sandals. For God's sake, didn't she have any proper dresses that covered more of her luscious curves and long lovely legs? He heard the collective sharp intake of breath from the businessmen at the sight.

And why shouldn't they gasp? Cleo looked as delectable as a piece of his crowberry crumble covered with whipping cream, and he suspected that the three were the kind of b'ys to lick off the cream and gobble up the sweet dessert underneath.

The men rose as one unit, and one said, "Evening, ma'am." If they'd had on hats, they would have tipped them, Max thought, enraged by their politeness.

Cleo was struck dumb by the sight of three large cheerful men on the porch above her, and in her surprise she posed prettily, a nervous smile turning up the corners of her mouth. She'd come looking for Max on a pretext she'd yet to think of, though she was certain something would occur to her. Max was her after-dinner drink, her chocolate on the pillow, her nightcap, and she had reached the point where she couldn't even contemplate going to sleep without her evening jousting match with him.

She had, predictably, dressed to torment, and now she found that strategy backfiring. She felt naked, even though the men's smiles were respectful. Then her glance went to Max and what she recognized as a look of jealous fury on his face. Excellent! She could not resist seizing the dagger hilt and turning the blade a twist or two. After all, if he'd come looking for her as he should have, this meeting never would have occurred, and they'd be necking happily in the seclusion of Squashberry Cottage's porch.

Summoning up her courage and trying not to simper like Scarlett O'Hara, she put one dainty scarlet-tipped foot on the porch step, thereby lifting her skirt a little higher and pulling it tighter around her sleek thighs. She caroled, "Hi! Am I interrupting anything?"

"No, ma'am, not at all," said one of the men heartily. "Are you a guest here?"

"Yes, I'm staying down the hill in Squashberry Cottage. I just came by to see if Max has . . . uh . . . a lemon."

"I'll get one for you," said Max through clenched teeth, turning toward the door.

"Don't rush away, ma'am. Won't you come and sit a bit with us? Wonderful sunset going on," said the largest and heartiest of the men, making a gesture towards the scarlet and lavender sky.

"Why, thank you." She made her way up the steps to a wicker chair that had been hastily vacated for her in the middle of the group.

"Could we get the lady a drink, Max?" said the large man. "What would you like, ma'am?"

"I know what she likes," snarled Max, earning himself a reproachful glance from Cleo, and he went inside, shoulders rigid in the attempt not to commit murder.

Cleo sat, and introductions were made all around. The

businessmen were Greg, Tim, and Don. Within five minutes
she'd gotten more information from them than Max had during
the entire three days of their stay. They were on a pleasure trip,
headed for Gros Morne National Park, where they hoped to take
in whales, icebergs, moose and anything else nature might care to
provide for them. They were united in praise of Newfoundland's
beauty. Greg, from Missouri, said it reminded him of the Ozarks,
with its pine forests and sparkling navy blue lakes, which, he said, a
Newfoundlander had told him were referred to as "ponds," regardless of their size.

All agreed that the province was beautifully unspoiled and
should remain so. Tim said he'd like to visit the province every
summer, and Don said he was contemplating buying property
here. He could get a nice house and a good piece of land for a rea-
sonable price, and fix it up for a summer vacation home for the
wife and kids; he liked handyman work. Fishing, boating, nature
walks, evenings spent singing around the piano or playing check-
ers, all good healthy pursuits for a family, and it would get them
away from city life, television and modern society's deleterious
effects.

In short, the men's motives were entirely honorable and above
board, a fact Max would have been pleased to hear, had he not
been so entirely preoccupied with Cleo's effect on the three. He
was so preoccupied, in fact, that he was careless with the liquor
bottle, and poured a drink that was twice as strong as he usually
made for Cleo.

She didn't realize that until she was nearly through with the
vodka tonic. She'd gulped it hastily for Dutch courage, because,
despite her outward savoir faire, the attention of three large,
admiring, self-assured men made her nervous. She wasn't used to
handling men en masse. Besides, her skirt had crept higher on her
thighs when she sat down, and it embarrassed her to have so much
flesh on display, since Max wasn't the viewer. But the drink was
helping her stay calm and sophisticated.

The voices on the porch rose and fell, interrupted by occasional peals of laughter. Max, in the kitchen, ground his teeth when he recognized the higher pitch of Cleo's laugh. He took all the spices out of the cupboard, arranged them in alphabetical order, and then jammed them back in helter-skelter in a chaos that would take him days to untangle.

When Greg's soft Southern voice came from the doorway, Max jumped, nearly slamming his head against the open cupboard door.

"Could we have another round, Max? And easy on the young lady's, please. I don't think she's used to real strong drinks."

Blindly Max fixed the drinks and brought them in on a tray, then stood just inside the door to hear the voices resume, quieter now, punctuated by Cleo's giggles. He slunk back into the kitchen, mad with jealousy.

On the porch a half-hour later, Tim stood and stretched. "Bed for me, guys. Busy day tomorrow." To Cleo he said, "Max has found a guy down in the village who'll take us fishing and he wants to get going around six. Some vacation, huh? Up at five. I get to sleep later at home before I have to get up for work."

Cleo rose, a little unsteadily, still feeling the effects of the first drink, and wondering why she'd drunk the second one. When Greg offered to escort her down to her cottage, she accepted gratefully, taking his arm at one point when she stumbled.

Max, skulking in the dining room near the front door, heard, to his considerable relief, that Greg had returned promptly. As lithe as an eel he slithered to the door and out, down the path to Squashberry Cottage to check on his nemesis.

She was standing on the cottage porch in a patch of moonlight so bright that it dazzled him. It silvered her brown hair and turned the garment she was wearing into a diaphanous fantasy that made Max's legs weak and another part of him hard.

He gulped, and growled, "Hi," as he gazed up at her.

"Hi yourself. What are you doing here?"

"I've come to make sure you're all right."

Cleo leaned forward unsteadily. "Why wouldn't I be all right? Though I'm a little drunk. Why did you make me such a strong drink?"

Max felt a pang of guilt. "Was it strong? I wasn't paying any attention. You're lucky it wasn't pure vodka. My mind was distracted by your giggles and the idea of all those guys ogling you in that get-up you almost had on."

She laughed and the sound sent a shiver down Max's spine. "The get-up, as you so poetically express it, was for you, honey. I didn't expect an audience. And they weren't ogling me. They were showing me pictures of their families, and telling stories about them, especially about their grandchildren. Don has three, Tim has two and Greg has one, the cutest little girl you could imagine."

Suspicion not entirely assuaged, Max demanded, "Why were you giggling?"

"Tim was telling jokes. He has quite a repertoire—all clean, by the way. Well, mostly clean."

Max was silent, reassured at last. He watched as a strap slid slowly down Cleo's softly rounded shoulder, gleaming white in the moonlight. He was uncomfortably, desperately, aware of the transparent garment the wind was wrapping gently around her, accentuating her shape. "What's that you're wearing?"

"It's my nightie. Pretty, isn't it." She giggled again, and Max's body tightened in response. "I love to stand out here on the porch to get cooled off just before I get into bed and snuggle under the covers." She said slyly, "Are you ogling me, Max?"

He made a choking sound in his throat.

"Sometimes if it's very late at night and there's no moon I stand out here naked. Why don't you come down and ogle me then?"

His mouth was so dry he could hardly speak, but he managed, "Can't. Have to get to work too early in the morning."

"Sorry, am I keeping you up?" She giggled insanely at the awkward double entendre.

"You know you are, you vixen," he growled. "Come down here to me."

"Can't, my feet are bare. Why don't you come up to me?"

"If I do I won't be in a hurry to leave. Are you ready for that?"

She considered, then shook her head. "No, I think I'm too drunk for sheninig . . . shaginigin . . . for fooling around."

"And I like my women sober."

Cleo laughed, and wiggled just to tease him, and the second strap fell off her shoulder. The nightgown began a slow descent. At the last minute she clutched at it, hugged it dramatically against her bosom, and eased the straps back into place.

Lust was making fierce, urgent inroads on Max's sorely tried self-control. "You are a shameless hussy, Cleo."

"I know. Isn't it fun? This wonderful moonlight and all that booze make me feel wild and sexy." She shimmied again and the straps fell down again. She hiccuped. "Oh, dear, I think I'd better go to bed. If you're not going to come up and tuck me in, at least give me a goodnight kiss, Maxie." She bent down towards him over the porch rail, into the moonlight, the nightgown dipping low between her breasts, coming to rest on her erect nipples. "Oh, it's so romantic, just like Romeo and Juliet, kissing on the balcony."

Max stretched upwards and one hand grabbed the hair that fell over her shoulder, then moved to clasp the back of her head. The other hand seized the front of her nightgown and his fingers slipped in to nestle into the warm valley inside it. He caressed the soft curve of her breast, his mind racing with possibilities.

He rose on the balls of his feet and pursed his lips up to hers. Cleo leaned further over the rail and pressed her mouth against his tenderly, then in drunken mischief licked his lips until he opened them, shocked, to receive her tongue.

Stunned with lust, Max lost his balance. For a moment it seemed that her nightgown would rip, her feet would leave the ground and she'd plunge over the porch rail to land on top of him, naked and willing. He managed to grab the railing to steady himself and seized her shoulder to push her upright.

"Oops-a-daisy!" Cleo said drunkenly. "That's enough for now, honey. I'm feeling a little dizzy. Must be that kiss."

"Sure you don't need help getting into bed?" he said, concern warring with desire.

"You know what that would lead to, and I thought you liked your women sober."

I'd like you any way I can get you, Max thought, and for a hot moment imagined himself sliding the nightgown off and filling his hands with Cleo. Then he made a supreme sacrifice. "Yeah, you're right. Go on to bed and we'll try this again another night."

"Maybe it'll be a night without a nightgown," Cleo said, and staggered to the cottage door, where she turned and waggled her fingers at him. "Nightie nightie nightgown, honey."

Max growled in frustration and cursed the demon alcohol all the way back to the Big House. The night had been a complete failure, thanks to the Yankee businessmen and his own carelessness with the vodka bottle, and once more he'd been denied the pleasure of making love with Cleo. He wasn't sure how much more of this he could stand.

He was beginning to fear that she was what all men publicly derided and privately desired: a tease. Derided, because men thought that teasing wasn't playing fair, and desired, because every man liked to imagine that he would be the one to finally break through a tease's defenses.

But that wasn't fair to Cleo, he decided. He'd done just as much teasing as she had; it had been a mutual effort at seduction. And he thought she was interested in the same outcome as he was and just as frustrated at their lack of progress.

He remembered, suddenly, that he hadn't set the tables for breakfast, and scurried inside to the dining room. I'se the b'y, he thought; it's all down to me. That was the problem with being the boss; he bore the total, complete responsibility for everything.

But it was worth it for the independence. If he'd wanted help, he could have stayed in Halifax and gotten on as chef at a posh restaurant. He'd have plenty of help, then, and could yell at them all he wanted, just like a real chef.

Oops, the cereal bowls were still in the dishwasher. He strolled into the kitchen to get them and noticed the bottle of tonic water sitting uncapped on the counter. Well, that's useless, he thought, all the fizz will be gone. Might as well finish it up. He got a glass and fixed himself a vodka tonic, and walked back into the dining room, drink in one hand, bowls in the other.

He made up his own version of a popular Newfoundland folk song, singing softly under his breath, "I'se the b'y that buys the grub, I'se the b'y that cooks it. I'se the b'y that makes the dough, and brings it home to . . ." Well, certainly not to Lizer. Not to anyone, in fact. Wasn't that a sad state of affairs?

He took a big slug of his drink, and allowed himself a moment of slightly drunken self-pity. Then he finished setting the table, and went off to a cold and lonely bed and uneasy dreams of a dancing, vaporous Cleo, always slipping away from his grasp.

Chapter Eight

You may talk of Clara Nolan's ball or anything you choose,
But it couldn't hold a snuffbox to the spree at Killigrews.
If you want your eyeballs straightened just come out next week with me,
And you'll have to wear your glasses at the Killigrews soiree.
There was birch rind, tar twine, cherry wine and turpentine
Jowls and cavalances, ginger beer and tea.
Pig's feet, cat's meat, dumplings bowled up in a sheet,
Dandelion and crackie's teeth at the Kelligrews Soiree.

"The Killigrews Soiree"
Johnny Burke

Cleo woke the next morning a little the worse for drink, ever so slightly hungover. She managed tea and toast for breakfast and two aspirin with a glass of orange juice. She decided a little housekeeping would get her head in order, so she tidied the kitchen, swept the floors and rinsed out some undies. Then she indulged herself in a long hot shower, washed her hair and stepped out of the shower, restored to health.

Was that knocking she heard over the noise of her hairdryer? She pulled on her terrycloth robe, wrapped a towel around her hair, and went into the living room, where she spied a slip of white paper under her door. It read, "Want to drive down into town with me? Come find me when you're up."

56

She rushed to the porch and spotted Max heading up the hill. She ran after him, the towel unraveling, and wet hair streaming out behind her. "When are you leaving?"

He turned. "Good day, Cleo. How are you?"

"Fine. I want to go to town with you. When are you leaving?"

He picked up a handful of her wet hair. "I was going to leave now."

"Can you wait twenty minutes for me to dry my hair and get dressed?"

"I'll wait for you as long as it takes, princess," he said, smiling. "Get yourself prettied up and come along to the Big House when you're ready."

She made it in twenty-five minutes, with her hair mostly dry and her body conservatively dressed in jeans and blouse for a trip to town, and they piled into Max's elderly mini-van, which was decorated with a logo reading "Experience True Rock Hospitality at Last Man Ashore B and B." The message was so long that the logo covered the entire door panel, and even then was hard to decipher.

Max turned the minivan onto the Trans-Canada Highway and headed down the long, straight road to the town of Last Man Ashore, talking briskly all the way. "Do you like pines? We've got a few here." He waved his hand toward the side of the road, which was completely enveloped in wave after wave of trees.

"It's like a giant Christmas tree plantation," Cleo observed.

"Pines and moose. You want 'em, we got 'em."

"Oh, I'd love to see a moose."

"Unless it runs out onto the road in front of you," said Max. "Then you'll wish you were dodging rush hour traffic back home in Minnesota."

"Do they really do that?" gasped Cleo.

"Oh, yeah. We've got thousands of them here and they're all crazy, the size of pickup trucks, and as unpredictable as cats in an alley fight. They have no fear of cars and they'll amble out of the woods, lurk by the road for an hour, and then waft onto the highway like a bad dream when a car comes by. Or one will lurch onto the road and stand motionless. They especially like to do that on the backside of a sharp curve on a mountain where you can't swerve to avoid them; the ditches on the sides of the road are too deep and you'd roll the car. Your only hope is to slow down as quickly as you can and hope that the moose will decide to stroll on across before you hit it."

On the right, a large pond of sparkling navy blue water flashed past while Cleo was silent, thinking about moose. Finally she said, "That sounds dangerous."

"Oh, it is, princess, it is. A moose weighs twelve hundred pounds and its skinny legs are so long that its body is level with the top of the car. The last thing you want is a half-ton of moose hurtling through your windscreen. The moose might win but the car's occupants are certain to lose. Keep an eye on the sides of the highway for me, will you?"

Cleo, thinking about a moose in her lap, nodded her head in vigorous agreement. "You betcha, boss." She spent the rest of the drive dutifully swiveling her head from left to right, trying to cover both sides of the road in case she needed to sound a moose alert.

Her neck was getting sore so it was a relief when they turned off the Trans-Canada and headed downhill on a narrow paved road that led into the small town of Little Last Man Ashore Cove. The square, old-fashioned houses that lined the main street all looked alike. They had front doors but not front steps, so that the door perched uneasily six to ten feet above ground. Max, anticipating Cleo's question, said, grinning, "We call that the mother-in-law entrance."

Cleo gave him a look of shock, but before she could question that remark, he pulled up and parked in front of Puddester's Restaurant, in the middle of a small group of elderly buildings that made up what Cleo supposed must be considered downtown. Across the street was a two-story frame building with a sign in fading paint proclaiming it "Brown's Hotel." "Want to see inside our town's hottest spot?" Max asked, following the direction of her glance.

"It doesn't look open," said Cleo dubiously, crossing the street beside him.

"It's not, so don't get any ideas about bolting down here for sanctuary next time you don't like the cut of my jib." Max fished in his pocket for a key, unlocked the building door and led her in.

Clearly the hotel had not been in business for several years, but it was reasonably clean and free of cobwebs. The reception desk was a massive affair of beautiful mahogany that dominated the front area, and next to it was a sweeping staircase to the upper floor. Sofas and chairs were arranged in cozy groups around the lobby as though waiting for long-dead conversations to resume momentarily.

Cleo stared. "It's beautiful. Why isn't it open?"

"Lack of guests. Used to be full of fishermen in the season but since the cod moratorium they don't come any more, and the lumberjacks stay in their camps. There's not enough tourists to re-open the place but I'm hoping one day that will change. I've got a couple of ideas to lure visitors, like holding a writers' conference here. Peaceful setting, comfortable accommodations, bar full of strong drink and a reasonably priced restaurant serving good food across the street. What more could a writer want, except inspiration?"

"Don't tell me you own this hotel," said Cleo.

He shrugged. "Bought her at a bargain price from the last owners, who hotfooted it back to Toronto where they belonged, cowardly old mainlanders. She's a fine building and I couldn't let her go to ruin, so I made an offer they were all too eager to accept. Couple of the local ladies come in every other week and keep her tidy. Do you get the sense that she's a queen in waiting for tourists to come and kiss her awake?" He smiled wistfully. "That's the extent of the Max Avalon empire: one B and B and a sad old hotel lost in dreams of past glory."

He reached over for Cleo's hand. "Let's get some grub, princess." They crossed the street and entered Puddester's Restaurant. It too had seen better days and wore that vaguely abandoned air that Cleo was coming to recognize as traditionally Newfoundland, but the woodwork inside was freshly polished, and the fifteen tables all sported white cloths and sparkling silverware in expectation of an on-rush of hungry diners.

A waitress rushed over to them. "Max, youse should have phoned up before youse came. Florence is right fussed dat youse is 'ere without warning."

He scowled. "How does she know I'm here?"

"Saw youse t'rough da window, and has been having kittens ever since because she doesn't 'ave anything special to offer youse."

"We don't want anything special. We'll order off the menu. Polly, this is my friend Cleo. She's a guest at the B and B."

The two women exchanged hellos and curious glances. Then Max and Cleo turned their attention to the menu, which was full of baffling items like figgy duff and Jiggs' dinner. "I don't know what to order," she said, frowning in perplexity.

"Try da fishcakes," advised Polly. "They're light as a feat'er." Then she turned to Max. "Florence is going to be a nervous wreck, whatever youse orders."

He gave a resigned sigh. "Tell Mrs. Puddester to fix for both of us the items on the menu that she thinks are her best work today." He gave Cleo a cunning glance. "Even if it's cods' tongues."

Cleo shuddered.

Polly said, "Now, Max, youse knows we don't serve cods' tongues except on our special Newfoundland sampler platter dat youse suggested we offers." Then she noticed Cleo's expression. "Oh, I gets it, youse is teasin' da lady. Be right back."

When Polly appeared with their first course, she said nervously, "'Ere's your seafood chowder, and Mrs. Puddester says I should tell you dat it's all right but it would 'ave been better if Clem Grant had gotten da 'addock to her an 'our sooner but he was gabbing with da other fishermen so da fish weren't as fresh as it should 'ave been."

Polly put the bowls in front of them and fled.

The chowder was exquisite, rich and creamy with chunks of fish, lobster and delicately minced clams. Cleo had to restrain herself from making loud slurping noises of ecstasy.

Polly appeared next with a basket of rolls, steamy and sweet-smelling, fresh from the oven. "Mrs. Puddester says she 'opes dese rolls is okay. She thinks her yeast might be a bit h'old but she 'asn't 'ad time to replace it."

Max nodded wearily. He said to Cleo, "Mrs. Puddester is suffering from what one of my cooking school professors called 'chef's inferiority complex.' She needs constant reassurance. Hell, she's a good cook and she knows it. She raised twelve children on her cooking, five still at home after the moratorium when money was tight, and all of them grew up to be smart, strong and healthy. But I can't get her to have confidence in her work and a good chef has to have that confidence, that arrogant faith in her work."

Cleo nodded her understanding, remembering some of her own students, and seized one of the fluffy rolls, regretting that there was only margarine with which to slather it. Bakery products like these cried out for rich yellow butter. Why was there no butter in Newfoundland? Was it part of a provincial struggle against heart disease or weren't there any cows on the Rock? Before she could ask Max, Polly reappeared.

She was carrying two plates piled with crispy fried fishcakes. As she served, she opened her mouth to relay more apologies from Mrs. Puddester.

Cleo said, "Thank you, Polly. Please convey Mr. Avalon's compliments to Mrs. Puddester and tell her that he wishes to hear no more excuses. He will judge her work entirely on its merits."

Polly gaped at her, then said, "Yes, ma'am," and scuttled back into the kitchen.

Max said, "Cleo, do you think that was wise?"

"Sure. You need to be firm with insecure students. Treat them as equals, show them respect, let them know you expect them to succeed and that you don't want to hear excuses. Give them a standard to work towards and teach them to realize and accept when they've done the best work they can." She smiled. "Trust me, pal, I'm a teacher."

"Hokay, teach. Helping Mrs. Puddester have confidence in her cooking is one of my goals in reviving the town, so it can offer a fine dining experience as well as a fine hotel stay. God knows there aren't many cooks who understand how to season food in Newfoundland; our provincial motto should be "plain is good, bland is better, tasteless is best." You can't lure tourists if you don't have good grub."

He grinned at her, and they dug into the platter of fishcakes, which were delicious, the outsides richly crunchy, the innards tender and flaky.

Mrs. Puddester herself, a tall thin woman with brown hair captured into a neat bun, appeared with their desserts. She sat down the pie plates, wiped her hands on her immaculate apron and cleared her throat in preparation for a lengthy speech of apology.

Cleo forestalled her. She rose and offered her hand. "You must be Mrs. Puddester; it's a pleasure to meet you. Won't you sit down and have a cup of coffee with us? You too, Polly."

`Mrs. Puddester said, "Don't mind if I do. Fetch da pot, Pol, and da china cups as was my mum's, and mind you don't drop da tray. And don't forget da sugar and a little pot of cream." As Polly dashed off into the kitchen, she lowered herself carefully into a chair and looked inquiringly at her guests.

Cleo said, "Lunch was delicious, Mrs. Puddester. However do you make your fishcakes so light and delicate?"

"It's all in 'ow you handles 'em," she said. "Beat da eggs first, then mix 'em into da fish with a fork, light and careful. Don't want to squat 'em; youse needs a tender hand when youse shapes them." She gave Cleo a shrewd look. "Liked 'em, did youse, me love?"

Cleo grinned. "I loved them and I wish I could take a vat of your chowder back home for long cold Minnesota winters. I'd never be cold again with that inside me."

Mrs. Puddester turned pink with pleasure, and to cover her embarrassment said, "Minnesota, dat's in the States. So youse is a Yankee?"

"I am indeed."

"Dey made a mistake back in de old days; Newfoundland shoulda been part of the States, it should. Dere'd be no foreign fishing boats in our waters den. A great big old Yankee gunship'd show up and fire a shot across 'er bows and dat'd be da h'end of it. Yankees don't take no nonsense," she said, and nodded her head wisely.

Unwilling to defend her country's sometimes bellicose response to challenges, Cleo smiled noncommittally.

Mrs. Puddester continued, "Youse're a long way from 'ome. Here for yer 'olidays?"

"I am."

"And what does youse think of Newfoundland?"

Cleo was experienced enough now to recognize that as a typical Newfoundlander greeting to visitors, and spent the next several minutes praising the Province's blue skies, pristine ponds and miles and miles of pine trees. She finished with, "But I haven't seen a moose yet. Max says there are a lot of them here. I'd love to see one."

Mrs. Puddester, Polly and Max all shook their heads. "Don't want to see dem fellers," said Mrs. Puddester firmly, and the other two nodded agreement. "They's right robustic. Lady next door to me, Lillian's 'er name, drove up 'er driveway one day last week, and a bad-tempered old boy moose stepped out of the shrubbery and charged 'er car."

"Must have been in rut," observed Max.

Mrs. Puddester gave a great laugh. "'E found out fast enough dat old Ford wasn't a lady moose. Lil hit 'er horn and 'e staggered off, shaking his 'ead and bellering fit to kill. Wish I'd'a been there to see it. At a safe distance, a' course."

Polly said shyly, "Once when I was a maid for a family in Deer Lake, da ten-year-old daughter was in the parlor practicin' da piano. All of a sudden us in the kitchen realized da music 'ad stopped, so we went out to see what 'ad 'appened. Da little girl was sittin' on da piano stool, not knowing whether to laugh or yell, starin' at a moose calf what 'ad stuck its 'ead in da window."

"Must have been a music lover," said Max.

"Long as it didn't get in da parlor, dat's the main t'ing," said Mrs. Puddester wisely.

Cleo looked from one to the other. Presumably the stories were true, she thought, not made up to bamboozle visitors as a technique of sly Newfoundland humor, although since she'd been in the Province several weeks and had yet to see a moose she found it hard to believe the critters were so omnipresent. Then she remembered something else that had puzzled her. "Mrs. Puddester, may I ask you a question?"

"Fire away, me love."

"I saw houses in the village that are built with the front door six to ten feet above the ground, with no steps. Why is that?"

The older woman eyed her shrewdly and said, "Ah, well, 'ere's the way it is. A young man'll be wantin' to get married and build a house for 'is bride. Maybe da first year 'e'll 'ave enough money to build da basement. Next year 'e'll 'ave enough to put up walls, with 'is family and friends 'elpin,' a course, and so on for a couple more years. When da 'ouse is finished, 'e'll do the landscapin.' After five years 'e'll have a house free and clear, not owing nothing to nobody.

"Maybe then 'e'll put in da front steps and maybe not. Don't need a front door, anyways, because everybody comes through da back door. Sits in da kitchen and 'as a cup of tea. That way nobody 'as to take der shoes off, unless they's been in da mud."

Cleo said accusingly, "Max said it was the mother-in-law entrance."

Mrs. Puddester gave her now familiar crack of laughter, and said, "Maybe 'e's right. You ever 'ave a mother-in-law, me love?"

Cleo remembered Charlie's formidable, bossy and often aggravating mama and smiled. "You betcha. Maybe Newfoundlanders have got hold of a good idea."

Later, on the way back to the B and B, Cleo realized how long they had sat talking with Mrs. Puddester and Polly, and decided that it was wise to make sure she had an hour or so to spare before engaging a Newfoundlander in conversation. Talking seemed to be the Province's favorite hobby.

Chapter Nine

Oh, there is an ancient party at the other end of town.
He keeps a little grocery store; the ancient's name is Brown.
He has an only daughter, such a beauty I never saw.
I only wish some day to be the old man's son-in-law.
Well, it's Old Brown's daughter is a proper sort of girl.
Old Brown's daughter is as fair as any pearl.
I wish I was a Lord Mayor, Marquis or an Earl,
And blow me if I wouldn't marry Old Brown's girl.

"Old Brown's Daughter"
Johnny Burke

Cleo, ever nosy, was curious about Maria, the housekeeper, who seemed to be both Max's bulwark and the thorn in his side. If she made friends with Maria, perhaps the woman would give her some background on Max and maybe a tip or two on how to bend him to her will. She mentally formulated a few opening remarks in her reasonably well remembered high school Spanish, and sauntered into the kitchen in search of the belligerent *señorita*.

Maria was chopping beef into cubes for Max's proposed dinner stew, and the sight of the enormous cleaver with which she was armed gave Cleo pause for thought, but she forged ahead bravely. "*Hola*, Maria."

"Hi," said Maria grouchily.

"*Es un dia hermoso,*" Cleo tried again. It's a beautiful day.

"Ees too hot."

"Maybe you're working too hard."

"*Señor* Max ees slave-driver. You lookin' for 'eem?" she added abruptly.

"Uh . . . no. I was just passing through. Does he ever let you cook dinner? I wouldn't mind some Mexican food one night."

"He don' let me cook. He say I too hot."

While Cleo digested that startling remark, Maria snapped, "An' I not Mexican. I Spanish, from Castile."

"Oh, sorry. Have you been in Canada long?"

"Too long."

"I suppose you're homesick for Spain."

Maria gave her an incredulous look. "No, not me. I never go back. Everybody poor in my village. They all losers. I wan' go to Weesconseen. You know where is Weesconseen?"

"Sure. It's right next to Minnesota, where I come from."

Maria wiped her hands on a paper towel and turned around. "I wan' go to Green Bay. *Toda mi familia es* in Green Bay. You Packers fan?"

"I don't care much for football."

"No wonder, eef you from Minnesota. Vikings are crap."

"Uh, yeah, whatever. What does your family do in Green Bay?"

'They run restaurant." Skewering Cleo with a steely look, she added, "Spanish restaurant. Not Mexican."

"Oh. So you do know how to cook?"

"No, I not like to cook. Ees too much sweating. I wan' be accountant. Go to Memorial University een St. John's, get degree, then be accountant for *mi familia y el* restaurant in Green Bay. They 'ave to listen to me, then. I be boss."

Ah, an ambitious woman, someone she could relate to. Sensing that the conversation had reached a dead end, Cleo tried another tack. "I wondered if maybe I could come and practice my Spanish with you sometimes."

Maria regarded her incredulously. "Why you wan' do that?"

"I'm a high school teacher in Minneapolis and there are a lot of Hispanic kids in my classes. I'd like to be able to communicate better with them."

"Keeds need to speak English. Spanish get them nowhere. They be losers."

Hearing the language of Cervantes and a large and lively minority of the population of the United States dismissed so casually grated on Cleo, but it didn't seem politic to argue the point. She persevered, "If I can speak Spanish with them, it would be easier to help them learn English."

"*Si*, ees good point. Hokay, you come, we talk. Unless slave-driver Max say no."

"I think I can get him to say it's all right, if I don't interfere with your work."

Maria fixed her with a shrewd eye. "He will say ees hokay eef you ask. He say hokay to mos' anythin' you wan'. He hot for you. Not had *una enamorada* for two, t'ree years. Ees sad case. *Esta el pobrecito, Señor* Maxwell."

Cleo had not thought of arrogant, self-confident Max in that light before. *El pobrecito,* the poor little guy, indeed. And no girlfriend for several years. What was wrong with all the women in Newfoundland?

Maria said, "He have Spanish book, tapes. Wan' to learn Spanish but no time. He lend them to you. You ask for anything, he say *si*. He look at you like you made of wheeped cream an' chocolate. *Pobre* Maxwell."

"Super. I'll ask him." She wandered to the door, bemused, then turned and said, "Be seeing you."

"*Hasta la vista*, baby," Maria said, and grinned.

Cleo stumbled out, thinking about Maria's comment: *he look at you like you made of wheeped cream an' chocolate.* That sounded pretty hot and confirmed her previous suspicions of Max's intense interest in her body. She strode out of the house and down the path to Squashberry Cottage.

The mouse crept out from behind the refrigerator and eyed Maria and her huge cleaver. An unsophisticated animal, she had never heard the nursery rhyme about the three blind mice and how they lost their tails. But she was wary. She gauged the distance between the refrigerator and the pantry, where delicious crumbs might lurk.

Being great with mice, she gave up the idea of a mad dash and retreated back to her hole behind the fridge.

When Max came through the door later, Maria said, "Cute leetle *señorita* lookin' for you, Max. You know she a schoolteacher? Maybe she got a lesson or two for you, and not out of book. You wan' to check eet out? I feenish up 'ere."

"Hmmm . . . hokay. *Muchas gracias*, Maria."

"*No es nada.* You remember eet when we talk about raise, Boss."

Max stopped in the hall to glance at himself in the mirror, and made an ineffectual attempt to tidy his unruly curls before he sloped off down to Squashberry Cottage. He had a few minutes to spare and he deserved a break, he rationalized to himself. It was good policy to keep in touch with the clientele, make sure they were happy. And satisfied. He didn't doubt his ability to keep the customers satisfied and looked forward to it, especially with this particular customer.

Down at the cottage, Cleo sat in the porch swing trying to stay awake, watching the sea gulls over the ocean and the four-inch-long dragonflies flitting around the pine trees. The weather had turned very warm, very suddenly, and the heat was making her sleepy. A high of twenty-seven Celsius was forecast for St. John's, twenty-six for Corner Brook. She figured those out, laboriously, to be in the high eighties Fahrenheit, the weather language she spoke. Finally she could fight drowsiness no longer, and decided to stretch out for a nap. After all, she was on vacation and could take it easy. Then she had a better idea; she'd work on her suntan. What was a vacation without a suntan?

She filched a bedspread from the second, unused, bedroom and put it on the floor of the porch in a promising patch of sunshine. She took a quick look around, realized she was not visible from below the cottage, succumbed to temptation, and pulled off her tee shirt and bra. Then she lay face down on the spread with a sigh of pleasure and let herself doze off in the sun.

Max sent up a silent prayer of thanks when he climbed the steps and saw her, bare except for a pair of shorts. Damned fine back, he thought, and the legs were first rate too. His body stirred in appreciation and he leaned back against the railing, admiring the view.

The noise of his shoes on the wooden steps roused Cleo and she moved sleepily.

Unable to keep silent any longer, Max said, "Ought to charge you extra for that."

Cleo yelped in surprise and nearly sat up, but remembered the lack of upper body covering just in time. She clutched the bedspread to her bosom and said crossly, "Charge me extra for what?"

"Spreading my best coverlet on the porch floor. Why couldn't you use a towel?"

"It's not your best; it's got a patch and the edges are frayed. A towel isn't long enough. I'd get splinters."

"I'm pretty good at removing splinters," he said, grinning.

"I'll bet you are. Thanks, but no thanks." She put her head back down and turned her face away from him. She ought to feel uncomfortable, having so much of her exposed to his gaze, but she didn't. It was stimulating, knowing that he was having a good look and enjoying it. She was enjoying his admiration.

"You're getting red," Max observed. "If you get sunburned I've got a remedy for that back at the Big House. Sal down in the village makes it up for me. Tourists are always fooled by how potent Newfoundland sun is and getting themselves burned." He moved to a more comfortable position against the railing. "I'd be happy to bring some down and rub it on your back."

"Regular little Nurse Betty, aren't you," she said. "Splinter removal and sunburn treatment."

"I try to keep my guests happy."

Cleo decided she needed some face-to-face contact; a flirtatious Max was well worth a closer look. "Turn your back," she ordered. "I want to sit up."

"Going to toast the other side, are you?" he asked hopefully.

"Ha, you wish. Turn around." She gave him a moment, then, unable to check whether or not he'd turned, she took a chance on it. She gathered the bedspread awkwardly around her chest and sat up.

He was looking out at the sea. "Damn, there's that eagle back again."

"Where?" she said eagerly.

He pointed and Cleo turned.

The giant bird was circling purposefully on its enormous wings over the ocean in front of them. Suddenly it dived and came back up, a struggling fish clenched in its beak.

Together they watched it soar and head back into the forest.

"That fish is almost as big as he is," observed Max.

"Oh, wow," said Cleo dreamily. "An eagle. Think of seeing one of those."

He turned, figuring it was safe, and was treated to the sight of Cleo, eyes shining with excitement, shoulders bare except for the hair that tumbled over them, the bedspread clutched to her breasts. She looked good enough to eat, innocent and somehow knowing at the same time. He groaned with pleasure and could not keep from staring.

Cleo let the bedspread slip a little lower accidentally on purpose, and blushed.

Mouth dry, he murmured, "Looks like you've got a little sun in front, too; you're all pink. Maybe I'd better go get that lotion and give you a good rubdown."

"Maybe you'd better turn your back and let me put my tee-shirt on."

"Maybe I'd better," he mumbled, and turned away reluctantly.

Cleo rummaged around for her bra and shirt and pulled them on, not letting the bedspread drop until she was covered. "Okay, you can turn around now."

"Liked you better the other way, I did," he said.

A miniscule animal, no bigger than a kitten, scampered up the steps and posed, paws against its chest, not more than six inches from Max's feet, utterly unafraid. It bent and nosed around on the porch floor. It found something to pick up in its paws and nibbled at it vigorously.

The humans watched without a sound, Cleo storing up every detail of the animal's appearance. Its fur was a shiny golden-red and its enormous eyes were like something out of a Disney cartoon. It turned suddenly, and ran across the floor, right past Cleo, close enough to touch. Then it disappeared off the side of the porch.

"Oh, what was that? It's darling," she breathed.

"Red squirrel. Very common. They're all over the place."

"I wish I had a crust of bread for it."

"Don't feed it. It'll come back every day if you do and it'll try to get into the cottage to look for food. Damned nuisance if it gets inside."

"But it's so cute," Cleo protested.

"Won't think it's so cute if you find it nibbling your slippers some morning. Or in your bed, sitting up on your pillow, staring at you."

"I suppose if I did find it in my bed you could take care of that, too," she said.

"Suppose I could. Maybe replace it with something more your size."

At that blatant suggestion Cleo gasped and retaliated the only way she could think of. "Don't you have something else to do?"

He gave her a long, slow look, taking in every detail of her appearance, face flushed, fists clenched, nipples subtly raising the surface of the tee shirt. Several suggestions of interesting things to do occurred to him and as their eyes met he knew they were occurring to her, too.

She remembered Maria's remark from that morning. Wheeped cream and chocolate, indeed. A little smile curled her lips.

Max had to grasp the porch to keep himself from moving forward in answer to that smile. But he truly did have other things to do, lots of them, and his time for dalliance in the daytime was strictly limited. He sighed, straightened up, and headed for the porch steps. "Be seeing you," he said, and was gone, but not so quickly that he missed the little flash of disappointment on her face.

He whistled "Jack Was Every Inch a Sailor" all the way back to the Big House. Deep water, he thought. You're getting in deep water, b'y, deep as the ocean off the Cove, getting all stirred up over a mainlander who'd be gone as quickly as that eagle.

But he hungered for female companionship and sex—why not give it its proper name? He'd not had a woman since his association with Ellen had ended by mutual consent, both of them exhausted by trying to keep up a relationship separated by half of a very large island.

For a long time he'd hoped that a tasty Yum-Yum or Pitti-Sing would turn up to join the Three Peninsulas Very Light Opera Company, but that hadn't happened. He'd even toyed with the idea of moving into St. John's in the winter in the hope of finding someone who'd fall madly in love with him, enough in love to come back to the B and B and live with him. But in the end the lure of Last Man Ashore Cove and the work he had to do there in the winter always kept him at home.

He greeted Cleo with a smile when she showed up for dinner that evening. "How's your sunburn?"

"Hurts," she admitted, wiggling her shoulders.

"I can see you didn't want to wear anything that might rub against it," he said, with a glance down at her bra-less chest.

She smiled. "Maybe I'll need some of your lotion treatment after all."

"Great. When?"

"How about right now?" She gave him a sly little glance.

"Now? But I'm . . ."

"Busy. Oh, well."

"How about later?"

"Oh, it probably won't hurt, later."

Damn it, she was teasing him. She knew quite well that he couldn't leave dinner to fix itself. He was tempted, though, by the idea of getting his hands on that soft, smooth, sun-reddened back. It was the thought of having to smuggle her past Maria that gave him pause. She'd say something like, "Where you going, Boss? Ragoǔt 'bout to burn its pants off. You, too, eet looks like."

He muttered a curse, then pulled out Cleo's chair for her and without thinking guided her into it with a hand on her back.

"Ouch!" she said, and winced away.

"Sorry." He bent and whispered, "Maybe we're going to have to take time out for that treatment after all."

"But I'm hungry," she said, and looked up at him through her long eyelashes.

"What are you hungry for, Cleo?" he sighed into her ear.

"What's on offer?"

This had to stop. He could see the other diners were looking at them curiously, wondering what was going on between the host and the pretty guest. Out of the corner of his eye he saw the kitchen door open and Maria appear.

"Pssst, Boss," she hissed in an exaggerated stage whisper.

Max ground his teeth and turned back to his duties. "What?" he demanded.

"Ragoǔt 'bout to bubble over. What I do next?"

Stir it down, he thought crossly as he entered the kitchen, but he'd tried often enough to teach Maria the basics of cooking and she'd stoutly resisted learning, so that she didn't have to take on any extra responsibility, he imagined. He dished up, and he and Maria carried the plates into the diners. He served Cleo himself. "Hope this takes care of your hunger," he said.

"Not for long," and she gave him that look again with the eyelashes.

Max was beginning to think that he'd met his match, and he was enjoying every minute of it.

Chapter Ten

I came upon a charming girl and Sarah is her name.
Her parents want a husband with riches, wealth and fame.
I haven't the riches, wealth and fame; they haven't come my way,
Until I crept up to her door and through the keyhole said:
Sarah, Sarah, won't you come out tonight?
Sarah, Sarah, the moon is shining bright.
Put your cap and jacket on,
Tell your mother you won't be long,
And I'll be waiting for you 'round the corner.

"Sarah"
Newfoundland folk song

Max's thoughts were full of Cleo nowadays. She was a smart woman, he was a smart guy. Why had they never had a serious conversation? He supposed it was because it was so much fun to tease her; to watch her go on the defensive and come up with a snappy answer that would throw the challenge back at him. A verbal tennis match—that was what they were engaged in when they weren't playing verbal sexual games.

He liked that, because he could toss smart remarks off effortlessly and so could she. It didn't take much time out of his busy day. But he was beginning to think that he could throw a little more effort Cleo's way. Maybe they could become friends and that might ease their way into being lovers. Might even make it more fun being lovers.

He'd like that. Long distance relationships might be a fact of life in sparsely populated, sprawling Newfoundland but they weren't his cup of tea. If he was going to take the trouble to invest time in a relationship with a woman, he wanted her around every day, for teasing, talking and lovemaking.

Cleo was around, and she was staying at the B and B for five more weeks. Plenty of time to get to know each other. He'd like that. Maybe she would, too. There could be more than just sex and sarcasm between them. Hell, maybe he'd even get a little bit infatuated with her. That might be fun, getting silly over a woman once more. He was starved for that kind of relationship.

What was she really like? He didn't know a thing about her, really; nothing about her likes and dislikes, musical preferences, books she read, or her opinion about politics.

Work on that tomorrow, b'y, he told himself. With that idea in the back of his busy mind, he looked at Cleo with new interest when she pushed the kitchen door open next morning and stuck her head in cautiously, unsure as always of her reception but unable to stay away. He was at the table, snapping the ends off green beans in a pan.

"Busy?" she asked.

"Not too busy for you," he said, with a wide smile. "Enter my lair, princess."

Suspecting a trick, Cleo slunk in.

He coaxed, "Can I have a kiss?"

"May I have a kiss," Cleo, ever the English teacher, corrected him. "Yes, you may." She walked over and bent down to brush her lips against his cheek.

"Very nice. I enjoyed that."

Cleo went to the other side of the table and planted herself in a chair. He enjoyed a mild kiss on the cheek? What was he up to?

She looked at him suspiciously. He gave her a wide, sunny smile and suddenly could not think of anything to say.

Sarcasm and flip answers came easily; meaningful conversation did not spring up out of thin air. How should he begin? What do you think of American foreign policy? Which do you prefer, Chopin or Debussy? What's the last good book you've read?

"What's your favorite color?" he blurted.

Astonished, she stared at him. "Uhhh... pink, I guess. Or maybe lavender. Yeah, that's the one. Lavender."

"Oh, great. I like purple, myself. We're on the same wave length."

"What are you planning to do, make grape Jell-O?"

"No, I was just curious."

"Oh. Anything else you'd like to know?"

Since she asked, Max realized that there was a lot he'd like to know. They were getting somewhere, even if his opening line had been stupid. What should he ask next? "Who's your favorite composer?" he blurted.

"Classical or pop?"

"Both."

"I like Charles Ives. And Cole Porter. The Beatles, of course, and the Kinks."

"I like Gilbert and Sullivan."

"Oh. That explains your musical choice the other night."

"I sing with the Three Peninsulas Very Light Opera Company. We do a Gilbert and Sullivan production every winter. Tour it around the north of the Rock."

"You have a wonderful voice," she offered.

"Thanks." Ooops, conversational dead end. He wracked his brain for another opening. Nothing was forthcoming.

Cleo began to sense, dimly, that he was making an effort to talk to her. That was nice, she decided. What could she contribute? She hadn't had any meaningful man to woman conversations lately, and she was a little out of practice. She was willing to try, though. "Umm . . . read any good books lately?"

He hadn't, actually; he'd missed the mobile library's previous stop in Last Man Ashore Cove and had been out of reading material for three weeks. "No, I've been too busy to go to the library."

Cleo couldn't imagine being without a book to read; she usually had several going at once, scattered through different rooms of the house, from bathroom to kitchen. "Maybe you should join a mail order book club."

'That's a good idea." Stymied again, he wondered what to say next.

They stared at each other. Cleo bravely took up the torch. He wanted to talk; she'd oblige him. "Tell me how you got started running a B and B in the heart of Newfoundland."

Max relaxed. She'd hit upon something he could talk about. "It was a family business, to begin with. My dad, my mother, and her brother John bought the B and B when Dad and Uncle John got laid off from the fishing fleet after the cod-fishing moratorium was imposed in 1992. The place was kind of run-down, and we all worked to fix it up and get it going again. The three of them ran it while I was in college, and I came here in the summers to work. Dad and Uncle John kept hoping they could go back to fishing, but when it became clear the cod weren't coming back and the moratorium wasn't going to be lifted, my parents sold their interest to Uncle John and retired to Florida.

"He ran the B and B until he got cancer. I came back from Nova Scotia to help him out and he left me the business in his will. It was his way of making sure I stayed in Newfoundland." Funny, Max thought, how both his life to date and his future could be summed up in so few words.

"That was nice of you to come and help. I imagine you gave up all kinds of opportunities to come back here."

He shrugged. "I like being here. I like cooking and here I can cook whatever I want, no chef or manager to tell me what to do, and I can run the B and B the way I please. I'm the boss." He said, "Your turn. Tell me about yourself."

Cleo obliged, and talked about her work as a teacher. By the time Maria came in to help with dinner prep, Max and Cleo had made awkward progress in getting to know each other.

Chapter Eleven

Eat, drink and be gay,
Banish all worry and sorrow,
Laugh gaily today,
Weep, if you're sorry, tomorrow!

The Sorcerer, Gilbert and Sullivan

Tonight Max was having a really good time at evening meal service. The roomful of diners had purred like kittens when he'd set the plates of steak *au poivre* or chicken fricassee in front of them. It was a reaction any chef would adore.

And back in the kitchen he had Cleo, who'd turned up early for dinner, inserted herself into dinner prep and was now working cheek by jowl with Maria, washing lettuce while the other woman made salads. She was practicing her Spanish at the same time, laughing with Maria whenever she made a mistake. It gave him a warm and cozy feeling, listening to the two women babbling companionably, and Cleo's latest tiny little outfit was giving him a warm and not in the least cozy feeling below the waistline of his jeans, despite his preoccupation with cooking.

His happiness was rudely dispelled when Mr. Number Eight appeared at the kitchen door. "Talk to you a minute, Mr. Avalon?" he said. "My son hates his dinner. Could he have something else?"

Taken aback, Max stared at him. He remembered the child in question. Seven years old, freckle-faced and redheaded, a kid with trouble written all over him. He had looked perfectly delighted when his steak *au poivre* was set in front of him. "What's wrong with his meal?"

"It has pepper on the meat. Eddie hates pepper."

Hell, he should have known better than to waste gourmet cooking on a kid. "Well, why don't you go back to the table and enjoy your meal, and I'll see what I can rustle up." Maybe a vat or two of Sugar Soaked Dinosaurs, Max thought bitterly, remembering how little Eddie had ignored his bacon, eggs and truly excellent crowberry muffins at breakfast. Instead he'd emptied several highly sweetened cereal packets, then spent the next hour buzzed up on sugar, zig-zagging furiously through Max's prized garden pretending he was a satellite orbiting Mars, nearly trampling the lettuce and spinach to little green tatters. He had sent Maria out to shoo the kid out of the garden in her garbled English; he'd been afraid he'd commit infanticide if he'd had to deal with him.

"Thanks," said Number Eight gratefully. "Margo and I think our dinners are amazing, by the way. But you know kids." Chuckling, he left.

Max did, and wished he had enough money and guts to declare Last Man Ashore a childfree zone. Tots were nothing but aggro and the older they got the more aggravating they got.

Cleo had overheard the discussion. She said, "Got any hamburger?"

"Why?"

"Kids love hamburger."

Maria whisked a package out of the fridge. "*Esta aqui.*"

"That's mooseburger, Maria," said Max patiently.

Cleo grinned. "Kid won't know the difference, if you serve it with lots of catsup. You have catsup, don't you?"

"Yes. Some morons like to ruin my hash browns with it."

"Wicked. Got any French fries?"

"I have potatoes, but it would take twenty minutes to get the fryer heated."

She shook her head. "Nah, I mean the frozen ones. Run them under the broiler for five minutes, give 'em a shake and lots of salt and you're all set to serve."

Max swelled up in indignation. "Why would I have those unspeakable plastic monstrosities in my kitchen?"

"They here, Boss. I hide in back of freezer," offered Maria.

Both women thought Max might explode. "What the hell . . . ?"

"Ees for emergencies, eef you run out of potatoes."

"Potatoes are grown in Last Man Ashore Cove, you Spanish lunatic. I could walk out the door and go down the road and dig up bushels."

Maria tossed her head. "Eef you don' want my help, you say eet an' I leave."

Cleo gave the housekeeper a big smile. "*Está bien, amiga.* Hand me a frying pan, light the broiler, Maxie, and get out of my way. If there's one thing I know how to cook, it's mooseburger and frozen French fries."

Max turned so pale they thought he might faint. "Sweet Mother of God, I've got a woman in my kitchen who thinks defrosting dead potato slabs is cooking."

"Outside, Max," said Cleo patiently. "Go into the dining room and chat up the customers. Try not to assault any of them. Smile. You know how to smile, don't you? Just open your mouth and bare your teeth."

After he had gone, muttering, Cleo fried a mooseburger and Maria broiled French fries. They slathered catsup liberally on the burger and garnished the whole works with parsley, so the kid could push it aside and his mom could pretend he was eating a vegetable.

Maria looked at the plate dubiously. "Ees 'orrible. No ees food. Even I know that and I no cook."

"I'd better take it in," Cleo said. "If Max sees it he'll go berserk." She picked up the plate and whisked it deftly out of sight as she slithered by Max, who was just re-entering the kitchen.

He turned and stared after her, noting her shapely behind in yet another short tight skirt, this one red, splashed with large yellow flowers. He'd taken careful note of her skirts; they seemed to be getting shorter every day. She must have brought dozens of them with her, he thought, bemused. And why not? They certainly wouldn't take up much room in a suitcase.

Cleo waltzed over to Number Eight's table and plopped the plate down in front of little Eddie, who glared first at it, then at her.

"What's this?" he demanded belligerently.

"Burger and fries, kid, just like at Wendy's." Then, to divert everyone's attention from the plate she grabbed a chair from the next table and plopped herself into it. "I don't think we've met. I'm Cleo. I'm a schoolteacher by trade."

"Yuck," said Eddie.

Eddie's mother began to sputter an apology but Cleo shook her head and leaned close to the boy. "Know what I think when I see a kid? Yuckedee-yuck-yuck-yuck."

The parental units looked alarmed but Eddie giggled.

Cleo knew that Mother Margo was about to urge her son to just taste the lovely meal the nice lady had prepared especially for him and that Eddie would react by pushing it away, just to be contrary. She forestalled that by saying, "Hey, Eddie, I'll bet you like school. What's your favorite subject?"

As Cleo had anticipated, like any child his age Eddie would rather die than tell anyone he liked anything about school. He picked up the burger sullenly and took a careful bite.

"More catsup?" Cleo fished the bottle out of her skirt pocket.

Eddie seized it and poured catsup over the fries.

Both parents were watching their son anxiously, awaiting his verdict on the substitute meal. Cleo sighed to herself. Ignore the kid for once, why don't you, she thought; he was on his way to being ruined by constant doting attention. She said brightly to the adults, "I'm from Minnesota. Where are you folks from?"

"Manitoba. Winnipeg."

"Wow, that's just five hundred miles north of where I live. Sure gets cold there in winter, doesn't it? Even colder than in Minnesota." She babbled on, watching Eddie out of the corner of her eye. The mooseburger was half eaten, and he'd started on the fries, stuffing them into his mouth four at a time. "What brings you to Newfoundland?"

"Family holiday," said Mr. Number Eight.

"How about you?" said Margo. "You've come a long way for a summer job."

"Oh, I don't work here, I'm a guest, just helping out tonight. Favor for a friend."

Margo grinned slyly. "I see. Well, I don't blame you. He's very attractive."

On the brink of denying any such devious female stratagems on her part, Cleo abruptly gave in. "Yeah, he's some cute," she said, and winked at Margo, woman to woman. Both smiled serenely, sharing a moment of female bonding.

In the absence of parental attention, Eddie had cleaned his plate. Cleo snatched it up, pocketed the ketchup, rose and turned to leave. "See ya, folks," she said brightly and scampered back to the kitchen to face Max's scowl.

"You realize, don't you," he began, "that if word gets out that I've served frozen French fries my reputation as a gourmet cook will be utterly destroyed."

"Lighten oop, Boss," said Maria.

Max looked from one woman to the other and surrendered to the inevitable. "Okay. But I'm making a note of Number Eight's name and they and that little monster are banned for life."

"Oh, I don't know," Cleo said thoughtfully. "Kids change quickly and he's only about seven. Next year he'll probably be a perfect little gentleman, holding the chair for his mom, eating everything you put before him, and asking politely for seconds."

Max said crossly, "Child psychology doesn't clear the tables and wash the dishes. Snap to it, Maria."

Later, after Maria had left and Max was in the dining room setting tables for breakfast, Cleo started washing the dirty wine glasses by hand, just for an excuse to hang around. On a whim, pretending that he was a chef at a really posh hotel, he had used his best glasses for his guests tonight, and he refused to put them in the dishwasher because the detergent would ruin them. The glasses were lovely crystal with a pattern of little thistles.

He came back into the kitchen. "You don't have to wash those. I'll do them."

"Nah, I don't mind. I like to play in hot soapy water."

For some reason that remark struck Max as having a definite sexual connotation. Maybe he was thinking about helping her out with her shower again. He came to stand very close behind her, so close that she could hear his soft breathing.

"You watching to make sure I wash them all right?"

"No." He hooked a finger in the knot of hair at the nape of her neck and worked it loose so the shiny brown locks spilled over her shoulders. He put his hands on her hips and smoothed them over the tight skirt. "I was wondering why you wear such sexy clothes."

His hands were hotter than the dishwater and she could feel his breath on her neck. "I'm a schoolteacher. Nine months of the year I have to dress like a nun. When summer comes I like to let it all hang out. Especially here, when I'm thousands of miles away from real life. What's the problem? You don't like my clothes?"

"I love your clothes, you little tart. I'd like them better if they were hanging on the back of a chair in my bedroom."

Cleo wiggled enticingly. "Whatever do you mean, Mr. Avalon?"

His hands moved higher. "Just what you think I mean. God, you've got a nice shape, even if you are too skinny. My hands almost meet around your waist."

"Call me Scarlett O'Hara, without the corset."

He growled, "I'd like to see you in a corset, and nothing else, except maybe long black stockings and stiletto heels." He kissed the side of her throat and was pleased to feel her shiver. "You've been nice to me tonight, what with little Eddie and washing glasses and stuff. I'm going to be nice to you now." His hands crept up over her ribcage. "Okay if I do this?" he whispered in her ear as he reached the bottoms of her breasts and curved his fingers upwards.

"Ees hokay." She leaned back against him. It was very sensuous, the way he was worshipping her body, and she was turned on by his leisurely approach. Nice to be seduced once again by an attractive, intelligent man who knew and cared about what a woman enjoyed. She relaxed against him, waiting for his next move.

Max was very glad he'd spent time yesterday digging his stash of condoms out from the bureau drawer where they'd lain undisturbed for two years. He'd moved them to the top drawer of the nightstand by his bed. He'd lusted after Number Nine for what seemed like eons, egged on by a few hot kisses, and now he was going to get lucky at last. Throwing caution aside, he let himself do what he'd been wanting to do.

His hands dropped to the bottom of her shirt and began to inch it upwards until he reached her bra. He buried his face against her neck while his hands encircled her breasts. "Ummm, nice. Just a little wisp of lace."

"I like lacy underwear."

"I'll bet you do, you vixen." He wiggled his fingers under the elastic so that he could feel the soft warm skin and the sweet curve of her breasts. He hadn't had his hands inside a woman's bra in well over two years and he was really enjoying himself.

Cleo cooed and pressed herself back against him. At last, things were heating up, and she didn't think this interlude would end in kisses alone.

"Does this unfasten in the back or the front?" he said, pulling on the bra.

"I don't remember. You'll have to look for it."

"Damn right, I will! Hmmm . . . it's not here, so it must be here." With a quick twist of his wrist, he unhooked the bra and her breasts spilled into his hands. "You are magnificently endowed, you luscious creature."

"They're kinda small," she said, enjoying his caressing fingers.

"I'm not complaining." He squeezed her breasts, licked her throat, and then kissed his way upward to nibble on her ear. She wiggled and moaned.

"I do believe you're hot for me, Ms English."

"I do believe you're right, Mr. Avalon. What do you suggest we do about it?"

"My apartment's right across the hall," he said. "I've got a king-size bed and a nice firm mattress. And a shower big enough for two." He bit her earlobe sharply.

Cleo purred.

Max stopped his explorations abruptly, hearing loud voices, male and female, in the dining room and heading for the kitchen. He pulled his hands free, yanked her shirt down in one quick motion, and strode towards the door, cursing. He turned around and said, "Don't move, and don't forget where we left off. I'll be right back."

"I'll finish washing the glasses," said Cleo happily.

But they were both doomed to disappointment. He came back into the kitchen a few minutes later, his expression gloomy. "Mrs. Number Six has dropped a diamond earring into the bathroom sink drain. Why was the silly bitch wearing diamonds in a Newfoundland B and B? I've got to take the pipe apart to retrieve it and pray it hasn't already washed down into Last Man Ashore Cove."

"Oh, hell. How long will it take?"

"That's the problem. Not only do I have to take it apart, I have to put it back together and mop up any mess I make. And straighten out the legal complications if I can't retrieve the earring.

It'll take hours. You'd better go back to your cottage. One of us may as well get some sleep."

Horribly disappointed, she stared at him. "Rats!"

"Yeah, I can't even take the time to walk you home. Time enough for this, though," and with a lightning move, he came close enough to sweep her into his arms and kiss her, running his hands up and down her bare back under the tee shirt.

His mouth could scorch paint off a wall, she thought, dazed. "I'm going to make a little voodoo doll of Mrs. Number Six, and spend the night sticking pins in it."

"Stick a dozen in it for me." He found the ends of her bra and hooked them together. "See you tomorrow, sexy."

"Nighty night, hot lips. Happy plumbing."

After he'd gone, Cleo sighed and turned to leave. Her glance fell on the mouse crouching by the side of the refrigerator. Her gaze sharpened. Surely the animal seemed fatter. "Oh, my God, you've gotten yourself knocked up. You're in trouble, Ms Mouse. Just couldn't say no, could you. I know how you feel. Only you got lucky, and I didn't."

She turned off the kitchen light. She made her way through the dark Big House and down the path to Squashberry Cottage and her cold bed, singing softly to herself, "I can't get no satisfaction," until she forgot the words.

Chapter Twelve

Hearts do not break!
They sting and ache
For old love's sake,
But do not die.
Though with each breath,
They long for death...

The Mikado, Gilbert and Sullivan

Cleo awoke the next morning to find her cheeks and her pillow wet. She had been crying in her sleep again. After a few moments, she remembered why. She had had her recurrent dream that she was an old woman living in a tiny apartment with only three cats to keep her company, a Siamese, a brown tabby and a calico. She was bent with painful arthritis, there was no one to help her out by taking her to the grocery store and she and the cats were desperate with hunger. The cats were crying too, long pitiful wails.

It was a dream about her deepest fear, that she would never again find love and would live the rest of her life alone. It wasn't one of her terrible, mad nightmares; it was just a sad fact of her existence since Charlie's death.

She could remember the apartment in the dream very well. It was a lost old lady's apartment, a place for the forlorn and the poor. Its kitchen was barely big enough to turn around in. The stovetop was stained, the burners were rusty, and the sink stood unsteadily on three legs. In the bathroom, the sink and toilet bowl were both cracked. The bedroom held a single, institutional style iron bedstead and an elderly dresser. The rest of the apartment was furnished with the ugly overstuffed furniture, now stained and threadbare, from the first apartment she'd shared with Charlie.

The dream apartment was obsessively neat. In the single cupboard over the sink, glasses were lined up like soldiers guarding the chipped china plates and cups. In the beat-up bedroom dresser her tattered underwear and sweaters were folded into precise piles, and in the closet three blouses, four skirts and a ratty jacket were organized with all of the hanger hooks facing the same way.

Cleo had always been a compulsively tidy person and it had meant a running battle with Charlie who was the exact opposite. He did not mean to bring disorder into her life; he simply could not help it. When he remembered to hang up his clothes, they fell off the hangers. When he emptied his pockets of change, coins always fell, unnoticed, to the floor and stayed there to cause a terrifying racket when Cleo, unsuspecting, ran the vacuum cleaner over the carpet.

Charlie, so kind and gentle, so sweet and caring, never, ever, meant to cause her extra work. If scolded, he would look ashamed and scurry around organizing his books and papers, picking up his piles of things, and stuffing clothes in the hamper. Then he would wrap his arms around her while she stood rigid in anger and nuzzle her neck, whispering soft apologies until she broke down and whispered her forgiveness.

She had often thought that he would have been absolutely perfect if only he had the slightest feeling for organization, order and neatness. It was virtually the only thing on which they disagreed. But who wanted a man who was perfect, anyway?

The day Charlie died, she walked back into her apartment and found it was exactly as she had left it three days before to sleep on a cot in his room as he neared the end. While he'd been in the hospice, she'd become even more obsessively tidy, straightening up the apartment every night before she went to bed, never leaving dishes unwashed in the sink, dusting every day.

The place was so clean it shone. There was no man's jacket draped over the dining room chair. No man's undershirt on the floor by the bed. No wet towel draped over the edge of the bathtub.

No Charlie.

He would never again leave a carton of milk to spoil on the table overnight, never again forget to wipe the whiskers off the bathroom sink, never again have to be nagged to hang up his clothes.

It had broken her. She'd gone to bed and cried for two days, getting up only when she heard her mother-in-law's urgent voice on the answering machine, telling her about the funeral arrangements she had made.

Now, on her vacation, three years later, she was having the same terrifying dreams of abandonment. They made her desperately anxious. What was happening to her? Perhaps this time she really was going insane.

She fought back against the fear and anxiety, and began to fixate on what had saved her the first time around: sex. She needed sex and Max Avalon was the obvious candidate. She hadn't had sex for ages, hadn't met a man she'd wanted. But there was no question in her mind that she wanted Max. Call it a summer fling, call it lust, he was gorgeous and hot and clever with his hands and she wanted him.

She wanted him and she was going to have him and he was going to save her from the nightmare.

Dressed to seduce in a midriff-baring top and her shortest, tightest skirt, she sauntered up to the Big House after breakfast and found Max deep in conversation with a tall curvy redhead and a short wiry blonde woman who had just checked in. Max seemed particularly attentive to them, as though they were old friends.

Cleo had always wanted to be a tall curvy redhead and having plain brown hair and what she perceived as a dearth of curves put her at a distinct disadvantage in her pursuit of Max's undivided attention, or so she thought. She eyed the two newcomers suspiciously, and hung around until they disappeared with him up to their room. She waited for him to return, and, plans for seduction foiled, stalked angrily off to her cottage when he didn't reappear after thirty minutes.

She didn't get another crack at him that day or the next. He was spending way too much time with Red and her pal, in Cleo's opinion, and it ate away at her soul to come into the Big House and find the three of them in the kitchen, heads bent over a map, planning the women's excursions for the day. Or she'd come up in the afternoon and find them all sitting on the big front porch having drinks and laughing. In both instances, she had turned and stalked away.

After a while she grew tired of it and sulked in her cottage.

Max wondered where she was and wanted desperately for her to appear on the scene in a short skirt and tight tee, eyeing him provocatively. They'd made good progress towards bed in the last few days and he was eager to take up where they'd left off. The dishwashing cuddle had stirred up every needy fiber in his body, and his dreams had taken a decidedly lustful and very enjoyable turn.

But he didn't have the time to go looking for her because he had a full house of unusually demanding guests occupying all his mental and physical energy. The two couples in Number Five were vegetarians, a concept which Maria pretended she didn't understand, and she kept trying to sneak chicken or beef bouillon cubes into the veggie soups and stews Max carefully prepared for them using his homemade herbal concoctions. "Is for flavor," she insisted. "Is nasty without."

Number Two's young baby had decided to cut a tooth, screamed all night and slept all day, so that his parents appeared chronically late for breakfast, upsetting the carefully paced routine of the Big House.

And Number Three was the type all B and B owners dread. He was an overweight New Yorker about forty-five, and he didn't like anything about Newfoundland ("too much scenery"), Last Man Ashore Cove ("too many waves"), and the B and B ("too many people and the food's too fancy").

All in all, Max had his hands full and longed crossly for Cleo to show up to brighten his mood and arouse his body.

In the bad, mad, sex-mad days after Charlie's death, when it seemed that passion was the only thing that reminded her she wasn't in the grave with him, one of the men Cleo had been with had proposed a *menage à trois* with a friend of his. She refused haughtily but graphic images of what might have been haunted her dreams for weeks.

Now she was being seared with jealousy at the idea of a threesome consisting of Max, the luscious redhead, and her wiry companion indulging themselves in one of the B and B's queen-sized beds. What the hell do you care? she asked herself angrily as she lounged on the Big House porch in the morning, waiting for Max with the cruel intensity of a stalking leopard. But she knew she cared; she hadn't seen him for two days, and couldn't stand the separation any longer. She'd been right on the brink of capturing him, and now he had wriggled away into the clutches of two other women. They hadn't invested the time and energy in Max Avalon that she had, and they didn't deserve to reap the benefits. It wasn't fair.

It was time to fight back using all her weapons of provocative clothing and sexy behavior. She needed what Max Avalon could provide and she was going to get him back or die of frustration trying.

He came out of the B and B at last, escorted by the redhead and the skinny one. Talking and laughing, whisking by Cleo as though she were invisible, the three swept across the porch and down to a waiting car.

She watched, full of thwarted fury, as he kissed first one, then the other, on the cheek, and loaded their luggage into the car's back seat.

When he started up the steps, he stopped in delighted surprise to see Cleo there. At last, he thought; and he actually had a window of opportunity this early in the afternoon to pursue her seduction. "Good day," he said in what he imagined to be a sexy voice, and he strolled across the porch to sit down by her on the wooden bench. "Long time no see."

He was close enough to touch. She gave him a veiled look full of dark suspicion and jealousy, tilted her nose in the air so high she got a kink in her neck, and stared off across the sea. "Hi."

Max wondered what was wrong with her. He knew what was wrong with him: petting her in the kitchen the other night had ignited the fires of hell in his body. He made it a rule not to get sexually involved with the clientele; it led to messy, unpleasant partings. But he burned for Cleo, really burned. It was pleasant and unpleasant by turns and right now was one of the pleasant times, when he felt himself minutes away from success.

"Losing a couple of guests, I see," she said at last.

Max was puzzled by the intonation in her voice. "Yeah, they're off to St. John's for a few days, then taking the ferry to Cape Breton Island."

"Nice girls?" she said nastily, visualizing the three of them rolling together, the redhead's glorious hair spilling over Max's muscular bare shoulder, the wiry one's glasses askew on her face.

"They're sweet kids, very nice. I was at MUN—Memorial University, that is—with Andrea, the redhead." He stretched lazily. "They're on their honeymoon."

"Huh?" Cleo straightened up and stared at him.

"Married in Toronto last week." Meeting her blank look he added, "It's legal in Canada." When she still looked baffled he explained patiently, "For gay couples to marry." She looked shocked. He wondered whether she was one of those righteous types who disapproved of gay relationships, and he had enough gay friends to resent that. He stared at her belligerently.

"They're . . ."

"Lesbians. You got a problem with that?"

She stared at him as though she'd just awakened from a dream. Oh, boy, how dumb could she be? She went red with embarrassment, remembering her wicked suspicions. Thank God, he couldn't read her mind.

"No. No, of course not." She jumped to her feet. "Be seeing you," she blurted, and stumbled down the steps back to her cottage, leaving Max bewildered.

What was the matter with her? Why was she playing hard to get? She'd seemed willing enough the last time he'd had a chance to pursue the issue with her. He'd been about to make a move but she'd left before he could set it up.

Rats! He got up reluctantly and wandered into his kitchen to bake brownies for tonight's dessert. Women were a puzzle, but at least cooking held no mysteries for him.

Chapter Thirteen

When Sunrays crown thy pine-clad hills,
And Summer spreads her hand,
When silvern voices tune thy rills,
We love thee smiling land,
We love thee, we love thee, we love thee, smiling land.

"Ode to Newfoundland"
Sir Cavendish Boyle

Cleo's chagrin lasted through the afternoon, until the thought of Max's cooking brought her out of her chastened mood and up to the Big House for dinner. It was not as if she had to apologize, she thought; he had no way of knowing about her evil suspicions. She would just sashay in and offer to help with dinner prep just as if everything had always been normal. She waltzed into the kitchen, a big "Hello" poised on her lips, but the room was empty.

A figure stepped out of the pantry carrying a basket full of cleaning supplies. She was a woman of indeterminate but advanced age, wearing a flowered blouse and skirt and a varied collection of sweaters. Her gray hair was curled into a knot skewered firmly on top of her head.

"Hi!" said Cleo. "I'm looking for Max."

"Yer not the first and ye'll not be the last," said the woman enigmatically. She looked Cleo up and down. "Dressed fer it, ye are."

Cleo interpreted that correctly as a comment on the length of her skirt and the tightness of her tee shirt and was annoyed to feel herself blushing. She snapped, "Where's Max?"

"'E's gone athirt 'is garten," said the woman, turning away.

Cleo was puzzling out that remark when Max came in, his hands full of carrots and turnips. "Hello, Mrs. Hoh, how are you today?"

"H'oh, h'I'm well, considerin.'" She jerked her head towards Cleo. "Yer doxy's lookin' fer ye."

"Well, really," said Cleo indignantly, but Max shook his head and grinned. "She's a guest, Mrs. Hoh; she's not my doxy."

"Not yet," snapped the old woman. "But she's thinkin' h'about it, fer she's 'ardly got a screed on 'er. Mind, ye could do worse, fer she's right clever-lookin.'" To Cleo she said, "H'I'll bet ye get h'up to all manner of shinanigin', don't ye, maid."

Cleo looked at Max helplessly, unsure of how to answer. Damn him, she thought; he was enjoying seeing her at a loss for words. It hadn't happened very often since they'd known each other. She said primly, "Of course not. I'm a schoolteacher."

"Mrs. Hoh, this is Cleo English," said Max. "Cleo, Mrs. O'Herlihy."

"You never says it right, Max, it's *H'oh*-er-li-ee."

"Hence Mrs. Hoh," said Max in an aside to Cleo.

Mrs. Hoh snapped, "Ye a marrit woman, maid?"

"I'm a widow," said Cleo.

"So'm h'I, twice over. First man was a fisherman an' 'e was lost at sea. Second took a 'eart h'attack and died on me. Third one just took h'off, and 'asn't been seen for h'eight years. H'I've given h'up on 'im, h'I 'as. Don't care h'if 'e comes back or not." She eyed Cleo. "Yer young h'enough to get yerself another man, maid."

"If I wanted one," said Cleo haughtily.

"Ye will, maid, ye will. H'every little dory wants a safe 'arbor fer the winter. Try yer luck with that laddio there," she said, indicating Max with a nod of her head. "He's no angishore an' 'e can't be jammed. 'E spent h'a lot of time on the mainland but 'e come back 'ome to the Rock where 'e belongs."

She bestowed an approving look on Max, then winked at Cleo. "But don't be countin' yer fish while yer still castin' yer line. 'E might just nibble at the bait and not take it. Well, h'I can't be standin' 'ere h'all morning talkin' balderdash; h'I've got me toilets to clean. H'I'll be h'off." She picked up her basket of cleaning supplies and stomped out the back door of the kitchen.

"Where is she from, to talk like that?" wondered Cleo.

"Oh, she's a liveyer, just like me. She's a charter member of LOLA."

"What?"

"LOLA, short for Let Our Language Live, started by a bunch of kids at MUN. Although it should properly be LODA, for Let Our Dialect live. Newfoundland English is a dialect, not a language. Mrs. Hoh likes to talk the way her parents did, keeping the old lingo alive, so she's a rare gem and the pride of LOLA."

"She sounds sort of Irish."

"You should have heard her third husband, Mr. Hoh. He sounded like you'd imagine a leprechaun would. He was from the Irish Loop, down south on the Avalon Peninsula. It was settled by Irish people and folks there have an Irish accent to this day."

"The Avalon Peninsula . . . named for your family, I suppose?"

"T'other way 'round, maid, as Mrs. Hoh might say. Sit down and have a cup of coffee, and I'll tell you a story."

When she had a steaming cup and two chocolate frosted brownies in front of her, he began. "One of the first permanent settlements in Newfoundland was in the early 1600's at what's now Ferryland on the Avalon Peninsula. It was financed by George Calvert, whom you'd know as Lord Baltimore. He founded your state of Maryland. He was quite an ambitious man. He wanted to start a new colony, rule it for King Charles I, and make it a safe place for Catholics to live, because it was a period of Catholic-Puritan strife in England. He named his colony after Avalon, King Arthur's final resting place. You know about that?"

"Of course. I'm an English teacher. I teach *Le Morte d'Arthur* to my junior classes."

"Right. Well, the colony was doing very well when Calvert came to live there, but his wife was delicate and couldn't stand the winters, so they went back to England. The colony kept going, run by another guy named Sir David Kirke. But it was attacked and burnt, first by the Dutch and next by the French who were contesting English control of the island. Then Lord Baltimore's people disputed Kirke's rule of Avalon and he was thrown in jail in England and died there.

"My people were from Cornwall, the Celtic county on the southwest tip of England, fishermen who were in the first batch of settlers. Our original name was Coffeyn, which is a very old Cornish name.

"Kirke was a harsh master. He took a huge share of whatever the fishermen earned for their catch. My folks got sick of it and moved up the coast to what became St. John's. At some point they struck off cross-country until they got to Last Man Ashore Cove and settled here. They added 'Avalon' to the family name to show that they were part of the original settlement of Newfoundland. And maybe so they could hide out if they'd been up to shady business."

Cleo, remembering something she'd been curious about, asked, "Where did the name Last Man Ashore Cove come from?"

Max laughed. "The place was called Brown's Cove until a whaler wrecked on the Devil's Fangs, those big sunkers just off-shore. The sea was very high the night of the wreck, and it was thought all on board the whaler had been lost, until the next day when a sailor washed up on the shore. He'd been clinging to a bit of wreckage, and by some miracle he hadn't frozen to death in the sea. Folks started telling the amazing story about the last man ashore, the survivor of the icy waves. So Brown's Cove gradually became to be known as Last Man Ashore Cove."

He added, "Newfoundland is full of interesting historical places you'd enjoy visiting. They're doing an archaeological dig at Ferryland and have uncovered a million artifacts so far. It's fascinating. You should go down and take a look someday."

"There's a lot here I'd like to see. Wish I had more time."

"Eight weeks isn't enough, is it. You'll have to come back again."

"Maybe I will," said Cleo thoughtfully.

Max grinned at her. "I'd like that, maid."

Chapter Fourteen

Oh! My name is John Wellington Wells,
I'm a dealer in magic and spells,
In blessings and curses
And ever-filled purses,
In prophecies, witches and knells.

The Sorcerer, Gilbert and Sullivan

Wild Ernie showed up at the back door of the Big House the next day with a string of two of the most delectable-looking speckled trout Max had seen in some time. Wild Ernie was six foot five inches of hair, beard and muscle and he had gotten his nickname not because of any disposition towards violent behavior, but because he was devoted to the preservation of the flora and fauna of the Rock's wilderness. He lived in a tin-roof shack hidden in the heart of Gros Morne National Park where he could keep an eye on everything that gurgled, rippled or slunk through the forest.

He knew every trout stream in his part of Newfoundland, and made it his personal responsibility to see that the trout population was kept in a healthy balance. He didn't think the government's Fisheries and Oceans people had a clue, so when he decided a particular stream's fish population needed thinning, he took action regardless of whatever fishing regulations were currently in force.

He liked Max's warped sense of humor, his blueberry pancakes, and his willingness to pay for a nice bit of fish without asking questions, so Max always got first dibs on whatever finny treat turned up on the end of his line.

Whenever Wild Ernie appeared, Max got out the pancake griddle, mixing bowls, and whatever berries were in season without a moment's thought, even if it meant giving the paying clientele the bum's rush for the nonce.

Now he stood leaning against the sink, arms folded, pancake flipper in easy reach, watching the enormous, stolid woodsman steadily demolishing lashin's of gandies and a dozen links of home-made moose sausage. He enjoyed watching a man with a hearty appetite eat his cooking, and Wild Ernie ate with fierce concentration and a daintiness unusual in a man so large.

Finally Ernie fastidiously wiped the grizzled beard that covered most of his face and stood up. "Good grub, b'y," he said, as he always did.

Max placed a number of loonies and twoonies in the out-stretched hand, said "Be seeing you," and his gigantic guest lumbered out the back door.

Max looked at his prizes and licked his lips in appreciation. Baked, he decided, with an herb stuffing. No, on second thought, these plump, stream-fresh little babies didn't need anything added to dilute their flavor. Split, rolled in crumbs with salt and pepper, fried in hot olive oil with a lump of butter for flavor; that was the ticket. Roasted potatoes on the side and green beans from his garden.

But there were only two trout and he had seven guests. An evil plan took shape in his cunning brain. Time for a little wheeling and dealing. He dialed up Hans Argetsinger, proprietor of Hans' Edelweiss Café, down the road from the B and B. Hans was

German and had come to Newfoundland a few years ago, determined to inflict the delights of sauerkraut and sauerbraten on an unsuspecting clientele innocent of German cooking.

Max had attended his restaurant's opening and had consumed enough cabbage to expand his trousers two sizes. He'd taken a course in gourmet German cooking (an oxymoron if there ever was one) in Halifax a few years ago, and knew that there were other permissible ingredients besides sour cabbage and bratwurst.

He wanted the restaurant to succeed, both because he wanted to help out a fellow entrepreneur and because it meant another place to get rid of dinner customers when he didn't want to be bothered with them. So he made friends with Hans and laid it on the line. "Lose the cabbage and the brats," he said. "Newfoundlanders and tourists have daintier appetites. Have you ever cooked rabbit in morel sauce *mit* spinach noodles?"

Hans had been contemplating adding his favorite dish, hamburger eel soup, to the menu and maybe *zwiebelkuchen*—onion pie—but he was not adverse to *das Hase*—hare. He did it roasted whole, smothered in gravy.

"*Nein, nein,*" said Max, when Hans mentioned that method of preparation. "Think dainty. Sauté the rabbit pieces in herbed olive oil, then simmer them in a delicate cream sauce with mushrooms added. *Hassenpfeffer*, only lighter."

Hans's moustache twitched, a sign that he was thinking hard. "*Und* vhat else you suggest?"

"Maybe veal with asparagus..."

"*Ja, ja, das Bayerisches Kalbfleisch mit Spargel. Sehr gut. Und das Kohlrouladen* on the side."

"*Gott im Himmel,*" said Max. "*Nichts mit das kohl.* I said, lose the cabbage. Do a nice beef *rouladen as* a main dish. Same idea, only chunks of steak instead of ground pork and cabbage. More *nouvelle* that way. What have you got for casseroles?"

"Ah," said Hans, and if he had been French he would have kissed his fingertips in ecstasy. "Is my specialty. *Apfel Quarkauflauf Mit Mandelkruste.*"

Max couldn't help wondering why German food always sounded as heavy as it tasted. "What's that when it's at home in Newfoundland, b'y?"

"Apple Cheese Casserole with Almond Crust."

Max felt his mouth water. "Now you're talking. Does it have any cabbage in it?"

"Vhat, you crazy? Is *nichts kohl,* is *apfel.*"

In the end, Max volunteered to spend a few Monday afternoons in Hans' kitchen when the restaurant was closed, helping him to work up *nouvelle* recipes for dainty Newfoundland appetites. It took time he didn't have, but it paid off: the restaurant succeeded and he'd made a friend for life out of Hans.

So he dialed up his pal. "Hey, Hans, vhat's on the menu tonight? I've got seven mouths to send you. Turgeson's has free-range chickens on sale. Can you do something *nouvellle mit* them?"

"*Ja,* I make a dainty chicken dish for your customers. Vhat else you vant?"

"A special price, to lure them in. *Und der Apfel Quarkpluf* for dessert."

"Is *Apfel Quarkauflauf, dümmling,* and is not dessert. Is casserole."

"*Ja,* vhatever. Price?"

"For your customers, $16.95 a head."

"*Sehr gut.* I send them over at six, *nicht wahr?* Throw in a couple of bottles of Blue Nun, with my discount."

"*Nein,* I don't buy that *Deutsch* stuff anymore. Got a deal on Nova Scotia wine."

Good one, b'y. Hans was finally becoming acclimated to the Maritime Provinces, Max thought as he hung up. He contemplated the trout. Hmmm, reverse tactics: use the fish as bait for a dainty little morsel he was hoping to gobble up. Humming his favorite patter song from *The Sorcerer*, he began to assemble ingredients for a fish fry.

When Cleo tripped in that afternoon, looking sexy and hopeful, he cast his spell. "Do you like fresh trout?"

A hungry look appeared on that kitten face. Fresh fish, prepared with Max's sure touch on the frying pan. "Ya, sure, you betcha, as we say in Minnesota. Pan-fried?"

"You got it. Your place, about six?"

"No dinner customers tonight?"

"Nah, I off-loaded them onto a pal of mine."

"Wicked. See you later." She sashayed out.

Wicked was the operative word for what he had in mind. Max smiled, and sang quietly to himself, "'I've a first-rate assortment of magic . . . love-philtre, I've quantities of it . . .'" Trout for a love-philtre. What a concept!

Cleo, sensing a showdown approaching at last, took special care with her *toilette* that afternoon. Shower, shampoo, shaving, dabs of perfume discreetly applied in appropriate areas, and a certain clingy top with "Princess" embroidered in sparkly letters across the front. And no bra. Definitely no bra.

His approving glance on arrival took in all of her in one gulp—"Princess," nipples, and tight little skirt. Hot times ahead, he thought.

The fish wasn't the only yummy treat laid on for tonight, thought Cleo in anticipation, eyeing the back of his jeans and watching the muscles ripple in his arms as he cooked expertly. The meal was magnificent. Trout, seasoned with exchanges of cozy talk, lustful glances and sexy innuendoes, and crowberry crumble for dessert. Just enough food to whet the appetite for the main course, two naked bodies in a warm bed. She whisked the dirty dishes off the table into the sink while Max packed up his favorite frying pan and cooking utensils.

Then Cleo offered, "Coffee on the porch? Excuse me for a

moment." She ducked into the bathroom and brushed her teeth.

When she came back he was at the kitchen sink, sliding his own toothbrush into his jeans pocket. "Let me help you with that," he said and picked up the coffee tray.

They'd had a lively conversation over dinner, and there wasn't much left to talk about as they sat across from each other in the wooden swing, drinking their coffee. Each was well aware of what was in the other's mind.

Max put his cup down and said abruptly, "I dreamed last night I held you naked in my arms."

Cleo shivered with excitement. Getting right to the point, thank God.

"In my dream I asked you if you wanted me to make love to you."

"What did I say?"

"I don't know. I woke up before you answered."

"Oh! Damn!"

"Funny dream, because I don't usually ask first. But if I were to ask you now . . ."

"I'd say . . . yes."

"Ah." He reached for her and she slipped willingly into his arms and submitted herself to his kiss. It was tender and seductive. When his tongue nudged her lips apart, she complied, and let him probe the inside of her mouth while she lay passive.

He drew back. "You don't want to?"

"I do. Ya, sure, you betcha!" she cried.

"Let's have at it, then, b'y." He pulled her close again, and this time his kiss was hot and demanding, forcing her to respond. She kissed him back with equal enthusiasm.

His hands went to the bottom of her little princess top, pulling it up and over her head, and he stared down at her breasts. "I knew you weren't wearing a bra, you vixen. Glimpses of your perky nipples have teased me all night."

"I meant it to be that way."

He muttered something low in his throat and tilted her back in his arms. "Is this what you were hoping for?" His mouth descended on her breast. He sucked, then nipped.

"Oh, wow," she moaned.

He grinned in triumph, then moved to her other breast. "Tell me you want me."

"I do, I do." She grasped frantically at the buttons of his shirt and tore them loose from the buttonholes. His shirt flew open and her hands possessed his chest, pulling on his chest hair.

His hand flew down her leg and yanked her skirt up. "No bra, but panties?"

"I thought you'd like to take them off."

"God, Cleo!" His lips grew more demanding until she moaned and arched toward him, shuddering with excitement.

"Witch," he said in triumph. "You're hot for me, aren't you?"

"Yes. Take what you want."

He stood her on her feet and pulled her skirt down and off. Then he eased her panties down very slowly, thumbs teasing her thighs, cheeks teasing her belly. She stepped out of them and stood silhouetted naked against the sea, feeling wild and free.

"I wonder if anyone is watching us. Maybe with binoculars, out on the sea in an expensive yacht. Leering at you without your clothes on, taking in every inch of your delectable body," he said, and smiled wickedly. "Let's go to bed."

His hands on her shoulders, he propelled her into the cottage and into the bedroom. He pushed her gently down on the bed and rose to kick off his shoes and slide down his jeans. He threw off his shirt and moved like a panther to cover her.

His body was lean and hard against hers and his mouth was demanding.

"I want you inside me," she gasped.

"In a hurry, are you?"

"I've wanted you since the first time I saw you. That's not in a hurry, is it?"

"No longer than I've wanted you." He lifted himself away, reached for his jeans, and drew a small package from a pocket.

"You came prepared."

"Are you surprised?"

"No, I've been expecting it."

"I've been carrying that around for days, just waiting for the perfect opportunity. I think this might be it." This time it was a slow, leisurely seduction with lips and hands while she wriggled urgently against him.

"Come into me," she whispered.

He laughed, low and sexy, and poised himself above her, teasing.

"Don't make me beg," she gasped.

"I want to hear you beg."

"All right, all right already, take me. I want you."

He thrust, his hips working furiously against hers.

She gasped.

"Do you like it?" he growled into her ear.

"What do you think?"

"I think you want more," he said, and pushed himself deeper.

She screamed this time and arched toward him in surrender.

Max smiled and took his time coming to his own release. Afterwards he let himself sink down upon her. "First course," he whispered into her ear. "Now for the entrée." Hard again, he suckled her breasts while he moved rhythmically in and out. She dissolved in pleasure and this time he let himself go right away.

"Why did I know it would be so good with you?" she moaned at last.

"Maybe you're psychic," he murmured. "I'd like a little dessert, now." He slid slowly down her body until he reached the junction of her thighs. He clamped his mouth over her and brought her to orgasm yet again.

Utterly destroyed, she lay limp on the bed, moaning.

With one abrupt motion, he lifted himself from her and stood up. "Gotta get back," he said. "Seven guests to cook breakfast for tomorrow." He would have liked to crawl back into bed and cuddle her sweet body for the rest of the night, and give her something to think about next morning. But there were those seven guests. He kissed her quickly and left, humming a happy little tune all the way back to the Big House. "'I'm a dealer in magic and spells . . .'"

Cleo slept, deeply and soundly, not a hint of a nightmare disturbing her slumber.

The next morning she woke, remembered the night before, and convinced herself it had been a dream, until she saw her princess tee shirt and skirt neatly piled on a chair, her panties artfully flared out on top of them. He'd picked them up from the porch and brought them into the bedroom while she slept. Nice touch, Max, she thought.

She showered and dressed, aware of a hot soreness between her legs. When she went into the kitchen, she found a basket holding croissants, fruit, and a thermos of coffee on the kitchen table. Max was taking care of his woman, she thought with satisfaction. Had he brought it down and stood over her, enjoying the sight of her naked, relaxed body? Or had he made Maria deliver it?

Either way, breakfast was almost as delicious as the evening before had been.

Chapter Fifteen

Sister Sue was always such a silly little goon;
She never really understood the proper way to swoon.
A young man asked her recently to sit upon his knee.
When she at last consented, she behaved so bashfully.
She's never been there before, she'd never been there before . . .

"Never Been There Before"
Newfoundland folk song

Max appeared later that afternoon when she was on the porch trying to concentrate on reading her bodice-ripper, all the while thinking that the hero, for all his muscles and hair, had nothing on her lover of last night.

All her senses sprang to quivering life at the sight of Max.

"Good day," he said. "How are you?"

"Fine. And you?"

"I could be better." He came up on the porch and extended his hand. They went inside and he pulled her close. His mouth hot on hers, he murmured, "Want to make me feel better?"

"How do I do that?" She wriggled seductively against him.

"I'll show you." He lifted her skirt and slipped his hands inside her panties to grasp her bottom.

Cleo whispered, "What do you think I am?"

"My mistress. My lover. My woman."

Your slave, she thought, and prayed he'd lift her and fill her where they stood.

But he was too careful for that. He eased her into the bedroom, sheathed himself in a condom and brought them both to an agonizingly sweet release.

"I've got to go," he whispered into her ear.

"I've got to come," she whispered back and rotated her hips against him until he gasped, "You hot little vixen," and took her again. Then he moved off of her, and they lay back on the bed, smiling at the ceiling, hands clasped.

At last he rose and pulled on his jeans. "Want to go out to dinner tonight? I'm tired of cooking and I'm giving myself another evening off. I'd like to share it with you."

"Okay." Then she said, "Will you spend the night with me?"

"Would you like that?"

"Yes. You'd like it too. I'd make sure you liked it."

"Witch." He bent and kissed her mouth. "We'll see."

After he'd left, she lay in bed, relaxed and happy, thinking about what had happened between them, and damned near about time, too. Glorious sex, and it was just what she wanted from the arrogant Mr. Avalon, plus a few laughs. No strings, no commitment. Just a summer fling with a great lover who was a nice guy with a great sense of humor, when he wasn't cranky. She thought she knew now what would cure the crankiness.

That night Max took her to the Edelweiss and introduced her to the joys of *nouvelle* German cooking and to Hans, who was profuse in his thanks for last night's bountiful harvest of tourists.

"They loved the *Kochrezept Salat mit Hühnerbruststreifen*, Max. You and Ms have dessert on the house. I have new recipe, Newfoundland recipe, crowberry crumble."

Max repressed a snort.

After dinner they returned to her cottage, shared another

round of dessert in each other's body, and fell asleep together. Max figured he'd be okay for his guests' breakfast as long as he rose by seven, and his internal clock always woke him on time. He could indulge himself in the pleasure of cuddling Cleo all through the night. It had been a long time since he'd enjoyed that pleasure, and he savored every moment. What a prize she was, he thought, and she'd just happened to come to his B and B. He was a lucky man.

He pulled her closer, enjoying every inch and nuance of her body. Her hair held the fragrance of all the wildflowers of the world in one garden. Her skin was silky and warm. And though she was on the skinny side, she possessed luscious curves that made him want to write a poem, compose a song, paint a beautiful painting. If he'd had any talent for art, he'd paint her nude, giving him the excuse to stare at her luscious self for hours. He nestled his face against her hair and breathed softly in her ear while they slept.

Sometime in the early morning, Cleo had a nightmare. In this one, she was a passenger in a speeding car headed for the edge of a deep canyon. She woke clutching the edge of the bed and crying, "Stop! Stop! Oh, please, stop!"

Max surfaced slowly; he'd been deeply asleep. "Huh? What's the matter?"

"Stop the car . . . the cliff . . ."

"What cliff? Cleo, you're dreaming."

She looked at him, dazed. "Are you sure?"

"Sure I'm sure." He kissed her, aware of tears on her cheeks. "See, that's real."

"Maybe." She shuddered. The dream was still in her mind and the hopelessness of the dream situation still tormented her. "I'm sorry I woke you. I was having a nightmare."

"Do you want to tell me about it?"

She did and she didn't, because she didn't want to relive it, but it was so clear in her mind she had to talk about it. "I was in a car about to go over the edge of a cliff."

"Were you driving?"

"No."

"Who was?"

"I don't know." She shuddered. "Something frightening . . . a hooded figure. It wouldn't listen when I begged it to stop the car. Oh, God, it was awful." The nightmare surged back over her again and she clutched his shoulders in sudden terror.

He straightened and looked down at her. "Okay, we're going to finish up your dream and make it turn out okay. Here's what you'll do. The driver is slowing down a little and you're going to use that to save yourself. Put your hand on the door handle."

She stared at him. "What?"

"Grab the door handle. You're going to throw the door open and hurl yourself out. Roll up in a ball and hit the ground on your shoulder and hip. Ready?"

She said, trembling, "Okay, I'm ready."

"On the count of three. Curl yourself as tightly as you can. One, two, three!"

He watched her face as she squeezed her eyes tightly shut. Her body tensed and thrust towards him. "Now you're on the ground and you're rolling away and the car is about to go over the cliff. There it goes! Hear the crash, Cleo, as it hits the bottom of the canyon. Get up now, and walk back along the road the way you came. There was a police car chasing you and now it's caught up. You're a little bruised and shaken up, but you're not badly hurt and the police car is going to take you to safety."

Her body relaxed and her eyes fluttered open. It had worked; he had dispelled the aura of the dream. She stared at him, suddenly embarrassed, imagining how frantic she must have seemed. "Thanks. I'm fine now."

He looked at her curiously. "Have those bad dreams often, do you?"

"They go in streaks. I've started having them again since I came here."

"Because you're relaxed physically but your mind hasn't caught up to your body."

"You think?"

"Yeah. Another couple of weeks of Newfie peace and Uncle Max's good loving and you'll sleep like a baby."

She giggled. "You mean sucking my thumb and wetting the bed?"

"Hey, you wet the bed, I'll have to charge you extra."

He was hovering over her, grinning. Cleo looked into his ice-blue eyes, at his mouth, his broad shoulders. She gave him a seductive look from under her lashes. "You don't have to leave just yet, do you?"

He glanced at the clock. "Nah, it's not even five-thirty. I can stay till seven."

She stroked his cheek. "I'd like to thank you for getting rid of the nightmare."

"'Zat right? I love having a beautiful woman indebted to me."

"You think I'm beautiful?"

"You're some cute, Cleo, honey. That's better than beautiful."

She curled her hand in his chest hair. "You're some cute too, you big hairy brute. Give me a kiss."

He did, and it began all over and they played until he had to leave, at seven.

Chapter Sixteen

Although we live by strife,
We're always sorry to begin it,
For what, we ask, is life
Without a touch of Poetry in it?

The Pirates of Penzance, Gilbert and Sullivan

Their sexual encounters became so frequent, so intense and so passionate that it was almost a relief to Cleo when her period came. It gave her a chance to stop and think about where this affair was going. After chewing over the situation, she decided it was only physical, but it was good for her. She could warm up on Max, sharpen her claws, so to speak, and it would clear her head so she could look for a real relationship when she got home. She'd use this interval to remind herself what it was like to be intimately involved with a man.

Max was getting something out of the affair, too. The way he looked at her with burning eyes and his ferocious mouth and eager hands when they made love told her that.

Now that they had to be celibate for a week, she thought she might as well try to expand their knowledge of each other. It was the civilized way to behave, chatting, telling intimate secrets, becoming pals. No reason they couldn't be pals as well as lovers.

They were sitting in the B and B kitchen watching each other uneasily, sexual tension simmering just below the surface. Cleo said, "I'd like to talk with you."

"What about?" he growled. He'd forgotten his earlier desire to get to know her better. Sex was all he could handle right now; he had a house full of demanding guests wearing him out. He wasn't interested in chitchat; what he needed was a nap.

"Oh . . . you know. Stuff. The meaning of life, maybe."

"There is no meaning to life."

Shocked, she stared at him. "You really believe that?"

He took a gulp of coffee. "Why not?"

It occurred to Cleo that she had never had a chat with him that hadn't become a verbal sparring match. He liked arguing, and didn't much care which side of an argument he was on, sometimes even changing sides in midstream. That was both frustrating and amusing for her, but now she was looking for something different. Maybe she could break through his defenses, for once, and have a normal conversation. "Tell me why you believe it."

He shrugged. "Read Nietzsche. Or Jean-Paul Sartre."

"I'm asking you."

"Asking is free, answers are expensive." He grinned smugly.

"Damn it, Max . . ." She could have said a lot more except that the doorbell rang. He unfolded himself from his chair and strolled out of the kitchen into the hall.

Cleo heard a woman's voice, low and coaxing. Who the hell is that, she thought, senses instantly alerted to competition. She rose, crept to the kitchen door, and peeked into the hall.

The voice belonged to a tall blonde woman, beautiful even in the dim light of the hall. She wore a tight low-necked turquoise sweater and matching knit skirt, with a glowing rose and blue scarf draped artfully over one shoulder. Her voice purred in contrast to Max's harsher, deeper tones. Her every movement was lush and seductive, even when she took the pen to sign the guests' register.

Cleo watched Max reach for the woman's suitcase and turn to guide her upstairs to Number Four. Did his hand touch her shoulder lightly as he indicated the way? Jealousy ripped through every inch of her, even prickling the hair on the back of her neck. She watched the clock angrily, counting the minutes he spent in the woman's bedroom.

When Max strolled back into the kitchen, he was greeted with a scowl. "New guest, huh? Pretty, is she?"

Max had been a little alarmed by the woman, to tell the truth. She'd given him a thorough looking-over, and decided she liked what she saw. She'd swung her hips provocatively as she climbed the stairs ahead of him. In her room, she'd drifted over to the queen-sized bed and requested another pillow. "There's a lot of room in this bed," she'd purred. "I need something to fill it up."

He'd turned on his heel and headed for the linen closet. When he returned with two huge pillows, he'd found her half-reclining on the bed, smoothing the quilt with a red-nailed hand. When she glanced up at him seductively, he thrust the pillows at her. "Let me know if you need anything else," he said.

"Oh, I certainly will," came the sultry answer.

He fled. Now, in the kitchen, he was met by Cleo's suspicious face. "Huh?" he said, having forgotten her question.

"I said, 'is she pretty?'" Cleo snarled.

Hot damn, she's jealous, Max thought, realizing that the idea filled him with great pleasure. Jealousy was the ultimate spice to a relationship. Maybe he could work it for some purpose of his own. She wouldn't let him into her bed this week, but maybe he could keep her from fading away and avoiding him like she'd done yesterday. For some dumb reason he liked having her close, even out of bed.

"See for yourself. Hang around and help me with dinner. I gave Maria the evening off. Some religious holiday or other; she said she wanted to go to evening Mass." He shrugged. "More likely she's got a new boyfriend she wants to spend the night with."

Cleo said suspiciously, "What would I have to do?" She wasn't used to helping in the kitchen without Maria as an interpreter of Max's whims and wishes.

He shrugged. "Anything I tell you to do." He rose like a panther, slunk around the table, and pulled her up into his arms. "You're good at taking orders, aren't you."

She remembered their encounter in bed two nights ago and turned red. For the first time he'd let her take the initiative in lovemaking and had given her very specific instructions on what he wanted her to do. It had brought out a wantonness in her that she'd never experienced before.

"Made you blush, haven't I, you little vixen," he growled triumphantly and ran a hand down her bottom to press her pelvis close to his.

Cleo wiggled, to tease him. "I mean, what do I have to do to help you with dinner?"

"Stir things," he said, and rotated his hips against hers. "Serve the guests. Keep me company. Keep me happy."

"Yeah, all right."

He let her go abruptly. "Go put on something plain, something that's not sexy. I don't want the male guests enjoying you instead of dinner. You'll have to wear a hairnet, too."

"I'm not wearing a damned hairnet."

He shrugged. "Maria won't, either. I'm dead meat if the health inspector shows up some night. Pull your hair back into a ponytail, then."

"Okay." She stalked out of the kitchen, determined to put on the sexiest items in her wardrobe just for the pleasure of seeing him scowl.

It turned out to be fun and a real challenge working in the kitchen with Max. He barked orders, impatient because he didn't have Maria there to read his mind. His tone gentled once Cleo got the hang of the routine, and they worked together in some semblance of harmony, though he kept glancing in mingled irritation and lust at her bosom in the tight tee shirt she'd pulled on over one of her trademark miniscule skirts.

When Cleo went into the dining room to serve the soup, she got a look at the competition from Number Four and her heart sank. The blonde was a beauty and knew it. She had on a sultry little black dress, her high, large, perfectly rounded breasts ornamented by a sparkling diamond pendant that dipped into the valley between them. Probably fake, Cleo thought crossly. The pendant, too.

Even the honeymooning couple noticed. The husband gave the blonde a startled, impressed look, and dropped his soup spoon into his lap. The wife's gaze was hostile. It warmed Cleo's heart to see that another woman had scented trouble, just as she had. She would have exchanged a look of cameraderie with her had not all the wife's attention been focused on her man's reactions.

Cleo forced herself to put the soup down gently in front of the blonde, who said, "Where's Max?"

"Mr. Avalon is in the kitchen, cooking," snarled Cleo, gentleness forgotten.

"Ask him if he'd like to come out and have coffee with me after dinner."

"He'll have the kitchen clean-up to do."

The blonde regarded her appraisingly. "Surely that's your job?"

Cleo stormed away, muttering under her breath, regretting that she hadn't dumped the soup onto the slinky dress and its inhabitant. In the kitchen she said dangerously, "Your blonde tootsie wants you to have coffee with her after dinner."

Max paid no attention, distracted because he couldn't get the final seasoning quite right in his spaghetti sauce.

Annoyed at being ignored, Cleo repeated the statement.

Ah, that was it. A little sugar to counter-balance the garlic. Damn, there'd be no vampires around the old campfire tonight; he'd put enough garlic in the sauce to slay thousands of them. He straightened up and looked vaguely at Cleo. "What? Who?"

"The blonde tart asked me if you would care to join her."

He was thinking about grating more aged Parmesan; it didn't look as though there was enough for seven plates, and he never skimped on quantity when the quality was so fine. "You mean Number Four? I'm busy. What the hell does she want?"

"Your body, I imagine."

That got his interest. "You think?" He smirked. "She's a looker, isn't she. Maybe I ought to give her extra attention since you're unavailable for a few days."

Cleo, furious with jealousy, stripped off her apron and flung it on the table, narrowly missing the pot of spaghetti sauce. "Maybe you should get her in here to help you with dinner."

His smirk grew wider. Before she could stalk out, he dropped the spaghetti sauce spoon, grabbed her shoulders and pulled her into his arms. "You think she might be better at it than you?" he murmured in her ear.

"Better at what? Damn it, Max, let go of me."

"Nah, I need a little nookie to warm me up for Number Four."

She would have slapped him but he had both her hands in one of his, clasped behind her back, pressing her hard against him. It was very erotic. He put his mouth over hers, surprisingly tender, and whispered, "Nobody's better than you, princess. In the kitchen and other places."

Cleo melted against him. "Is that for me or Number Four?" she said, pushing herself at his arousal.

"You're here, aren't you? I guess it's for you if you want it. You do want it, don't you, vixen?"

He kissed her hotly just as the door swung open, giving the guests in the dining room a little cabaret with their dinners. Maria flounced in, muttering under her breath.

Max let Cleo go in a hurry and she staggered when he released her. "What are you doing here? I thought you were going to Mass."

Maria muttered something in Spanish, grabbed the apron from the table and wrapped it around herself. She demanded,

"Entrée not ready yet? They finished wit' soup. Be bangin' spoons on plates soon, eef you don' get a move on."

Max sighed, faced with yet another hostile woman. "Yeah, all right."

Grinning, Cleo sat down in a chair to watch the fun, jealous thoughts of the sultry blonde gone from her brain.

When he walked Cleo home, Max said, "You have any idea what was wrong with Maria? She was scouring pots so fiercely I thought she was going to rip the bottoms out."

"I heard her mumbling something about *un hombre repugnante*. I don't know that word, but I can guess what it means. Maybe she's run into a tender, lovable Newfoundland man, like I have."

He stopped and looked down at her by the light of the moon. "What's that supposed to mean?"

"What do you think it means?" muttered Cleo, ashamed that she had to resort to such childish tactics.

"No wonder women used to be locked up in huts at their time of the month. Damn, you're bitchy tonight."

"I'm not."

"You are." He yanked her into his arms and kissed her, the full treatment, hot mouth and exploring hands, a real knee-trembler.

Maybe I am, thought Cleo, and succumbed. She was always needy during her period, wanting cuddling but too proud to ask for it, and sex, which she was too embarrassed to initiate.

She kissed him back, her mouth as hot as his, until he growled, "How about it?"

"No! Go away."

He did, much to her disappointment.

Chapter Seventeen

Oh, there's lots of fish in Bonavist' Harbour,
Lots of fish right in around here;
Boys and girls are fishin' together,
Forty-five from Carbonear.
Oh, catch-a-hold this one, catch-a-hold that one,
Swing around this one, swing around she;
Dance around this one, dance around that one,
Diddle dum this one, diddle dum-dee.

"The Feller from Fortune"
Newfoundland folk song

For Max, life was simple. He now had a companion who was sex personified in bed with a wicked sense of humor that complemented his own, someone to whom he could vent about the frustrations and pleasures of running a B and B in the high season. Vibrant and lively, Cleo radiated good health and energy and she was giving Max the time of his life. Even the pleasant aspects of his often-troubled marriage had not been this good.

For Cleo, life was simple. Her relationship with Max was open and honest, no devious subplots, no trickery, no emotional involvement. Nothing in it took her back to the bad old days when she'd used sex to find relief from the pain of Charlie's death. She felt strong, womanly and competent, free of worry for the first time in years. The tension knots were gone from her neck and shoulders, her fingernails were long, pink and unbroken, her skin was soft from the lotion Max rubbed in whenever she got sunburn.

Happiness was in everything she did, whether it was sleeping late and fixing breakfast in the little cottage kitchen, or stumbling over the rocks down to the pebble beach to wet her feet in the cold waters of the bay, or bending and stooping in Max's garden digging up carrots and plump purple turnips for his stews.

Or lying luxuriously naked on her front porch in the bright sun, the ocean breezes caressing her. No one could see her from the path and the only person who ever came up on the porch was Max, who chortled with glee at the sight of his lover's lithe body turning golden from the sun. "You look good enough to eat," he said once after catching her sunbathing. "As delicious as a Tim Horton's toasted bagel dripping with butter."

"What's a Tim Horton's?"

"Our Canadian fast food joint, started forty years ago by, who else in Canada, an ex-hockey player. Difference between Tim's and other joints is that the food is actually good, even by my standards. Bagels, donuts, sandwiches and excellent coffee."

She had little interest in fast food but a lot of interest in sweet talk, so she purred in response, stretched and moved so sensuously in the sun's warm rays that his mouth went dry. He'd thought he was getting almost as much pleasure from watching her show off her body as from the moments that inevitably followed such a display.

Cleo was finally accepting that nothing she could have done would have saved Charlie, not even urging him to the doctor sooner when he'd started feeling so inexplicably exhausted. His was the type of leukemia that was fast and fatal, and nothing and no one could have saved him. This realization was bringing her the deep peace she'd craved since he died. Closure, at last. Charlie would always be with her, a warm and comforting spirit, no longer a reminder of what might have been.

Halfway through her vacation, Cleo was rejuvenated in body, mind and spirit. It was what she had come to Newfoundland to find, and she had found it. No wonder the province was called "the smiling land," she thought. It was making her smile again.

Now, relaxed, she was able to think seriously about her life and future. She assessed her teaching career, the progress she'd made, and what she had yet to achieve. She thought about the students she'd helped and those she hadn't, and took quiet satisfaction from the one and tried to find the lessons in the other. She was preparing herself for the challenges of the year of school ahead, but trying also to look beyond it. Should she keep on teaching? She liked working with kids but was there some other way to be of use to them? Maybe some day she'd have her own child, she thought longingly; someone who belonged to her, someone to benefit from her teaching skills.

And the Newfoundland summer continued its predictably unpredictable course. Sunny days were interspersed with those of heavy overcast, when fat gray cloud puffs moved vigorously across the sky, alternating bursts of rain and bursts of sunshine. On one of those days Cleo dressed warmly and headed down the rocky hill to the rocky beach. The fierce howling wind tried to blow her back from the shore, plastering her clothes against her until she looked like the Statue of Liberty.

She imagined herself a Newfoundland woman of old, facing into the wind and watching the whitecaps grow higher and higher. Worrying about her man out in a small boat on the great big sea. Wondering whether a storm was coming, and whether she had enough salt fish and hardtack stowed away to last out a spell of bad weather. What would that life have been like? It had been hard; she was sure of that. Had it been harder than life today, with its own challenges?

Chilled, she tore herself away at last from her fantasies, and climbed the hill.

Max was waiting for her at the top. He took in every detail of her appearance, her wild, windblown hair standing out at right angles to her skull, her reddened cheeks, and the heaving of her delectable bosom from the climb. He smiled and said, "What's the news from the sea, b'y?"

"Oh, Max, it's gorgeous and so wild. The waves are enormous and the wind is howling like a 747. Is a storm coming?"

"Well, it might pelt down buckets, as Mrs. Hoh would say, or it might blow over. You never know about Newfie weather; it changes every fifteen minutes on schedule like the Number Five bus. You're shivering."

"I got cold down by the sea."

"Come into the kitchen. I brought a thermos of coffee and some brownies."

Later, over her cup, she smiled at him and said, "I can almost imagine what it must be like here in the winter."

"It gives Mexico a certain appeal."

"I like winter, though as a Minnesotan I'm supposed to whine incessantly about it."

"Same here. I hole up in this big old house and talk to the spirits of my ancestors, or rather, shout at them over the roar of the wind. I build huge fires in the fireplace and cook up dishes I'm working on for next year's season. Drink a lot of wine, read a lot of books, write my memoirs, stuff like that."

"It sounds heavenly," said Cleo wistfully.

"Cozy as a rat in a garbage dump," he said, smiling at her. "When Christmas comes, I cut down a pine tree . . . there's millions of them on the Rock, in case you hadn't noticed . . . stick it up in the parlor and decorate it. Write a batch of cards, especially to former customers I'd like to have return. Cook an elegant Christmas dinner for friends."

He paused, then, catching her off balance, said, "God, it's lonely here that time of year. Why don't you come up and spend Christmas with me, as my guest?"

Cleo looked up in surprise. "Could I?"

"Why not?"

"I could, couldn't I."

"Of course it wouldn't be much of a vacation for you, going from bitter cold weather and snow to bitterer cold weather and even more snow."

"I don't care about the weather as long as I don't have to go out in it. Staying in with a fire and great food and wine would be wonderful."

"Music from my CD collection. And a warm king-sized bed."

"You didn't mention that one before."

"Didn't I?" he said innocently. "Guess there are a lot of advantages to a visit, maybe some we haven't even thought of. Will you come to me for Christmas, Cleo? But you can't stay in Squashberry Cottage; it's not winterized and I don't plow the drive. It'd cost me five loonies a square yard to replace the gravel I'd plow up. You'd have to stay in the Big House. In my apartment." He looked at her, fearing the intimacy of living together, even for a couple of weeks, would make her change her mind.

But she was growing increasingly enthusiastic. Christmas away from her lonely apartment, where the most she could hope for in gaiety was the teachers' holiday party.

Christmas away from a home she hadn't had the heart to decorate since Charlie's death. She used to make a big deal about the holidays. Buy a tree from the Boy Scout lot, string lights, decorate, shop for gifts, bake cookies. They were never very good cookies, but it was the principle that counted One year she and Charlie went door to door with friends singing Christmas carols, and would have done it again had he not been ill. Sad thoughts loomed, and she said hastily, "Do you put up decorations in the Big House?"

"Oh, yes, got to have those. I give a big party for my staff and friends. Maria even comes from St. John's for it. If you were here, we'd have a screeching-in for you."

"A what?"

"It's a Newfoundland initiation ceremony. It involves drinking a very potent local rum of questionable taste and kissing the backside of a dead cod, or if you prefer, biting the head off a capelin, which is like a herring. Then the screeching-in officer says, "Is you a Newfie now?' And you say, 'Deed I is, you old trout, and long may your big jig draw.' Which means that you hope his sails will always be full of wind."

Cleo stared. "You've got to be kidding."

"Come up for Christmas and find out, me old trout," Max said, grinning.

"Well, I'm game for anything. So since I'll be coming up for the holiday, what would you like for Christmas?"

The familiar leer appeared on his face.

"Besides that," she added hastily.

"Nothing, princess," he said softly. "Nothing but you."

Absurdly pleased, Cleo blushed to the tip of her scarlet toenails.

"Hey!" he said suddenly. "You can help me pick out presents for my women."

"What? What women?" she snapped, suddenly alert to the possibility of competition.

"Maria, Mrs. Hoh, Polly and Mrs. Puddester. Usually I just order something from a catalog but I never know if it's right."

"I'd be glad to help. But you have to begin early to get good gift ideas, notice what color each one prefers, their sizes, what books they like to read . . ."

Max looked at her as if she had grown three heads. "I'm supposed to find out what sort of books Mrs. Puddester reads? What should I do, go down to Whitbourne and interrogate Heather the librarian?"

Cleo smiled shrewdly. "Use your imagination. How about a cookbook?"

"A cookbook," said Max in wonder. "That's brilliant, that is. I'd never have thought of that. Say, why don't I give you my gift list and you can start working on it now."

Cleo just laughed.

Chapter Eighteen

Poor wandering one!
Though thou hast surely strayed,
Take heart of grace,
Thy steps retrace!
Poor wandering one!

The Pirates of Penzance, Gilbert and Sullivan

The next time Max stayed overnight, he made love to her in the morning until she wept with the excruciating pleasure of it. They lay twined together, relaxed and happy. Then he said, "I forgot to tell you. You have to be out of the cottage by eleven AM."

Shocked, she gasped, "What are you talking about?"

"The cottage is rented to someone else. Emergency booking. You have to move out by eleven so that I have time to clean it." He glanced at the clock. "But there's time enough for a quickie," he said, moved on top and buried himself inside her.

Too stunned to resist, she lay passive beneath him. So it's over, she thought, despite all that talk about spending Christmas together. She'd imagined it might end abruptly, but she'd never expected he would be cruel enough to throw her out once he'd had his way with her. Since when had a man gotten tired of her so fast? Usually she was the one who said goodbye. Tears of shock and humiliation trickled down her cheeks.

He looked down at her in surprise, puzzled by her lack of response. "What's wrong? Why are you crying?"

I won't give him the satisfaction of knowing he's hurt me, she thought angrily, and snapped, "Because I love this cottage and I hate to leave it."

"I have a better place for you to stay. Up in the Big House."

"What? Where?"

"In my apartment." He smiled as her eyes widened.

"You want me to move into your apartment?"

"Why not?"

Torn between anger and relief, she hesitated. Who did he think he was, to assume she'd make herself available so easily? "Suppose I don't want to. Suppose we don't like living together."

"You can move back into the cottage when the emergency booking leaves."

Got it all figured out, haven't you, she thought crossly. Somehow he was making her seem the unreasonable one. "I'll come up to the Big House because I've still got lots of vacation left and I'm not ready to go home to Minneapolis, but I want my own room."

He said, "What if I don't have another room?"

Devil, she thought furiously. "Then I'll leave."

"Ah, you wouldn't do that, would you?" He bent and nibbled her throat.

"Maybe."

"Maybe I'll change your mind."

God help me, she thought, even as she began to moan with pleasure in response to his teasing mouth. He had all the answers and she wasn't even sure of the questions.

Afterwards she packed her suitcases while he waited impatiently. "Get a move on. I've got a lot to do to get this place ready."

"I'll help you clean it since it's such a big deal."

"Start by dusting." He tossed her a dustcloth. "I want the place spotless."

She said sarcastically, "Someone important must be moving in."

"Very important. My daughter."

"You have a daughter?" She stared at him in shock.

"Seventeen years old and I haven't seen her for seven years."

"You're married."

He growled, "You think I'd be rolling in the hay with you if I were married? I've been divorced for nine years."

"Oh." She blushed, feeling foolish. "But you haven't seen your daughter . . ."

"She and her mother lived in Halifax for five years after Sharon left me. It wasn't too bad even after the divorce; I could get down to see her at least twice a month. Then Sharon met a new guy. They got married and took Angela away, down to the States. A violation of our joint custody agreement but there was nothing I could do. I couldn't press charges and have my daughter's mother put in jail. I couldn't even find them because she took her new husband's name, which I didn't know, and didn't send me her address. I thought about having a private detective trace them but didn't have the money.

"Four months ago they moved to Florida and Sharon made contact with my parents who are retired and living in Sarasota. She thought Angela should get to know her grandparents. Mom let me know about it right away."

His voice was bitter. "I don't know why Angela's coming. She wrote me a letter announcing her imminent arrival. Coming to tell me off for abandoning her, I suppose."

"But you didn't . . ."

"Tell that to a kid."

Cleo could not think of anything else to say so she dusted

furiously, wondering what had gone wrong between Max and his ex and unable to figure out how to ask.

Finally she ventured, "Your wife didn't like it here."

He gave her a suspicious look. "How did you know that?"

Too nosy, Cleo, she told herself, and hurried to cover her tracks. "Just a guess."

"Yeah. She's Newfoundland born and bred, though; she'll come back eventually. Newfies always do."

"Did you hope she'd return to you?"

Max sighed. "No, it was over, the flame was out. Wasn't much of a flame, anyway; we just made a mistake and got pregnant when we were seventeen. Tried to keep it going, but we weren't meant to be together for life. At least we got Angela out of the deal, and she's a good kid. At least she was the last time I saw her."

Cleo absorbed the information, the most Max had ever shared with her, and said nothing, but thought deeply.

After they finished cleaning, he helped her get settled in a room too small for paying guests that he took care to point out was just across the hall from his apartment.

"Why didn't you put your daughter in this room?" Cleo growsed.

"Sharon told her about the cottage and she insisted on having it. Liked the independence, and didn't want to be too close to her old man, I guess."

Cleo wasn't sure she wanted to be that close to him, either. It made late night *tête-a-têtes* all too terrifyingly possible. It was one thing to entertain her lover on her own ground where she was in control. It was quite another to be right on his doorstep, at his convenience whenever he got the urge. Knowing Max, he would probably get the urge with alarming frequency.

As it happened he got stuck in the kitchen for hours that first night working on a new bakeapple muffin recipe, dropped a jar of jam and had to mop the entire floor. The mouse came out and watched him, sitting back on her haunches with her little paws folded against her belly. It reminded him, depressingly, of his B and B guests waiting for breakfast, and sent him to bed in an exhausted funk.

Cleo, waiting for him in her flimsiest nightgown, freshly showered and hot to trot, finally fell asleep, disgruntled.

He woke her early the next morning with kisses, and brought her breakfast in bed, a big plate of blueberry pancakes with homemade syrup and moose sausage. Once she stopped complaining about the lack of butter and ate herself into a good humor, he persuaded her to drive to Gander with him to pick up his daughter at the airport. He was leery of having to get reacquainted with the girl without reinforcements.

Daughter Angela was a pop princess in a tight tee shirt with a rude saying on it, navel exposed by low-riding jeans, ears, eyebrow and nose pierced and ringed, fierce blue velvet eyes heavily made up. Her hair, a gelled pastiche of stiff tendrils rising above her forehead, was the same color as Max's except for the gray in his and the purple and gold streaks in hers. It even had the same hint of curl.

She scowled at Max and ignored Cleo. "Hi," she said coldly. "You Max?"

"I'm your father."

"Long time no see, Pop. I'd forgotten what you look like." She turned and hoisted her backpack on her shoulder.

"I'll take that for you," Max said.

"Nah, it's kinda heavy for an old guy. I'd better do it."

Max scowled fiercely.

Cleo looked from one to the other. Same hair, same eyes, they looked very much alike. They even scowl in the same way, she decided, amused; and thought maybe Max had met his match, at last. The girl looked ready to take on the world, let alone one hapless father.

Max attempted in his bumbling way to point out the sights as they drove from Gander to Last Man Ashore Cove.

Angela affected a profound disinterest and asked if either of them had a cigarette.

Max exclaimed in horror, "You're a smoker? Don't you know cigarette smoking causes lung cancer and heart disease?"

Angela shrugged her shoulders, and having successfully upset her father, refused to say anything else for the rest of the ride.

Cleo, high-school-teacher-wise in the ways of teenagers, kept her mouth shut.

When they arrived at the B and B, Cleo left Max alone to settle his daughter into Squashberry Cottage which she still jealously regarded as her own. She was tired of being ignored by a cranky kid and she didn't even have the satisfaction of being able to send her to the principal's office.

If she were ever lucky enough to have children, she thought, as soon as they became teenagers off they'd go to boarding school. Or to a cage.

Chapter Nineteen

Everything is a source of fun.
Nobody's safe, for we care for none!
Life is a joke that's just begun!

The Mikado, Gilbert and Sullivan

Sulky Angela occupied most of Max's thoughts. He couldn't keep up with her moods. At one breakfast, she denounced his muffins as too fattening; the next day she whined because he'd provided only toast. She'd demanded a CD player, and now loud weird music issued from the cottage at odd hours of the day and night, and a customer complained after his eardrums were assaulted on his way down to the beach. Max didn't dare speak to Angela about it; she'd proved she had the ability to destroy him with a single withering glance. He hadn't seen her for too many years, had no experience with her as a teenager, and he was out of practice in playing the heavy father role.

He was almost too distracted to sneak into Cleo's room and make love to her. On the third night, he forgot the condoms and had to skulk back naked across the corridor to his own rooms to get them while Cleo lay in bed, tapping her fingers impatiently.

This had to end, she thought. She wasn't exactly jealous of Angela, but she disliked seeing Max in such a state; he wasn't much fun, in or out of bed. The edge was even off his sarcastic wit, and he went around mumbling and glum. She'd stayed away from his confrontations with his daughter because her high school teacher's soul was appalled by the idea of a teenager always getting the upper hand. But now it was time for her to intervene.

Maybe she should make friends with the girl, dubious as that proposition sounded.

She concocted an excuse: she'd pretend she'd lost an earring in the cottage and would inquire politely if Angela had found it. That should get her on the porch, and once there she'd plant her bottom on the swing and refuse to budge until she'd had a chat and gotten a handle on the girl's personality. Maybe then she could give Max tips on how to tame a savage teenager.

Rounding the corner of the cottage, Cleo caught a whiff of a once-familiar odor. Angie was sitting on the swing and when she caught sight of her visitor she hastily lowered her hand from her mouth and hid it beside her chair. "Hiya," she growled in a "get lost" tone of voice.

Ah, a righteous opening, and never mind the earring. Cleo stood at the foot of the steps, hands on her hips. "You'd better not let your father catch you with that."

"With what?" Angela assumed an innocent look.

"Give me a hit of that joint and I might not tell him." Cleo climbed the steps and held out her hand.

"You a doper?"

"I haven't had any since my husband died." She sank down in a chair, her hand still extended. "That was almost three years ago."

Angie held out the joint.

Cleo brought it to her mouth and inhaled. In seconds the old warmth spread through her and with it, a flood of memories, some pleasant, some dreadful.

Angie watched her. "Was your husband a dealer or something?"

"He had cancer. I used to get weed from friends for him, sneak it into the hospice, lock the door of his room, and put a towel across the doorsill while he smoked. It helped with the nausea, it made him want to eat and in his last days it helped him relax. He didn't need as much pain medication when he was high."

Angie regarded her with new respect. "I've heard that. You smoked with him?"

"He insisted. Said it would help me relax, too." She inhaled again and handed the joint back. "He was right. We had a few laughs when we were stoned. God knows there wasn't many other reasons to laugh."

"What kind of cancer did he have?" Angie took a hit.

"Leukemia. The fast kind. He died five months after his diagnosis."

"Oh. Bummer."

"Major bummer." Cleo looked out across the sea. The marijuana was hitting her gently and the water was suddenly a shimmering blue against the vivid green of the trees. Wildflowers sprinkled in the deep emerald lawn vibrated with color like neon lights. She exhaled slowly. "How'd you get the stuff past the border inspectors?"

"They're too busy looking for terrorists to spend time on grass. The dope-sniffing dogs have been replaced with explosive-sniffing dogs."

"Ha, you wish. You were just lucky."

"Yeah, I guess I was. I hid it inside sachets pinned in my panties in my suitcase."

"Taking a real chance, weren't you?"

She grinned. "I figured if I got busted my dad would get me sprung. He owes me big time. One more hit?"

Get her sprung, indeed. Typical teenager magical thinking. Cleo took the tiny remnant of the joint, carefully inserted it between her lips, inhaled, and held her breath. Then she said, "Why does he owe you?"

"You know. For leaving my mom and me. All that stuff."

"That's not the way he sees it. Better get his side of the story."

Angie stretched lazily. "Nah, no sweat. Most kids I know have divorced parents. Who cares what excuses a bunch of old people make for ruining their lives?"

"Your father is thirty-three or thirty-four. That's not old."

"Whatever." The girl shrugged and changed the subject abruptly. "You sleeping with him?"

Cleo had expected that question but not phrased quite so bluntly. She was proud of herself for not flinching. "Not that it's any of your business, but yes, I am."

"He any good in bed?"

Cleo gave her a steely-eyed look. "Define good."

"Well . . . you know." The girl blushed, suddenly and hotly. "Does he make you, like, you know, happy?"

"Yes. Very happy."

"Guys I've been with only care about making themselves happy."

"I've met some like that."

"'Zat right? What did you do?"

"I wised up." When the girl looked puzzled, Cleo said, "There was a time after my husband died when I looked for comfort anywhere I could find it, and some of it was physical. After a while I came to my senses and quit sleeping around. Max is the first guy I've had sex with in two years." She glanced at Angie, who was listening, wide-eyed. "So the moral of the story is find a nice guy or sleep alone. Your father is a nice guy. Arrogant and grouchy but basically decent."

Angie considered. "Yeah, I guess he is. You going to marry him?"

"Why would I do that?" Cleo rose; she'd had enough of playing the mentor. "You got anything to eat? I'm starved. Reason number sixty-five not to smoke grass; you eat a lot and gain a ton of weight."

Angie rose to her feet. "You going to tell Pop about the dope?"

Cleo grinned. "Hey, you don't tell on me, I don't tell on you."

"Deal." Angie extended her hand and the two women shook on it. "I've got cookies and chocolate ice cream I made Pop buy me. And a stash of peanut butter and crackers."

"Super. Let's eat, drink and be merry, for tomorrow we diet."

The old joke tickled Angie, and she laughed out loud for the first time since Cleo had met her.

Max came around to the cottage about thirty minutes later and heard the sound of hip-hop music cascading out of the windows. Then it stopped. As he walked up on the porch, he heard Cleo say, "God, that's terrible. How can you listen to that junk?"

"Because old people don't dig it. It bugs them, just like it bugs you."

"It's crap. That guy was singing about 'slapping his bitch around.' Sexist crap."

"So what do you listen to, wrinklies like Mick Jagger?"

"I like the Kinks." Stoned, Cleo began to sing, "'Lo-la! L-O-L-A, Lo-la.'"

"Hey, I know that one. It's cool." Angie chimed in. "'Lo-la! L-O-L-A, Lo-la!'"

"'I met her in a bar down in old Soho where they drink champagne and it tastes just like Coca-Cola,'" warbled Cleo in her best imitation of Ray Davies. They sang "L-O-L-A!" again and exploded in giggles.

What the hell? thought Max. He stomped up on the porch and flung the kitchen door open, ready to denounce Cleo, that irresponsible witch, for getting his innocent seventeen-year-old daughter drunk. And she's a teacher, too, he thought indignantly.

The two women stopped singing and stared at him. Then they giggled dementedly again.

"Hi, Pop," said Angie, who was giggling so hard she could scarcely talk.

"Hi, Maxwell, baby," said Cleo, making a ridiculous effort to plaster a serious expression on her face.

"Bang, bang, Maxwell's silver hammer came down upon our heads," chanted Angela, relishing her father's baffled expression.

He growled, "What's going on here?"

"We're eating peanut butter and crackers. Want some? I haven't licked this yet." Angela waved the knife at him.

"We're listening to music. If you can call it music."

"Lighten oop, Cleo," said Angie. "You sound like an old lady."

"I am an old lady, next to you, kid. Old and wise, and so totally well preserved." Cleo stuck out her tongue.

Stunned, Max stared from one of them to the other. There were no wine bottles on the table so he couldn't imagine what was wrong with them. The appalling effects of hip-hop music, perhaps. He said stiffly, "I came to take you both out to dinner. If you're not too stuffed with peanut butter and crackers, that is."

"Oh, wow, dinner," said Cleo. "I'm so hungry I could eat a horse."

Angie said, "I want a burger and fries. Is there a MacDonald's anywhere in this Newfie dump, Pop?"

Max scowled. "We're going to a proper restaurant, not a nasty fast food joint. I'll meet you at the Big House in ten minutes." He started to stomp out, then snapped, "And get some decent clothes on so you don't embarrass me. Take off that tarty tee shirt, Angela. You too, Cleo, you look like something the cat dragged in."

Behind him as he clomped down the cottage steps he heard a chorus of "meow, meow, meow!" He ground his teeth in frustration. Damned women, he thought.

The damned women had straightened up quite a bit by the time the three of them were seated for dinner in Puddester's restaurant, although Angie and Cleo still giggled now and then and exchanged glances brimming with merriment. Both had put on mini-skirts and low cut, strappy tops, just to irritate Max.

He was, indeed, irritated. He blurted, at last, "What's so damned funny?'

"You are, Pop," said Angie, and grinned when a look of fury appeared on his face.

"Shut up, Angie," said Cleo. "Leave your father alone. He does the best he can. Show a little respect for his age."

"Yo, teach," said Angie, smirking.

Max stared from one of them to the other, completely befuddled.

For revenge he whisked the menus out of both sets of hands. "I'll order for us," he said smoothly and did so despite their indignant sputterings. For Cleo he ordered a Jiggs dinner—salt beef with vegetables—and for Angie a mooseburger.

Both examined their meals with the greatest care.

"Looks like beef stew," said Cleo. "Tastes like corned beef and cabbage."

"Yum, nice rare hamburger, the way I like it. Lots of blood," Angie said.

"It's moose," said Max furiously, pushing his own delicately grilled herbed salmon around on his plate.

"'Zat right? Wait till I tell the kids back home I ate a moose."

"Better tell them it was a mooseburger," said Cleo, who knew teenagers, "or you'll never hear the end of it. They'll call you Moosie, Moose-gobbler, Moose Girl."

"You are so right." Angie took another huge bite.

Max ate glumly, wondering if he'd ever get the better of them. When the crowberry crumble arrived, he cheered up considerably because his version was better, even though he'd given Mrs. Puddester the recipe.

At the cottage, Angie and Cleo high-fived at parting to Max's annoyance.

"Night, old lady," said Angie.

"Sleep tight, Moosie Girl," said Cleo.

Max stared, and decided to give up on understanding women. He bid Cleo a haughty good night and stalked off to sleep alone, to teach her she wouldn't get any nookie if she laughed at him.

Chapter Twenty

Far away from toil and care,
Revelling in fresh sea air,
Here we live and reign alone
In a world that's all our own.

The Pirates of Penzance, Gilbert and Sullivan

The next day, after she'd straightened out, Cleo felt a little guilty. She knew she'd been naughty, smoking grass with a teenager. She should have confiscated the joint and given Angie a stern lecture about the perils of ingesting dope. She was a schoolteacher, after all; she had responsibilities. She was the grown-up. Trouble was, she hadn't felt the least bit grown-up. Marijuana always did that to her; it made her feel as giddy and irresponsible as a child.

She figured she owed the Evil Weed a vote of thanks for getting her through the dark days with Charlie, and she could never regard its use with the horror that normal people did. Still, if she was going to build bridges with Angela, she needed to establish a relationship with the girl that wasn't based on getting high. That was kid stuff.

She swung by Squashberry Cottage and hailed the teenager. "Hey, Angie, want to go down to the beach?"

"What for?" Angela was back in her sullen persona.

"For laughs. To hang out. Throw stones at seagulls, I don't know."

"That's a terrible idea. You shouldn't throw stones at birds," said Angie primly, re-inventing herself as a responsible person.

"You'd better come along, then, and make sure I don't."

"Yeah, okay. Why not? I'm bored out of my gourd here, anyway."

"So what did you expect, a three-ring circus?"

"I wanted to spend some time with my father." The girl assumed a put-upon look. "But he's too busy to care about me, I guess."

"He's too busy for me, too," said Cleo, thinking if you can't beat 'em, join 'em.

Angie stared at her, then switched sides just to be contrary, another way in which she resembled Max. "Well, he does have a B and B to run, you know. It takes a lot of time. All that cooking he does takes hours."

Cleo wisely declined to argue the point. "You might want to put on sturdier shoes," she advised. "The beach is rocky before you get to the sandy part."

"Yuck. Sturdy shoes are for losers and sports freaks," said Angie, and defiantly stomped away in her flip-flops ahead of Cleo on the path to the beach.

She had to give the girl credit, Cleo thought. Angie slipped and wobbled over the rocks without a word of complaint. But once onto the sandy shore, the teenager relaxed. "This is kind of pretty. Wow, the waves are huge!" She kicked off the flip-flops and waded into the shallows. "Jeez, it's cold! Hey, Cleo, don't be a wuss, come on in."

Cleo sat down on a large rock to pull off her sandals.

"Told ya flip-flops were best," taunted Angie, splashing up and down along the shore. She bent and examined the sand. "Cool shells," she said, and began to gather them in her hands. "All different colors and shapes."

Cleo waded into the water and stood staring out at the sea. What a beautiful place this was, she thought, and wondered why she'd chosen to live in a landlocked state like Minnesota. Here, the sea was alive and lively. The waves sparkled in the sunlight like Christmas tree lights, flickering and shimmering. The vista constantly changed, and she could spend all day watching the ocean and never see the same wave twice.

She'd always loved big bodies of water. She and Charlie had had a favorite cabin on Lake Superior that they rented for two weeks every summer and escaped to on weekends whenever they could. They'd dreamed about buying property on the North Shore, some day when their ship came in. Cleo hadn't been Up North since Charlie's death and she'd missed it enormously.

She waded out a little further, enjoying the cool water slapping against her calves. When a big wave flooded in, its magnitude catching her by surprise, she retreated hastily, but not fast enough to keep her shorts from getting wet on the bottom. She grinned and hitched them up and waded further into the sea.

Angie returned from her wander down the beach. "Hey, Cleo, look at what I found." She opened her hands, full of treasures: wave-scoured pieces of glass, shells, rocks, driftwood, even a lobster claw. "There were plastic bottles down there and I pulled them out. When we go we'll have to take them with us."

She looked out at the sea. "What kind of morons throw junk like that into the water? Everybody knows it isn't biodegradable. My science teacher taught us a whole unit about plastic and water pollution."

"My husband was gung-ho on that stuff, too," said Cleo. "It drove him nuts if I got lazy and put a plastic bottle in the garbage. He said we had to recycle or the planet would die."

"Well, he was right on." Angie glanced at Cleo. "One of the good guys, huh?"

"The best." Cleo brushed her hand over her eyes and forced herself to smile.

"Sorry. Hurts to remember him?"

"Sometimes."

Angie said suddenly, "Do you think my dad is one of the good guys?"

Cleo restrained herself from a quick pat answer and gave the matter serious thought. "Well," she said at last, "he's opinionated, impatient, arrogant and a worrier. But basically I think he's okay."

Angie looked thoughtful. "That's what my mom said."

"So why did she leave him?" Cleo knew she was pushing the boundaries by asking that, but if she could get Angie to talk, she might pick up inside information on the mysterious Mr. Avalon and his failed marriage.

"Mom didn't want to run a B and B here. She thought it was Nowheresville. She couldn't figure out why Dad would get a college education and take those special classes in cooking, and waste it all on dumb tourists in Newfie-land. She says he's a great cook and a really smart guy. He could have gotten a super job in Halifax, chef, restaurant manager, something like that, but he came back here instead and bailed out his Uncle John when he got too sick to run the place." She shrugged. "Kinda dumb, but nice. Loyalty is a good thing, I think."

"Umm." Still curious about Max's ex, Cleo asked, "What's your mom like?"

"She's the Bitch Goddess."

Cleo looked at her in shock, and her teacher instincts sprang to alertness. "Sorry, but is that an appropriate way to talk about her?"

Angie tossed her head and began to reel off a string of complaints. Her mother didn't want her to pierce any part of her body even though all the kids were doing it and it was her body, wasn't it? Her mother bought her old lady clothes and Angie had to work at a fast food joint to get money for the cool stuff she needed so she didn't look like a freak. Her mother hated her friends and tried to forbid her to see them but they were the only ones who understood her and she could talk to them about all kinds of things which she couldn't do with her mom.

Her mother was, in short, both bossy and bitchy, and thought she was always right and her daughter always wrong. And the Evil Stepfather was worse: he backed up his wife in everything relating to Angie, even though he wasn't her real dad and it was none of his business what she did so why didn't he just button up?

"Is that why you came to Max? Are you going to ask to stay with him?"

"Are you kidding?" said Angie incredulously. "Stay here in Newfie Nowheresville? There's nobody my age for miles and I bet there's no club scene, no decent bands or any raves, no weed. What am I supposed to do on the weekends, polish the silver? Shine the customers' shoes? Besides, my mom would miss me." She shrugged. "I'd miss her, too."

Cleo relaxed. Angie was a normal teenager, but she wasn't going to tell her that. She'd tell Max, though. Get him to lighten up and enjoy being with the kid.

Chapter Twenty-one

Come get your duds in order
For we're going to leave tomorrow.
Heave away, me jollies, heave away.
Come get your duds in order
For we're going across the water.
Heave away, me jolly boys,
We're all bound away!

"Heave Away"
Newfoundland folk song

It dawned on Cleo one day that while she was having a good time hanging out at the B and B and enjoying the sensual and social attentions of her host, she wasn't seeing much of Newfoundland, her childhood dream place. It would be a shame to go back to Minnesota having seen nothing of the Rock but Last Man Ashore Cove, fascinating though that was. She decided she'd better get right on the sightseeing gig, so she hauled out her tourist information and made a list of places she'd like to visit.

Her premier choice was L'Anse aux Meadows, where the Vikings had made their first landfall in North America. There was an extensive archaeological dig there that would be well worth seeing. And the route to get there went through Gros Morne National Park, an UNESCO World Heritage Site that sounded spectacularly beautiful, so she could knock off two tourist goals with one trip.

When she announced her plans to Max, he was appalled. "You can't go all the way up the Northern Peninsula by yourself."

Cleo looked at him in surprise. "But I want to."

He said, his face turning red with exasperation, "Well, you can't. I forbid it."

"You what? You can't forbid me to do something. You're not the boss of me."

Max inhaled and said all in one long breath, "I'm your lover and your friend and your B and B host and I'm telling you it's too far and too dangerous for you to drive alone. It's a hundred or more kilometers between gas stations, and there's a moose behind every tree waiting to leap out in front of your car and make you smash into it. It's wild country."

"Well, I'm a wild woman and I'm going to do it."

"Not alone," he growled, glaring at her. "And I can't leave the B and B for several days to take you."

Defiant, Cleo clutched at the most outrageous idea she could think of and snapped, "I'll ask Angie to go with me, then. She can remind me about stopping for gas and she can keep a lookout for moose. And if I have a flat tire she can hike to the nearest gas station. Or help me change it."

"Angela? Are you out of your mind?" Max looked at her, astonished.

"Why not? I like her and she likes me. We get along great."

Sure that his daughter would turn down the invitation to spend three days driving around Newfoundland with an adult, an English teacher no less, he turned conciliatory. "Okay. If Angela goes with you, I withdraw my objections."

His objections, indeed. Who the hell did he think he was, Cleo thought in fury, telling her what she could and couldn't do?

She was almost thirty and a responsible adult. She flounced angrily out of the kitchen and stomped down to Squashberry Cottage. "Hey, Angie, want to take a trip with me?"

"Where?" asked the teenager suspiciously.

"Up the Northern Peninsula to L'Anse aux Meadows. It's . . ."

"The place where the Vikings landed. Any good clubs up there?"

"I don't know . . ."

"Just kidding. Yeah, that would be cool. I am soooo bored here. How long will we be gone?"

"We'll go through Gros Morne National Park and we might want to spend some time in it because it's supposed to be beautiful, so I don't know how long it will take."

"Gros Morne? Hey, I've been reading about that. You can see whales and icebergs and take boat trips on fjords. We'd better spend a bunch of time and have a good look around."

"If your dad will let us be gone that long. He thinks it's too dangerous a trip for a couple of women. He thinks we'll run the car headfirst into a moose or something."

"Parents," said Angie with an exaggerated sigh. "Honestly, you'd think we were twelve years old, the way they act."

Cleo was startled to be included in the anti-parents league, but decided it gave her an advantage. She pressed it. "I brought tourist info. Let's figure out an itinerary."

Max was dumbfounded when they announced their plans. He had been so sure Angela would say no to the idea that his carefully reasoned arguments flew right out of his head, and the defiant stares of both women dared him to say anything negative. He was in a quandary. He could forbid Angela to go—he had that right, as her father and her temporary caregiver—but it would result in a sullen, combative teenager, a prospect he'd encountered earlier in her visit and which he dreaded with all his soul. And he wouldn't gain anything by it: Cleo would go on her own, and he had to prevent that as well.

He sighed dramatically. "Okay. If you're sure the two of you are up to it, bring your maps and brochures to the kitchen this afternoon and we'll have a briefing session."

Cleo rolled her eyes. He made it sound as though they were embarking on the invasion of Normandy. Briefing session indeed; what he intended to do was give them their marching orders. But she complied, and that afternoon the three of them were seated around the kitchen table, maps spread out in front of them, while Max lectured on the hazards of driving the Northern Peninsula. "Make sure you fill up around Gros Morne, and use the washroom, for obvious reasons. You don't want to have to go into the woods to go, if you know what I mean."

"Take a leak, you mean, Dad," said Angie, grinning.

He considered the remark indelicate, and ignored her. "And the most important thing to be careful about is moose. There's eight thousand of them in Gros Morne alone, and they are as unpredictable as hell."

"I know," said Cleo patiently. She'd been in Newfoundland for several weeks and had yet to see a moose. She was beginning to think they were a figment of the province's collective imagination, or a story made up to scare tourists. But to humor him, she said, "We have the same trouble with deer up on the North Shore in Minnesota by Lake Superior."

He fixed her with a steely stare. "A deer doesn't weigh twelve hundred pounds. A moose does." Turning to Angie, he said, "It will be your responsibility to watch the road every minute while Cleo is driving. And make sure you watch it carefully. Moose are dark brown and they blend into the trees and bushes around the road."

The teenager yawned, and Max was annoyed. "Are you listening to me, Angela?"

"Sure, Pop." Then she changed the subject, in the disconcerting way that kids have. "How come you always call me Angela? Everyone else calls me Angie."

"Because . . ." Max drew a deep breath. "We hadn't picked out a name for you before you were born, but the moment I saw you I thought you looked like a little angel." His voice was unexpectedly tender. "You still do to me. That's why."

The teenager was, for once, at a loss for words, but she turned pink with pleasure.

Cleo grinned at both of them. She loved these unexpected parent-kid bonding moments; she'd seen them in after-school parent-teacher conferences, and she'd wondered if she'd ever experience it with a child of her own. Angie wasn't hers and neither was Max, but she could take a vicarious pleasure in what had just happened.

For the next several days Max went around muttering words of doom and destruction, and making lists for them of things they had to take. On the morning of their departure, he looked them both up and down, noting with profound disapproval their shorts and tight tee shirts, and growled, "You can't go up the Northern Peninsula dressed like a pair of tarts. What if you have car trouble? You're more likely to be hit on than helped."

Angie drawled, "You are such a drag, Pop."

"I'm a realist," he snapped. Then he moved in for the kill. "I suppose neither of you checked the weather reports for the area. It might interest you to know that it gets cold up there and storms move in without warning. Remember the snow in June, Cleo? On the Northern Peninsula, you're right across the Strait of Belle Isle from Labrador." He moved closer and hissed in her ear, "What if you get sick? A woman with a red nose and fluids pouring from every facial outlet won't be welcome in my bed. I don't have time to catch a cold, I've got too much work to do."

Cleo glared at him, but said, "Your dad's right, damn it. Let's put on jeans and throw a couple of sweatshirts in the car." Angie nodded reluctantly, and the two retired to change their clothes.

When they returned, it was to find Max stuffing a huge picnic basket in the back seat. He had reverted to an area of the trip he could control: their diet. "I packed fried chicken, lobster rolls, and potato salad so you'll have enough food for lunch and dinner. That should take you to Rocky Harbor and a nice B and B that's clean and comfortable with a good nourishing breakfast. I phoned Mrs. Parsons and made reservations for you."

Angie and Cleo exchanged glances. Angie had hoped to stay in a cool little hotel she'd read about in the tourist brochure that had a club offering music till 2 AM. Cleo had agreed with reluctance, but figured she could keep the teenager out of trouble for a couple of nights. But a B and B booked by Max was a *fait accompli,* and it was a relief not to have to worry about the hotel. She said, to distract Angie from complaining, "Did you pack any brownies, Max?"

"Half a dozen. Angela's favorite, with nuts and lemon cream cheese frosting."

Distracted by the idea of brownies, Angie decided not to argue about the B and B. Reservations could always be cancelled, after all, or just plain ignored. Arguing would only delay their departure and she was seething with impatience to get gone. She climbed into the passenger seat, Cleo took the wheel and turned on the motor, and they were off.

Max waved goodbye, a worried frown settling between his eyebrows, there to reside until the women returned home.

As soon as they pulled out of the B and B driveway, Angie yanked her backpack up from the floor, took out her headphones, put them on and turned on her MP3 player. Soon she was staring at the tiny screen, undulating gently in her seat and mouthing lyrics, occasionally singing them aloud to the muffled racket issuing from the headphones.

Cleo stood it as long as she could. Then she reached over and tapped Angie firmly on the knee.

"What?" said the girl loudly.

Cleo motioned for her to take off the headphones.

She did, and said again, "What?"

"You need to talk to me while I'm driving."

"Why?"

"Because," said Cleo patiently, "we got up early today, and I get drowsy driving, and if you don't keep me distracted, I'll fall asleep and drive into the path of a big truck and we will be, like, dead. Squashed under the giant tires of a humungous eighteen-wheeler. Not the nicest way to die."

"Jeez," said Angie in a martyred tone. "I thought this trip was going to be fun."

"Fun for you, work for me. How about this? An hour of music, an hour of talk. But you have to stay on moose watch even when you're listening to music."

"Yeah, all right," said Angie, resigned. Then she brightened. "Could we, like, listen to my music on the car CD player?"

"What have you got?"

Angie rattled off a string of artists' names, mostly unfamiliar to Cleo and the ones she recognized made her shudder. "No thanks. That kind of music rots my brain."

"Shoulda brought the wrinkly Kinklies," said Angie with a sideways grin. "Maybe next time, right?"

Bemused by the idea that Angie thought there might be a next time, Cleo nodded. "We'll raid your father's CD collection. I'll bet he's got some good music."

"Oh, yeah, terrific, like the Beatles and the Stones."

"Classics, every one," said Cleo. The subject of Max had been introduced and, woman-like, she felt a burning urge to talk about her lover, but could not think of a way to work him into the conversation.

Angie did it for her. "Dad's kind of cute, in a retro way."

"What does that mean?"

"You know, old-fashioned, like a father in those Victorian novels we have to read in English. Like, he disapproves of my clothes but doesn't have the nerve to tell me so." She glanced at the other. "You wear the same kind of stuff, and he likes it on you."

"Well, that's different, isn't it?"

"I don't get why. Of course you look pretty good in mini-skirts and tees for your age, that is. You've got a nice build. Really good breasts. Wish I had a pair like yours." Then she spoiled it by adding, "You're kind of hippy, though."

Cleo said, "Tell that to your father. He keeps trying to fatten me up."

Angie giggled. "Yeah, me too. All those muffins, you know? They are so, like, death. Might as well rub them on your hips as eat them." She lowered her voice to a conspiratorial whisper. "He makes them with butter."

What? He'd been holding out on her. Was she staying at the only place in Newfoundland that harbored a secret stash of butter, and she wasn't getting any of it? Cleo said, "Is that right?"

"Yeah. I've been hanging out in the kitchen watching him cook. He uses real cream, too."

"Maybe that's why everything he cooks tastes so good. Fat adds flavor."

"My mom will like it if I gain weight. She thinks I'm anorexic."

"Are you?" asked Cleo, alarmed and suddenly wary at the idea of spending several days in close confinement with a teenager who refused to eat, or even worse, pigged out and threw up. She'd seen anorexic and bulimic girls at her school and it was not a pretty sight.

"Nah, that's dumb. Friend of mine was, though. Her mom and dad got really hyper about it and stuck her into a psycho ward for kids with eating disorders. It didn't do any good, though."

"It didn't?"

"Nah. She died."

"Oh, my God, that's terrible. A girl in one of my classes was anorexic, but she got help in time and she's in recovery now."

"Anorexia is so uncool. I tried to get Bette to smoke pot with me—you know how hungry that makes you—but she wouldn't do it. She went down to ninety pounds and still thought she was

fat, and she was afraid smoking dope would make her want to eat."
Angie shook her head sadly. "It was awful when she died. I cried
for two weeks."

Cleo patted the teenager's knee. "I'm so sorry."

"I was really bummed because I couldn't help her."

"It's hard to watch someone you love die." Cleo's memories of
Charlie flashed to full alert and she sighed deeply.

"Especially when it's for such a dumb reason. I didn't get why
she thought she was fat when she was just skin and bones, like a
skeleton. You know, like those pictures of concentration camp
inmates they make us look at in history class."

"Yes," said Cleo, and they were quiet for a few moments, thinking about death.

The peaceful landscape soothed them as the Trans-Canada
rolled along over gentle hills. The sun was by turns very bright,
then suddenly covered with clouds rapidly moving over the sky
in the changeable weather characteristic of the province. The
wind had picked up, and on the occasional flagpoles they passed
the Newfoundland flag stood out straight and proud, its red and
blue design pierced by a stylized yellow arrow glowing against the
white background. Some poles flew the old pre-Confederation
flag of pink, white and green, a symbol of Newfie disdain for the
central Canadian government.

Garden plots edged the side of the road, little patches of
ground planted with potatoes, root vegetables and cabbages, surrounded by pole fences to keep out moose and caribou. Cleo
remembered Max telling her that the gardens had been made possible by the disturbance of the ground during road building years
ago, and that some of the plots had been in the possession of the
same families for years. And he'd added that though the garden
patches were isolated from the homes of those that owned them,
no Newfoundlander would raid another's plot; that was an unwritten rule. Newfoundlanders might be poor, but they were honest.

On both sides of the road, pine trees swayed gently back and forth in the breeze as the road swung closer to Notre Dame Bay. Seagulls drifted over them, riding the currents, unfazed by the unpredictable wind. They were nearing Gros Morne National Park.

An abrupt, driving shower splatted the windshield with large raindrops. Cleo tightened her hands on the steering wheel and leaned forward in concentration. When a roadside gift shop appeared she slowed and pulled into its parking lot to wait for a break in the weather. Holed up in the car, they rummaged in Max's picnic basket and gobbled up part of his sumptuous lunch. He'd been right to pack food for them, Cleo thought; she hadn't seen one restaurant in all the miles they'd driven. Score for you, Maxie, she admitted to herself with reluctance.

Afterwards they ran into the gift shop to use the bathroom and look for souvenirs. Angie's search for a new sweatshirt seemed to Cleo to take hours, as the girl dithered among the variety of colors and designs. None of them had rude sayings, to Cleo's relief, so she wouldn't be faced with playing the heavy mother figure. But time was passing and night was fast approaching. Cleo nudged Angie and tapped her watch.

"Okay, okay, I'm coming," said the teen, turning over another pile of shirts.

Fifteen minutes later Cleo said, "We've really got to go. It'll be twilight in an hour and your father said not to drive then. He said there's lots of moose on the roads at dusk in Gros Morne and they blend into the scenery so you can't spot them."

"Nah, I think he made that up so we'd stop early and get to bed early."

Such trickery would be just like Max, the all-knowing, all-controlling, ever present fellow traveler, Cleo thought, but she couldn't be sure and didn't want to take a chance. "Come on anyway."

"Okay, gotta find my size first." She rifled through another pile.

The stalemate ended with Cleo snapping, "It's getting dark and we're leaving," and stomping out, Angie trailing sulkily along behind her without having made a purchase. They settled into the car again, turning north at Deer Lake towards Rocky Harbor and Gros Morne National Park, past the shimmering waters of Sandy Lake.

"What color would you call that pond?" marveled Cleo, forgetting her irritation in the glory of the scenery.

"Tahlo Blue, with a touch of Payne's Gray," mused Angie dreamily. Art was her favorite class in high school, and she loved working with pastels and watercolors. She stared at the scenery, storing up images to paint when she got home.

A pale violet twilight was descending, the setting sun's brilliant pink rays enveloping the flat-topped mountains on their right in clouds of lavender. It was glorious, spectacular, and it pierced straight into Cleo's soul, distracting her from driving.

Angie gasped in sudden horror, "Moose!"

Cleo's head snapped towards her, then back to the road. Dead in front of them in the road's center was an enormous mud-brown animal, barely visible in the dusk. Its huge lugubrious face, crowned with antlers like airplane wings, rushed towards them at a terrifying pace, thanks to the car's speed. Its bulk loomed closer and ever closer, and the closer they got, the bigger it seemed. Terror ripped through both women.

The moose stared at them stolidly, completely motionless.

Cleo jammed her foot on the brake. Angie screamed, "Stop! Stop!"

They were doomed. There was no chance of stopping the car in time to avoid hitting the moose and she didn't dare swerve on the narrow road, not knowing what lurked in the dark on either side. Cleo threw her right arm across Angie in a vain protective gesture and braced herself for the impact. "Max was right, again," was her first thought, and "We're going to die," her second.

The moose stirred in one fluid motion and its ghostly figure drifted across the road like a patch of smoke and disappeared into the underbrush. The car shuddered to a halt a few feet beyond where it had stood.

The two women sat, gasping, hearts pounding. Neither spoke.

Then Cleo took her foot off the brake and drove forward slowly, hands clamped to the wheel, eyes riveted on the road ahead. Beside her, Angie leaned forward tensely, her gaze swiveling from one side of the road to another in search of further road hazards.

The outskirts of the town of Rocky Harbor appeared, and the ubiquitous sign announcing a Tim Horton's. Cleo pulled into the parking lot, jumped from the car, and stomped into the fast food joint. Angie followed her, puzzled, arriving at the counter just in time to hear Cleo's order for a half-dozen mixed donuts.

They found a table and sat down. Cleo ate a chocolate frosted donut, then a caramel glazed, then a butterscotch-frosted, all without saying a word. Then she got up, went to the counter again, and returned with a cup of coffee and a box of donut holes known as Timbits, each one flavored and frosted like its larger cousins.

Finishing her first donut, Angie watched in awe as a chocolate Timbit disappeared whole into Cleo's mouth. "Wow, you're really shook up. I've never seen a woman eat that many donuts in one sitting," she marveled.

Cleo selected a toasted coconut Timbit and stared at it morosely. "My blood sugar's dropped to zero; I'm really freaked. I keep hearing your father's voice in my ears, yelling at me about my careless driving. He'll be furious. He'll probably throw me out. I may as well go back to the B and B and start packing." She put the Timbit in her mouth and chewed.

"Sure, he'll be freaked that we almost ran into a moose, but why would he be mad at you?"

"For endangering his daughter's life."

"You didn't endanger my life. It was my fault for screwing around so long with those sweatshirts. I didn't know it would get that dark that fast. And I didn't believe that a stupid moose would actually be dumb enough to stand right in the middle of the road. Jeez, what a brainless waste of space those things are."

Cleo selected a maple Timbit, popped it into her mouth and said around it, "Doesn't matter. It's my fault. I'm the responsible adult."

"Hey, just because I'm only seventeen doesn't mean I'm not responsible. I mean, that's like, ageism or something."

Cleo only shook her head and stared glumly at the box of Timbits, contemplating which one to gobble next.

After a short pause, Angie said, "So what if we don't tell him?"

Cleo looked at her hopefully. "You think?"

"Sure. We'd be doing him a favor, keeping his blood pressure down and stuff."

Cleo shook her head in despair. "It's no good. All he'll have to do is ask me how the drive went and I'll blurt it all out and then he'll throw me out."

Angie said, "Why don't we just tell him part of it? I spotted a moose on the road and you slowed down and it ran away. That's the truth. We don't have to tell him we were driving after dark."

Cleo considered, a ray of hope dawning. "It might work."

"Sure! You've forgotten basic strategy in dealing with the 'rents. Tell them only what they need to know, leave out details that might worry them. It's for their own good."

Angie grinned and picked up the last donut, while Cleo sat back in her chair and mused that now once again she was on the kids' side, not the side of the responsible adults. It was an odd place to be, but oddly comforting.

She got up, tucked the box of Timbits under her arm for future comfort and the two went back to the car. They drove slowly into Rocky Harbor. The town, stretched along the side of the bay, seemed to go on forever. In its center was the hotel Angie had day-dreamed about. "There it is! Let's stop."

"What about our reservation at Mrs. What's-her-name's B and B?"

"Find a phone, call her and make some excuse. Tell her we were delayed or something."

Cleo considered. They were in front of the hotel, after all, and her appetite for driving had disappeared back on the road with the moose. She parked, they got out, and walked to the hotel entrance. Men lounging on the porch glanced at them with curiosity, and one man nudged another in appreciation. Noting the gesture, Cleo realized that Max had been right about their clothes, too. Damn it, was there anything he hadn't anticipated?

The lobby was tatty and full of more men draped across overstuffed chairs. To their right was the entrance to the night club, out of which drifted a thick cloud of smoke and the raucous sound of a band tuning up. Cleo's desire for a safe haven rose abruptly, and she turned on her heels and stalked out. She'd had enough excitement for one day.

"What's the matter?" whined Angie, following close behind.

"We're going to the B and B. It's just a little further down the street."

Angie muttered, but did not argue. She too had been a little alarmed by the stares.

Tucked into their beds in the B and B, neither woman could fall asleep right away after their nerve-racking day. Their hostess, Mrs. Parsons, fussed over them in a motherly Newfoundland way and offered to fix them bowls of chowder. Stuffed with donuts, they hadn't been hungry either for chowder or for the lobster rolls left in Max's basket, and the stress of the drive had left them both tense and nervy. Mrs. Parsons had nodded at their refusal of her offer and said, "All righty. Youse go on to bed now and get a good night's sleep. Dat's the main t'ing when youse is travelling; get plenty of sleep so youse can drive safe. Plenty of moose on da road and youse don't see dem if youse is tired."

But once in their beds, they couldn't sleep. At last Angie punched her pillow into a more comfortable shape, turned toward Cleo and said, "Do you want to talk?"

"What about?"

"I dunno. Sex, maybe."

Cleo repressed a groan.

Angie said, "Have you noticed that cute guy that works in Max's garden?"

"You mean the tall skinny kid with the curly brown hair? The one with the sexpot girlfriend that hangs around and distracts him from weeding the turnips?"

"Yeah, him. I kind of like him. Do you think I should, like, make a play for him?"

"His girlfriend's very possessive. She'll eviscerate you if you get too friendly."

Angie sighed. "I guess. Anyway, maybe it wouldn't be fair to make him fall in love with me when I'm only going to be at the B and B three more weeks. I shouldn't break his heart," she added virtuously.

Cleo felt a pang of guilt. Was that what she was doing with Max? Dallying mercilessly with him when she knew she'd be leaving at the end of August?

"What's it like?" Angie blurted out of the blue.

"What's what like?" said Cleo evasively, anticipating and dreading the answer.

"Sex. You know, making love."

"Angie, the relationship between your father and me is private."

"Not him," said Angie impatiently. "Like I want to know what you and my Dad get up to. Gross. Can't you just give me some general information?"

"I suppose," said Cleo, musing on Max's reaction if he learned that she had now assumed the role of chief counselor in intimate matters to his teenage daughter. "What do you want to know?"

"How it works."

"Jeez, kid, you've had sex ed classes in school."

"I know the mechanics, but I don't know what it's like to be with a guy."

"Why are you asking me?"

Angie blurted impatiently, "Because I've never done it and if I get some details from you I won't have to do it and I won't look so dumb when the other girls talk about being with their boyfriends. I can't ask my mom. She'd spaz out to know I was even thinking about it."

Cleo sighed, and decided to give it a try. She was going to skip the intimate details, however. "Well, you should really like the guy. Love him, if possible. Never get pressured into sex, because a boy who has feelings for you won't try to make you have sex if you don't want it, and besides, that's rape. Always insist the guy use a condom. Don't go to bed with somebody to keep him from dumping you, because he'll dump you anyway, and tell everyone you're a slut."

There was nothing original about Cleo's advice but the girl was listening avidly. It was not like being lectured at in health class, and it was worth paying attention to someone she respected as a woman of the world. She said, "Yeah, I had a boyfriend like that once. I finally made up my mind to do it with him; then I found out he'd been screwing around with another girl, the weasel."

"Narrow escape. And remember that guys don't like to be used and discarded any more than women do. Develop a relationship before you go to bed. My husband Charlie and I went out for six months before we became lovers. We were each other's first."

Angie said, "That's really cool."

"Yes, it was, and we were deeply in love. When you come right down to it, I don't think sex without love is a good thing."

Angie demanded, "Are you in love with my father?"

Uh-oh, thought Cleo; right to the heart of her deepest insecurity, the looming elephant in the room she'd been avoiding. "I don't know, I haven't thought about it." Right. She'd pushed it out of her mind whenever the idea had cropped up.

"But you're having sex with him."

Cleo turned her gaze to the high ceiling. "I don't have all the answers, honey."

"I think Dad's in love with you."

Cleo was silent, pondering that.

Angie said, "If you two want to get married, it's okay with me."

"Thanks," said Cleo, unable to think of any other reply.

"If you do, I'll come up and visit in the summer and we can take another trip some place. It'll be Angie and Cleo's excellent adventure number two, since this is Angie and Cleo's excellent adventure number one." She chuckled, then yawned. "I'm getting sleepy. 'Night, Cleo."

"Good night, Angie." Before she fell asleep, Cleo became uneasily aware that she now was becoming a role model to Angela. It was not an unfamiliar situation. Every year two or three of her female students decided that she was the kind of woman they wanted to become, and took to hanging around her classroom after school, doing whatever little jobs she needed done. If the school had used chalk and erasers on its boards instead of dry markers, the girls would have vied for the privilege of clapping them.

She usually acquired several young men with crushes on her, too. They stared at her longingly in class, and competed for the more masculine jobs of lifting heavy packages and opening boxes. There was always at least one boy per period who could be relied upon to return her books to the school library or go to the supply room for her.

One year she'd even had a bespectacled young poet so mad about her that he'd asked her, shyly, to read and critique his poetry which he'd never before showed to anyone. Cleo was flattered, and walked a fine line between criticism and encouragement.

All this was part of being a teacher, and she understood and accepted it. She'd never expected Angie to feel that way about her, but this trip together was bringing out undeniable symptoms of hero worship in the girl. She'd have to make clear that she was not Angie's mother, she was not her teacher, she was not even a wise elder sister.

Maybe they could just be friends.

And she wasn't even going to think about Angie's ideas about the state of Max's heart.

Chapter Twenty-two

Oh, it was last Monday morning
And the day being calm and fine,
For the Harbour Grace excursion
With the boys to have a time,
And just before the sailor
Put the gangway on the pier,
I saw some fellow haul me wife
On board the Volunteer.

"Excursion Round the Bay"
Newfoundland folk song

Cleo woke early the next morning. She groaned when she saw 5:30 on the clock radio, knowing that breakfast was not until 8:30 and that she'd never be able to go back to sleep. She punched the pillow, tossed and turned, snuggled into the warmest spot in the bed, but remained violently awake.

She'd dreamed of the moose encounter only vaguely, as a huge shadowy figure popping out from behind a tree. It hadn't disturbed her sleep, only left her feeling anxious this morning. Perhaps that was why she couldn't drop off into slumber again.

Bowing to the inevitable, she rose and pulled on underwear and socks. In the other bed Angie still slept, curled into a fetal shape, and Cleo, feeling maternal, pulled over the girl the covers she'd thrown off during the night. Then she went to the large window in the front of the room, tiptoed the curtains open, and found herself gazing at the best view in Rocky Harbor. The sea stretched before her, made golden by the rising sun, each wave tipped by a foam frosting like whipped cream. The sky was enormous and rapidly turning blue as the sun rose higher, losing the bright orange and reds of its rising.

Entranced, Cleo stood and stared until the day was successfully launched. Then she realized that she was standing in front of a picture window wearing only bra and panties, and turned away hastily to finish dressing.

Angie stirred and moaned.

"Good morning," said Cleo.

"Ummph," said Angie, and burrowed her head under the pillow.

"Beautiful sunrise," said Cleo.

Angie emerged from beneath the pillow and demanded, "What time is it? Why are you up so early? Do you get up this early every day?"

"It's 6:30. I'd rather have slept later but I couldn't go back to sleep once I woke."

Angie turned over and pretended to drop off to sleep again.

Cleo sighed and searched the bookcase for something—anything—to read. Some time later she was happily settled with a tattered copy of *Gone with the Wind*, when Angie snorted abruptly and jumped out of bed. She rushed into the bathroom and turned on the shower full blast, emerging wrapped in a towel and looking marginally more humanoid.

"Jeez, I'm hungry," she announced. "Did we bring in Dad's basket of goodies? I could kill for a brownie."

"No, but in a half hour we can go down for breakfast. Reluctantly she consigned Scarlett to Twelve Oaks and Ashley's betrayal, got up and finished dressing.

"Let's go down now. Maybe the coffee's ready."

It was, strong, black and very hot. Mrs. Parsons emerged from the kitchen with a tray of muffins and the inevitable saucer of foil packets of margarine. "My, youse are right early risers. Sit yerself down and I'll bring in da porridge." She put down the tray and bustled back into the kitchen.

"Do you think she'd fix me a hard-boiled egg?" whined Angie, but when the porridge appeared with brown sugar and maple syrup, she attacked it greedily.

Cleo ate it too, and between them they demolished three pecan muffins, juice and several cups of coffee. Angie asked for and got another serving of porridge. Mrs. Parsons pulled up a chair, poured herself a cup of coffee and began talking, like any good Newfoundlander with a captive audience. "Where are youse headed today?" Told that they were going to explore Gros Morne Park and hoped to ride the boat that went into Western Brook Pond, a fresh water fjord trapped between billion-year-old glacial cliffs, she volunteered to make their reservations. By the time she returned, they'd finished their breakfast and were itching to get started on the day's adventures.

"Youse're booked for da one o'clock sailing and youse should be there at 12:30, else they'll give yer seats to somebody else. It's right busy this time a year. Make sure youse take jackets because it's cold on da water."

They left the breakfast room with more motherly admonitions hurled at their departing backs, the last being, "Take head scarves against the wind and mittens if youse has got 'em."

The boat tour was given a bit of spice by the fact that they got lost and almost missed the departure time. The boat's captain was looking for them anxiously and fussed as they lined up for the walk to the boat that he'd been right worried when they hadn't shown up. "Tourists are always getting lost," he said. "Youse should have compasses surgically implanted before youse leave home." Everybody calmed down on the forty-minute walk to the boat and the captain told stories about what they were going to see. He told them that the valley surrounding Western Brook Pond was carved out by glaciers during the last ice age, that the water in it was pure and contained salmon, trout and char, and that many unusual birds nested on the cliffs.

Nothing he said could have prepared them for the spectacular sight of waterfalls coursing down the green shrub-covered cliffs, dissolving into blue-tinged spray as they splashed into the clear cold water of the Pond. There were so many colors in sky and water that Cleo wanted to count them, and she heard Angie muttering under her breath in a dazed way, "Cobalt, ultramarine, phthalo, cerulean, turquoise . . . there's veridian . . . violet . . ." That was the only thing she said during the trip. Cleo was not any more vocal.

They were still bemused by the splendors of Gros Morne National Park when they set out the next day to drive the Northern Peninsula to its very tip, to L'Anse aux Meadows, the only authenticated Viking site in North America. They emerged from the Museum full of information, such as the fact that two Norwegians, the explorer Helge Marcus Ingstad and his archaeologist wife, Anne Stine Ingstad, had discovered the site, and worked diligently to prove that it was settled by Vikings around the year 1000.

It did not look like much, on first sight, wide green fields with bumps rising above the ground where buildings had once stood. But then they discovered the sod-roofed replica of Norstead, the Norse village, populated by costumed, chatty reenactors, and they got to handle battleaxes. Both Angie and Cleo were indignant to learn that in Viking mythology only men went to Valhalla; women went to Hel. Angie said, "So who made all those dumb dead Vikings their supper if there were no women?"

"Ah," said the male re-enactor, "that's what Valkyries were for, to serve the heroes mead and the meat of the boar Särimner, a special boar that could be slaughtered every night."

"What a deal," said Angie sarcastically. "I suppose the Valkyries had to wash the dishes, too."

"Of course," said the re-enactor smugly. "That's women's role."

Angie might have said more, except for the cry of "Whale!" that came from outside the longhouse. She and Cleo rushed out in time to see a huge silvery-blue body crest the surface of the water, leap into the air and splash back down again.

They stood together, watching in silent satisfaction and savoring the moment, then turned to begin the search for a meal in nearby St. Anthony. They'd nibbled at the rest of Max's provender all day, but were still starved by 6 PM. Cleo hoped for lobster rolls, Angie yearned for pizza, but they found themselves at a small café called the Harbour End, reminiscent of Puddester's in Last Man Ashore Cove. Cleo, remembering Max's complaint about the lack of gourmet cooking on the Rock, ordered fried cod and Angie had a hamburger. Both were plainly seasoned but filling and surprisingly tasty.

Cleo slept better that night and didn't wake until 8 the next morning. They scrambled down for more porridge and muffins, squashberry this time, and made plans for the long drive home. Max intruded into Cleo's brain again, making her feel like a puppet on a string. This time he was reminding her about the dearth of gas stations, so she obediently filled up the gas tank in St. Anthony before beginning the long drive down the Northern Peninsula, and both women used the bathroom.

They were quite at ease with each other now after the moose escapade, the donut gobbling, the thrilling boat ride and the whale sighting. Angie maintained a dutiful moose-watch and chatted to Cleo about school, her favorite classes, the boys she liked and didn't like and why, and occasionally about her mother and stepfather, casting them in a much more favorable light than previously. Despite her years as a teacher, Cleo had never had an opportunity for such an intense one-on-one interaction with a teenager, and she filled her mind with useful tips on teen thoughts and attitudes. The girl chattered relentlessly, and by the time they'd passed Gros Morne on the way home, Cleo's ears were ringing.

But it was not an unpleasant sensation. She'd discovered she genuinely liked Angie. She was, as Max had said, a nice kid.

Cleo and Angie walked into the Big House radiating quiet triumph. They had done it. They had successfully completed a long trip through the wilds of Newfoundland, they had seen three of the province's scenic wonders, and they had not been running on empty, assaulted, insulted, or murdered by a moose, although the last one had been a near thing.

Max was stirring something in a large pot on the stove when they walked in. He dropped the spoon and rushed forward to take them both into a surprisingly unrestrained hug of welcome. Then he drew back, and Max-like, launched into a litany of complaints, the chief of which was, "What took you so long to get home? I've been worried sick."

Cleo was wise enough to deflect the complaints by changing the subject. "Got any coffee, Max? I'm dying for caffeine. What Newfoundland needs is a Caribou on every corner and I don't mean the four-legged kind."

Angie chimed in, "Yeah, and have you got anything to eat? I'm starved."

They'd successfully yanked his chain. Requests for food and drink always grabbed Max's instant attention, and he bustled around with percolator, cups, and refrigerator dishes. Soon Cleo and Angie were seated at the table in front of plates full of sandwiches and salad. He said, "I'm sorry, this is the best I can do at such short notice. If you'd phoned that you were close to home . . ."

"Chef's inferiority complex," said Cleo. "Just like Mrs. Puddester. Relax, Max."

He grinned reluctantly and threw himself down into a chair facing them. "Tell me all about your trip."

Angie said, "Gros Morne was gorgeous. L'Anse aux Meadows was interesting but the guides were sexist . . ."

Cleo said, "But historically accurate. And we saw a whale . . ."

"It jumped up out of the water right in front of us . . ."

"I almost got its picture but I couldn't get the camera out of the case in time . . ."

"The only thing we didn't see was an iceberg but people said it was too late in the season . . .

"We went on a boat trip on Western Brook Pond . . ."

"And there was a moose on the road," Angie threw in casually.

Cleo swallowed hard, waiting for questions, threats, recriminations.

Angie added in a matter-of-fact voice, "Cleo slowed down and the moose ran away."

Max said, "So now you believe me."

"Oh, yes," said Cleo.

"Definitely for sure," said Angie.

"We'll never doubt you from now on," said Cleo, relieved at having successfully avoided further interrogation.

Proved right yet again, Max smiled and urged more coffee and sandwiches on them. "I made white chocolate chip cookies this morning," he said, sure of a positive response.

The two women grinned at each other, happy to be home.

Chapter Twenty-three

I hear the soft note of the echoing voice
Of an old, old love, long dead . . .

Patience, Gilbert and Sullivan

July faded into August and August neared its closing days. Angie went home to Florida to get ready for the start of school, presenting Cleo with the remainder of her dope stash when Max wasn't around to witness the transfer. "You're right," she said. "Don't want to be nabbed by customs guys. Besides, I can score plenty at home."

She grinned at Cleo. "Why don't you get Pop to smoke some with you? He's so hyper it would do him good." Cleo grinned back, thinking about what kind of persuasion would be necessary to get uptight Max to smoke marijuana.

She moved back into Squashberry Cottage, and once she was on her own ground her affair with Max became even more torrid. They couldn't get enough of one another. It was the best sex either had ever had and now, suddenly, it wasn't enough. Something was missing.

Cleo recognized it first, alerted by Angie's comments about the state of Max's heart. He wanted something from her besides sex.

He wanted something she'd not given a man since Charlie, something she wasn't sure she still had to give, wasn't sure she wanted to give. He wanted a friend, and maybe even more than that.

He wanted companionship; he was desperate for someone to talk to. He wanted a sympathetic audience for his B and B woes. He was even starting to talk to her after they'd made love, becoming positively chatty at a time when most men would roll over and start snoring. "You have the prettiest hair," he'd whispered the night before, burying his face against her neck. "Don't ever cut it." She'd lain there uneasily, absorbing his compliments, only half believing them. He sounded perfectly sincere, but was she as special as he thought? She couldn't believe it.

Another night he lamented that he couldn't take her off to explore the wonders of Newfoundland beyond what she'd seen with Angela. "There's Ferryland and the archaeological dig, and Twillingate and Tickle Bridge, and the new Beothuk Museum... You haven't even been into St. John's. Maybe I could take next Monday off—no, there's a coach party coming in. Tuesday? No..." He was still trying to find a free day when they both fell asleep, his voice trailing off in her ear.

Neither would let the idea of love to enter their minds, Max because he was too overworked to think seriously about anything but the B and B, and Cleo because it seemed unfair to Charlie's memory.

Ah, Charlie's memory. She got his picture out of her billfold where it lived and sat on the cottage porch looking at it, dreaming of old times. It was her favorite picture of him, one she'd taken on a camping trip that had celebrated their fourth anniversary, just a few months before he'd been diagnosed.

His flyaway blond hair had been even more rumpled than usual in the high wind blowing through the trees. The sunlight had ricocheted off his glasses, and he'd given his trademark goofy, loving grin for her camera. That night they'd spread their sleeping bags under the stars of the Boundary Waters Canoe Area in northern Minnesota, and made love slowly and sweetly, as sweet as though it were the first time.

They'd lain in each other's arms afterwards. Charlie had talked about the bright students in his biology classes and how he planned to challenge them with special projects in the coming year. Cleo had talked about *Romeo and Juliet* because she was teaching it fall semester. They'd challenged each other to exchange Shakespearean quotations, and he'd fallen asleep while Cleo was reciting from *Hamlet,* "'Good night, sweet prince, and flights of angels sing thee to thy rest.'"

He'd loved hearing her read Shakespeare. Utterly drained of tears, she'd read him sonnets while he lay dying, and he'd smiled at her for the last time.

The vast unfairness of it all swept over her yet again. Charlie had been a fine person, a great teacher, a wonderful husband, and he would have been a wonderful father to the child they'd talked about having next year. He'd been cut down in his prime, as the saying went, with scarcely enough time to say goodbye. Good night, sweet prince.

If she didn't have his picture, she might not be able to remember exactly what he looked like, his likeness growing faint and blurred in her mind like a fading photo. The idea terrified her, and she clung to every memory with an iron grip. She couldn't let go of Charlie; she had to keep him alive. She'd tried so hard when he was sick and she'd failed. Memory was all there was left of him, and that had to survive.

She had a little weep, then tried to cheer herself up with the thought of Max sliding into her bed in a few hours. Life didn't seem quite as desperate whenever she was with Max. He was handsome, he was witty, he was passionate. She felt safe in his arms and nervy and high-strung without him. The shell she'd built around herself was cracking, letting in nightmares, tears and raw emotion. Her earlier feeling of peace and contentment was gone, and apprehension had taken its place.

She wasn't as tough as she thought she was, as tough as she'd been with her other lovers. Sensible modern thinking told her she didn't need a man to feel secure but her emotions told her the reverse. She wanted to cling and be cuddled and indulged like a child. She was developing what she had to regard as an unhealthy attachment to Max Avalon. Worse, the long suppressed thought was creeping into her head that she was falling in love with him, and that road was signposted for a broken heart.

It annoyed the hell out of Cleo. Why couldn't life be simple, and sex be enough? Why couldn't she have a summer romance like a normal woman? Why was she suddenly so needy, wanting comfort and reassurance, always wanting, wanting, wanting?

She wasn't sure she could go on living if her heart was broken again. She could not let it happen, she would wrap her mind around the idea of going home soon where she'd be safe from impossible yearnings. If she could keep her emotions under control for two more weeks she could return to Minneapolis with great memories of her Newfoundland summer and her hot Newfoundland lover.

A summer fling, that's what it should be, as much a part of summer as bikinis, ice cream cones, and trips to the lake. Fun and games to spice up her vacation, nothing permanent.

She would go home revitalized, ready to move bravely forward into a future full of hope, where she could make friends and go out on dates and maybe find a new relationship that would last a lifetime.

Max would just be a memory, she decided, and wondered why that realization didn't make her feel any better.

Chapter Twenty-four

A Newfoundland sailor was walking on the strand.
He met a pretty fair maid and took her by the hand.
Saying, "Will you come to Newfoundland, along with me?" he cried,
And the answer that she gave to him was "Oh, no, not I."

"Oh, No, Not I"
Newfoundland folk song

Max was chopping onions that night when Cleo sashayed into the kitchen. He stopped in mid-chop to stare at her in admiration. Determined to put her heart back on an even keel, she'd pulled herself together and made herself focus on the fun and games aspect of their relationship. She was his gal pal and temporary bed partner, nothing more complicated than that. She'd even dressed the part in the princess t-shirt from the night of their first sexual encounter, this time with a bra, and it fit her like the paper on the wall.

It worked on Max like a charm. He felt a predictable stirring in his nether reasons. "Good day, princess," he said.

"Hiya," she answered and slithered over to him. "How about a kiss?"

"You betcha," he said, speaking Minnesotan for the first time. "But my hands are onion-y so you'll have to do the grabbing."

She grinned, took his face in both hands, and gave him a hot, wet kiss.

"You vixen, you really know how to suck face."

"Because you taste so good," she said, running her tongue across his lips until he shuddered with excitement. "Shall I help with dinner?"

"Nah, just sit down and let me look at you." His hands resumed chopping before his eyes went back to the onions and he came within a hair's breath of slicing himself. "Maybe you'd better help with these after all. I almost lost a thumb."

He pushed the chopping board over to her and watched as she lifted the cleaver with care, arranged the onion slices into a neat pile and began delicately to chop them into pieces of exactly the same size. "Do a lot of cooking, do you?" he asked, amused.

"Not much. It takes such a long time to prepare food from scratch," she said, and made another careful slice across the onion pile.

"Ummm," said Max, who chopped vegetables so fast that stray bits flew around the kitchen like machine gun bullets. Good thing I don't need those onions until the last minute, he thought. "What do you like to cook?"

Her face brightened into a smile that left Max dazzled. "I make a wonderful macaroni and cheese from my mother's recipe. Charlie loved it. He'd make hamburgers and we'd have a feast for about two bucks a person. We were always short of money back then, when we were students," she said wistfully.

Max wondered what her Charlie had been like and wondered if it would be okay to ask, when the kitchen door opened and Maria came in. "Why you sit down, Boss? Lotsa work to do." Then she noticed Cleo, carefully chopping. "*Ay, caramba*, you got somebody else to do the work. You got another slave."

"That's right," said Cleo, looking seductively at Max from under her lashes, and licking her lips. "I'm his slave, all right."

Max's eyes grew wide with anticipation.

"You lookin' or cookin', Maxwell?" demanded Maria. "'Cause meatballs don' make themselves." She was taking a risk, calling him by his despised full Christian name, but she thought she could get away with it because he was so enraptured, watching Cleo. She didn't dare go too far in teasing him for fear of retaliation. If sufficiently annoyed, he might call her bluff by getting rid of Mrs. Hoh, and make Maria clean the toilets as part of her duties. She hated cleaning toilets even more than she hated cooking.

She couldn't afford to quit because she was saving money to go to school next winter in St. John's to learn to be an accountant, so she had to stay sweet with Max, no matter how much she yearned to tease him until he sputtered and turned red with aggravation. "You got meatball mix made or you wan' me to do eet?"

"You? You've got hands like pile drivers. Meatballs need to be made with a delicate touch or they'll be as hard as cannonballs."

"Hokay." She grinned. Another messy, disagreeable task evaded. "You do eet, Boss; then it be perfect. But hurry oop because guests circling dining room like vultures."

Max sighed, knowing who was the slave at Last Man Ashore Cove. In a better world, he would have been able to sit and stare longingly at Cleo for as long as he liked. Maybe share a glass of wine and watch each other while passion grew slowly and surely. Lean forward across the table to exchange a kiss. Rise, join hands and drift off to bed. Afterwards, take all the time they wanted to talk and laugh and share confidences. He was surprised by these ideas, then realized he was feeling romantic and that was a tip-off that something was happening in his head. If only he had time to explore what it was.

He sighed again.

Ah, well, he'd have her in his arms tonight, hot and hungry. Lust never sleeps. Right now he had to concentrate on another type of hunger. He took the meatball ingredients from the refrigerator, dumped them in a big bowl and plunged his hands into the mixture. "When you're finished chopping, Cleo, pour the onions in here."

"Hokay, I done now," Cleo said, unconsciously imitating Maria. "Here they come." Her hands, wet with onion juice, and his, covered with meatball mix, touched as she scraped the onions off the chopping block into the bowl, and this time both sighed and stared into each other's eyes.

Maria watched them with satisfaction. When she'd first come to work for Max, there had been a flicker of sexual interest between them that had quickly dissipated after the first clash of their all-too-similar personalities. Each put the other's back up, and they squabbled like cats that were meeting for the first time. After a while, the conflict had settled into a sort of truce, with occasional skirmishes over duties and time off.

She thought Max was a pretty nice *hombre*, all things considered, and she was pleased that he and Cleo had gotten together. It had improved her boss's temper one hundred percent, too. All he had needed was a little hot loving to lose the grouchiness, and it appeared that he was getting plenty of that. She would do whatever she could to nudge the affair along to a permanent resolution, like marriage, because she liked Cleo and she liked having a kinder, gentler Max around the B and B. And she had a bit of romance in her practical Spanish soul.

She said, dripping sugar, "I serve tonight if you want, Boss, and you can 'ave a leetle private 'oliday in kitchen with slave. Maybe 'ave a leetle sweet dessert."

"Not noted for subtlety, are you, Maria?" said Cleo.

Max, to the amusement of both women, was blushing. He growled, "Business before pleasure, and work before play . . ."

"Vegetables before dessert," added Cleo helpfully.

"And fruit before nuts," he snapped, glaring at the grinning women. "Check the table settings, Maria. Last night you forgot the dessert forks and they had to eat their crowberry crumble with their knives."

"Hokay. Be sure you wash hands before you touch anythin',

Max; you don't want to get meatballs on slave's leettle skirt." She grinned and flounced into the dining room.

"She's a smart mouth, for someone who just learned English nine months ago," Max grumbled.

"She's a hoot. She likes to tell me funny stories."

"Mostly about me, I suppose."

"Some of them." Cleo grinned smugly. She and Maria had had an amusing conversation the other day about Newfoundland men. Maria had said, "They like cavemen, all hair and big hands and brains in *pene*."

"*Pene?*"

"You know. Down there." She made a significant gesture.

"Is that an old Spanish saying?"

"Hell, no. Is what my friend Isabel say. She having hot affair with Newfie guy. He wan' marry her an' carry her off to his cave."

"Cave?"

Maria nodded. "He live at Dark Tickle. Population seventy-four *hombres*, three hundred moose."

"Does he really live in a cave?"

"No, ees figure of speech. He own beeg apartment building that ees full of fishermen and laborers all summer, empty all winter. Hees apartment look like cave, stuffed moose head and moose skin rug and lotta First People art. He collect that stuff. Isabel say he loaded wit' dough, and helluva lover."

"Why doesn't she marry him?"

Maria grinned. "She goin' to. Right now she tell heem she thinkin' about eet. You gotta make men wait for answer; then they think they really got a prize when you make up mind to say yes."

Cleo pondered that advice in her heart. She hadn't made Max wait very long before she gave him everything he wanted. But then she wasn't angling for a proposal of marriage, like Isabel; she just wanted a hot summer romance. Or was that all she wanted? No, don't go there, don't think about it. But she couldn't stop herself from daydreaming about a more lasting arrangement. She eyed Max, scrubbing his hands briskly under a stream of hot water. "What's Newfoundland like in winter?" she asked abruptly.

"Colder than a witch's tit and snow up the wazoo." He looked at her with interest. Maybe she was considering extending her stay, a pleasing prospect. Never mind just coming for Christmas, how about staying for several months? They could have a cozy winter together if she did stay, with lots of sex to keep them warm and his excellent cooking and fine wine cellar. The idea had real possibilities. Hmmm, he thought; he could use a good recipe for macaroni and cheese. Wonder if she'd share hers?

Maria pushed the door to the kitchen open with elaborate caution. "Ees hokay I come in?"

Max cursed under his breath. A thoughtful, good-natured Maria was even more annoying than an obstreperous one.

Cleo grinned and said, "*Si,* sure, ees hokay."

The three enjoyed plates of meatballs and spaghetti for dinner while the guests were feeding, and they washed up companionably. Then Cleo and Max went back to Squashberry Cottage and had a wild night together, and when he left in the morning he was stumbling and talking to himself all the way back to the Big House. He sang bits of Gilbert and Sullivan patter songs while he cooked breakfast, and greeted Maria with such a warm and friendly smile she was instantly suspicious.

"Don' forget, I off early tonight," she warned him, in case he was buttering her up to try to wheedle her into working extra. "I 'ave to go to church."

"Oh, that's right. I remember you said that."

"Ees hokay?"

"Is very hokay."

"I not be here to help with washing-up."

"Not a problem. I'll get Cleo to keep me company in the kitchen." He smiled serenely. "Work always goes faster when you have someone to chat with."

"Ees called chat, huh, Boss? Hokay, eef you say eet."

"Oh, I do. I do say it, indeed." He gave her a wide grin and tossed her a hot pad. "Get the rolls out of the oven for me, Maria, my little hot tamale."

Maria grinned back. Boss's romance lookin' good, she thought. He happier than a sea gull with its beak full of fish.

The first rays of dawn in the bedroom window of Squashberry Cottage woke Max early the next morning. Cleo lay sound asleep, nestled against him. The sun painted her body a pale gold and struck sparks of fire from the brown strands of her hair. She sighed and turned over, leaving a cold place on his shoulder where her head had been.

He glanced at the clock, realized that he didn't have to get up for an hour, and turned his attention to Cleo, lying soft and vulnerable against him. He pulled down the sheet to give himself the luxury of looking at her closely, when for once he was not consumed with passion.

Her eyelashes were very dark, almost black, and very long, curling tenderly against her cheeks. Her nose was slightly turned up at the end, something he hadn't realized before. That was why it was so effective when she stuck her nose in the air to snub him, he thought.

There was a tiny beauty mark of a mole on the outside curve of her right breast and her nipples lay relaxed against her breasts like rosebuds drooping in the summer heat.

Her legs were wonderful, long and sleekly curved, but the rest of her was too skinny, he thought, preferring like most men an abundance of curves. He ran a gentle finger over her ribcage and decided that she needed fattening up, and he was just the b'y to do it, with his fine cooking. Rich, velvety cream soups. Yeasty rolls, fresh from the oven. Crowberry crumble with a pitcher of cream to pour on top. He'd even share the butter from his secret stash with her.

He wouldn't get a chance, because she'd be leaving Last Man Ashore Cove at the end of the summer. The thought sent alarm coursing through him. He didn't want her to leave. He didn't want to lose his lover, his friend. His woman.

He knew suddenly and beyond doubt that he had hit the nail on the head. His woman. Cleo English belonged at Last Man Ashore Cove, belonged with, belonged to Max Avalon. And why was that? Because he loved her. Wow. What a concept.

A powerful wave of emotion rumbled through him; lust combined with love, a heady mixture that made him growl, "You're mine," in her ear. He bent and kissed the beauty mark on her breast, then her nipples, awakening them. Then he took her mouth.

Cleo woke to his hot, hard lovemaking. *The guy is insatiable,* she thought happily, and let herself be kissed and caressed until she was thoroughly aroused. "Come on," she whispered, and wrapped her hands around his slim hips to pull him into her.

His entry jolted her as though she'd grasped a hot wire, and his muttering made her crazy. "What are you saying?" she gasped.

"You're my woman," he said distinctly, and took her so fiercely that she hadn't the breath to scream. She felt his shuddering climax deep inside her. "You betcha," she sighed and lapsed into a semi-conscious heap. *What a way to wake up,* she thought.

Max stared down at her, wondering what had just happened to him. Then he realized that he wasn't wearing a condom. It was the first time he'd not been careful since he'd gotten his girlfriend pregnant when they were both seventeen. He'd been plenty careful after that. Sharon hadn't wanted another kid and had gone on the Pill promptly after Angela had quit nursing, and he'd kept himself protected in any sex he'd had since their divorce. Using a condom had become second nature to him.

And he hadn't even thought about it, a few minutes ago, his need to possess her so deep that it had wiped everything from his mind.

Was his sperm even now making its blind way up inside her, seeking the bliss of an egg to fertilize? Was he on the brink of making her pregnant? What would they do if she were to become pregnant?

These were dangerous, important ideas. He lay back down and thought hard about the situation until he had to get up and cook breakfast for six up in the Big House.

Chapter Twenty-five

To sleep, perchance to dream.

Hamlet, William Shakespeare

When Max left that morning, Cleo fell back asleep, straight into a nightmare. People were gathered around her, pointing their fingers. "Whore," they hissed. "Your husband's hardly in his grave and you're screwing other men."

She awoke from that one in a cold sweat. Where had it come from? She knew almost immediately: a sense of guilt over the series of affairs she'd had the year after Charlie's death had suddenly surfaced, after being buried for a year and a half. She'd not felt guilt before; she'd had only a profound feeling of relief at having avoided the serious consequences of unbridled sex. She'd thought she'd gotten away with the whole fiasco, but perhaps people had noticed after all, and had been whispering about her behind her back. Perhaps they'd thought she'd betrayed poor dead Charlie.

Perhaps she had. What kind of a woman was she, to have behaved that way? Didn't she have any loyalty to her husband's memory? What was she doing now, taking a casual lover on her vacation? A summer fling? Ha! Call it by its right name: slutty behavior. Perhaps she was heading back to that same pattern of uncommitted sex. She shuddered with self-loathing at the thought.

Guilt, ugly and cruel and long dormant, raged in her and depression entered in guilt's wake. She buried her face in her pillow and wept.

Max, happily working in his kitchen, had no such problems. Today had become a major turning point in his life, and satisfaction from the morning's revelation had stayed with him all the while he cooked. He loved Cleo English and thought there was a good chance that she might love him too, and that she might be receptive to an invitation to share their lives. Think about this logically, b'y, he advised himself. What have you got to offer her besides terrific sex and great cooking?

He wasn't a rich man, but he was doing all right. The B and B was prosperous and he owned it outright, thanks to Uncle John's generosity in leaving him the property as thanks for keeping everything together while he fought cancer. He'd lost that battle and Max had gained the B and B, and realized months later that he'd played right into his uncle's hands.

"Too many Newfies leaving, going down to Halifax, or out west to Toronto. Need to keep our people here," his uncle had said. "Need to have jobs for them, keep the communities alive. Need our bright young folks to stay here on The Rock."

And Max had stayed. His wife had left, taking their daughter, looking for a better life in some place that wasn't a tiny Newfoundland outport.

How would Cleo feel about living here? He'd have to sweeten the offer to get her to stay, and that meant marriage. What a wonderful idea. He'd enjoyed large chunks of his previous marriage, deranged as it had been with guilt, shame and a baby coming into his life before he turned seventeen. He'd loved waking up early and finding Sharon nestled close beside him. He'd wake her with kisses and caresses and they'd have glorious early morning sex. Then one of them would crawl out of bed and get Angela and bring her back to their bed. They'd play baby games with her, like pattycake and this little piggie, until it was time to get up.

Max had worked at the B and B in summer and Sharon had been the maid. They and Uncle John had shared baby Angela's care. Max had loved summers, especially after he'd been allowed to take over some of the B and B cooking, and he and Sharon had plenty of time for beach picnics, playing with Angela and romps in bed. He'd had the time of his life, and he couldn't imagine why anyone would ever want to live any place other than Newfoundland or live any other kind of life than the one he was living.

Until Sharon told him that she couldn't stand it any more. She was tired of cleaning toilets and making beds in the summer, tired of the dumb jobs she had to get in the winter to support them while he was in school, tired of wasting her life. He was smart and talented and so was she, and they could have a better life than anything they could find in Newfoundland. She was going to leave him if he didn't leave the Rock.

He didn't, and she did. She took Angela and went to Halifax in Nova Scotia and never returned. Their divorce was amicable, even to the terms of sharing their child. Then she'd married another man and fled with Angela, leaving no forwarding address, knowing Max would fight her going so far away, and would probably win.

Now he was about to take a monumental chance on asking someone else, a Yank no less, to marry him and live in Newfoundland. The Rock wasn't everyone's cup of tea. How would Cleo feel about living there?

Most important of all, did she love him? And if she did, would it be enough to convince her to share what he freely admitted was an insulated, isolated life? There was only one way to find out—ask her.

That was settled, he decided; he'd ask her and coax her into saying yes, if necessary. Thinking about Cleo as his wife made him outrageously happy and he reveled in it, and pushed the associated problems out of his mind. He whistled and sang and teased Maria while he cooked, and joked with the guests when he served them.

What a charming man, they all thought, and began making mental plans to return next year to Last Man Ashore Cove B and B.

After breakfast he whizzed through the rest of the morning's work, and made for himself a window of opportunity to go to Squashberry Cottage. He'd probe a little about how Cleo felt about Newfoundland, so he could plan his marriage marketing strategy. And he'd try to get a clue about how she'd feel about joining her life with his.

He'd be subtle and clever. They'd have a laugh, to start with. A guest had told him a funny story, quite naughty, and he looked forward to sharing it with her and hearing her delighted, shocked giggles. That would loosen her up for an intimate talk about their future.

She was not on the porch reading the new romance novel he'd found in the back of the bookshelves yesterday, a novel that had been so hot and graphic he thought she'd really get off on it, and maybe acquire some interesting new ideas. She was not in the kitchen or the living room. "Cleo?" he called tentatively. "Where are you, princess?"

Cleo heard him and buried her head deeper in the covers.

At last he tracked her to the bedroom. "Ah, waiting for me in bed, are you. Just what I'd hoped for. I don't have much time, but we can have a quickie . . ." He began to unbutton his shirt, and stopped when she raised her head and he got a good look at her.

There were tears on her cheeks and her eyes were red and swollen.

He moved toward the bed, then stopped at the tortured expression on her face. God, he hadn't frightened her this morning with the intensity of his passion, had he?

"What's wrong, Cleo?"

Mute, she shook her head.

He sat on the edge of the bed and rubbed her back, wincing when she pulled away from him and curled up into a little ball in the center of the bed. He begged, "Tell me what's the matter, princess." Then he got it. "You had another bad dream, didn't you."

She mumbled something.

"What?"

The nightmare voices zinged in her head. She said, "I'm a whore."

"I thought you were a schoolteacher," he said stupidly.

She glared at him. "It's not a joke."

"I didn't mean it as a joke, Cleo. I don't understand what's wrong."

"I'm a whore. I sleep around. I had an affair before Charlie was dead a year and then I had four more in eight months."

He tried to assimilate that information. "Why?"

"Why? Because it made me feel better. Because it helped me to forget Charlie."

He said, "You weren't having sex with married men or with your students?"

"What? I'd never do that. What do you think I am?"

"Well, that's what we're trying to figure out. Are you a whore or aren't you?"

She burst into tears.

"Aw, don't cry, Cleo. You're not a bad girl. You told me you hadn't made love with anyone for two years. You stopped after those guys, didn't you."

"Yes," she sobbed.

"And I'm your first lover since them."

"Yes."

"There's nothing wrong with seeking comfort in sex after the terrible experience you had with Charlie's illness and death. People find comfort in all sorts of weird ways." He rubbed her shoulder. "Have you had breakfast?"

She shook her head.

"I'll fix you something to eat. You'll feel better with something in your belly." Food, the ultimate remedy for Max, something he could control absolutely. He went to the bathroom and came back with a warm wet washcloth. "Here. Put this over your eyes."

He returned a few minutes later with a cup of tea and a plate of toast. "Sit up. Otherwise you'll spill crumbs all down your front and then your bed will be all crackly tonight when we're making love. I'll cook you some scrambled eggs."

She sipped the tea and nibbled on a piece of toast. "I can't eat anything else, Max. This is enough."

Tears were still in her eyes and he knew she needed more comforting and more food. He wanted to crawl into bed with her and cuddle her until she stopped weeping and then get up and fix her a plate of eggs and sausages and more toast, with butter this time. He stole a surreptious look at his watch. Damn. It was only an hour until four new guests were due to check in, he still had beds to make, and he'd sent Maria to the grocery store with a long list that she might or might not pay attention to. He had to leave right now and take charge or the whole shaky edifice that was Last Man Ashore B and B would crash down in ruins.

She'd finished the tea and toast and he took the dishes from her. "You need sleep, Cleo. A nap will make you feel better. I'll bring lunch down to you later."

No man had been that kind to her since Charlie, who was always kind and gentle, and her eyes filled with grateful tears. Max understood how she felt and he was going to help her. She really needed that help; she was limp and weak and stupid, but at least he'd reassured her that she wasn't a slut. Obediently she slid down in the bed. He pulled the covers up and kissed her cheek. "Have a good sleep, with no nightmares."

If only, thought Cleo despairingly as she heard the front door shut. She was desperately tired but afraid to go to sleep because the nightmares might return. She tossed restlessly, then sat up, swung her legs over the edge of the bed and rose. She was okay, just a little shaky, and she was determined to make it to the bathroom to brush her teeth.

The bathroom mirror image was not flattering. Her hair was a tangled mess, there were dark circles under her eyes and her eyes were red. She looked every one of her thirty years, and worn out.

And Max had seen her in this condition. He probably won't come back, she thought gloomily. She dressed in a horrible baggy sweatshirt and jeans she'd brought for hiking, and went to the kitchen to make herself another cup of tea.

After a while she was nodding uncontrollably. Maybe she could sleep now.

But back in bed she could feel another nightmare coming just as she slipped into deeper sleep. Odd, she thought drowsily, that now she could tell when they were starting, like an epileptic could sense a seizure coming on. Maybe something was wrong with her head, like a brain tumor or schizophrenia or terminal depression.

Max saved her again. Coming in with a tray of minestrone, garlic bread and cheese ravioli, he heard her crying out. Uh-oh, he thought, set the tray down and rushed to the bed. It was a bad nightmare: she thrashed against his hands and pushed him away when he tried to hold her. He couldn't understand what she was saying. "Cleo, wake up!"

"Oh, damn," she said groggily. "It happened again."

"What was this one about?"

"I don't remember. I think it was about death." She drooped against his shoulder and began to cry. "Oh, God, I think I'm having a nervous breakdown."

"No, you're not," he said firmly. "I won't let you." What can I do, he thought, how can I help? He certainly didn't intend to leave her alone in the state she was in. He pulled her gently to her feet, surveying the baggy sweatshirt and pants with alarm. Cleo, always so fastidious about her appearance, must really be wrecked to wear such an ugly outfit. "Eat your lunch, then comb your hair and put on some pretty clothes. You're coming up to the Big House with Maria and me. You need company."

She obeyed him to the letter, but felt awkward in the kitchen with Maria sneaking glances at her red eyes, and Max urging her into a chair. "Sit and talk to us."

"What about?" she said in such a dispirited tone that Maria and Max glanced at each other, worried.

"Tell me what eet's like in the U. S," said Maria. "What you know about Weesconseen?"

"Well, it has a lot of trees and it's cold," Cleo began. "And it gets tons of snow."

"Ha! Ees like Newfoundland. I goin' to like eet there. Maybe get fur coat to swank around in when eet snows. What else you know about eet?"

Cleo racked her brain for more tidbits and gradually began to snap out of her depression in the cameraderie of the kitchen and with Max's good cooking warming her belly.

Max, skinning chicken breasts, sensed she was running out of stories, and he wanted to keep her talking because she was beginning to sound happy again. Besides, he was on an intelligence-gathering mission, finding out all he could about Ms English so he could shape his plans for her. But this was no time for intimate questions. He asked instead, "What's your teaching job like?"

She said slowly, "It's a difficult school. The focus is on troubled, smart kids who are underachievers. A lot of our job is motivation. I teach English and creative writing. I like it, but it wears me down. Two to three years is the standard stay for teachers at my school because they burn out. And of course, some of the kids drop out, too. Those are the ones that break your heart."

"We have a high dropout rate at our local school, too," said Max as he made a wine sauce. "There's so much unemployment in Newfoundland that it's hard to convince kids it's worth staying in school, because there aren't jobs for them if they do graduate. Our economy was built on fishing. Newfoundland waters used to be so thick with cod that you could walk across the water on their backs and scoop them up in buckets. Then the fish started disappearing and in 1992 the government banned cod fishing altogether.

"Cod ruled here for hundreds of years and most of the population worked the fish. Now their livelihoods are gone. Thousands of fishermen out of work since 1992 and an unemployment rate of twenty to thirty per cent. It's a damned shame. The cod haven't come back even with the moratorium and nobody knows why.

Some people say they're back, but reserved for the large foreign boats. The large boats, foreign or Newfie, rule the industry. It costs a least a million to build a fishing boat these days, not something your everyday fisherman can afford."

"That's terrible. How are people going to earn a living?"

"Well, there's oil and logging, mining and crab fishing. I think tourism is a good bet," said Max. "But maybe I'm prejudiced." He layered the chicken breasts in a baking pan and poured the wine sauce over them. "Gives people work during the summer, anyway."

He slid the chicken into the oven and turned back to the women. "Hokay, ladies, let's cook vegetables. Who's peeling potatoes?" God, he loved cooking and he loved having Cleo in the kitchen with him; it felt so right. Even Maria was mellower now; she and Cleo got along like buddies from way back.

And Cleo seemed to be hokay now. Maybe his proposed arrangement would work out. The nightmares showed she needed him, and damned if he didn't need her, too.

Chapter Twenty-six

Sorry her lot who loves too well,
Heavy the heart that hopes but vainly...

H.M.S. Pinafore, Gilbert and Sullivan

Max's terrible, horrible, no good, very bad day started when he awoke next to Cleo in bed in Squashberry Cottage. Last night he'd made her happy so many times that he'd lost count; it had been an epic performance, one for the ages. She'd finally curled up in surrender, satiated and whimpering. He'd swept her hair away and bit the back of her neck as a mark of possession. Her damp skin smelled sweetly of sex and flowers and he'd licked it, wanting to devour her completely. Instead, he'd wrapped himself around her, an arm and a leg flung over her body so that she fell asleep trapped under him, her hand clutching the side of the bed to keep from being completely swallowed up. Max's last thought before sleep was that he was making excellent progress in winning his woman. I'se the b'y that gets the girl, he told himself in drowsy satisfaction.

Cleo awoke abruptly. This time it wasn't Charlie trapped in a coffin, trying frantically to get out; she was the one entombed. She struggled desperately, weeping, clawing at the lid as it closed over her.

Her agonized thrashing and cries woke Max. "What's wrong?" he gasped.

"Trapped . . . please, please, let me out!" she cried.

He pulled her against him. "Wake up, Cleo. You're having another nightmare."

She fought him until he loosened his grip. He rose over her. The first rays of the rising sun slanted through the window and illuminated his face, grim with determination, his eyes narrowed into two chips of blue ice.

Cleo clutched at his shoulders. "Help me, save me!"

"I'll help you, Cleo. Tell me about it."

"I dreamed I was trapped in a coffin, still alive. Like Charlie."

"Honey, he's dead. He wasn't buried alive and neither will you be. I'll make sure of that."

She stared up at him. "Promise?"

"I promise."

"It was so real . . ."

"It wasn't real, it was a bad dream. Go back to sleep, Cleo." He bent and kissed the tip of her nose. "You're hokay, princess. You're safe with me." Now, and for the rest of their lives, he thought with determination.

The thought she'd repressed, the thought that this was more than a summer fling, came back into her head and would not be dislodged. He'd promised to keep her safe. He must have feelings for her, and now she allowed herself to realize that she had feelings for him. Tenderness overwhelmed her and she reached up to stroke his cheek. They smiled at each other, and reassured, she fell asleep again, her body relaxing against his.

He'd intended to stay only until she'd gone back to sleep, but her sweet touch had melted his heart and sent him drifting into a glorious dream, like the cheerful finale of a Gilbert and Sullivan operetta. Newfoundland in winter, the B and B cut off from civilization by a blizzard of epic proportions. The entire Big House his to command, with no guests underfoot, whining and demanding.

His refrigerator full of food, his cellar full of wine, a blazing fireplace, and Cleo in his arms on the sofa, the two of them laughing, talking and cuddling. In his dream he was nuzzling her lovely naked shoulder, and he awoke to find himself doing just that.

Soft Newfoundland summer morning sunlight poured through the window. Dream merged slowly with reality, colored with a promise expressed in mental shorthand. Cleo, smart, cute, feisty Cleo, his woman forever. He'd make sure she had no more nightmares. They'd run the B and B together in the summer. If she wanted to teach, there were always vacancies in the local schools, and if she wanted a challenge, there was plenty there.

He loved her, and he was almost certain she loved him. It was going to work; he'd make it work. Organized as always, he began to plan his approach. He couldn't do anything about arranging things now because he was so busy until . . . he counted days in his mind. Nine days till the last Saturday in August when the B and B was entirely booked with a busload of tourists. They were going off all day on a sightseeing trip beginning Saturday morning after breakfast, and they wouldn't be back till very late that night. A whole day without responsibilities, after he and Maria had cleaned up the breakfast dishes and changed all the bedding and towels.

Max, a closet romantic, began to dream about his proposal. He'd fix Cleo a wonderful dinner in his apartment, served on his beautiful maple pedestal dining room table, which he'd polish till it shone. Something superb from his private wine collection, in sparkling crystal thistle glasses. Flowers and scented candles burning, romantic music on his CD player, all the accoutrements a woman would like.

He'd have to get her an engagement ring and he had no time to go to St. John's to a jewelry store. He'd ask Silvia, the silver worker at The Rock gift shop in Little Last Man Ashore Cove, to make something pretty. If Cleo wanted a diamond they'd go to St. John's together to pick it out when the fall tourist rush was over. He couldn't afford a big stone but he'd get her something she liked even if he had to mortgage the B and B. Nothing was too good for his woman.

He'd finish up the proposal dinner with lemon *crème brulée* and a dram of Glenmorangie. Then he'd get down on his knees, take her hands, and pop the question. Dearest Cleo, I love you. Will you be my wife?

It all fell together in his mind like a completed jigsaw puzzle. She'd say yes and he would gain a wife, a helpmate, a lover. Maybe they'd have kids after a while. Maybe she was pregnant even now, since he'd forgotten the condom a few nights ago. A family, himself, Cleo, kids. Just nine days to wait until he could seal the deal.

Lost in planning, he forgot that she was due to leave in eight days.

His future life settled, he turned flat on his back and pounded the bed with his fists in satisfaction. Then he caught sight of the clock. Six AM.

Damn. Damn. Damn it all to hell. He had intended to get up at five because he had six guests who had requested an early breakfast so that they could hot foot it to Port aux Basques to catch the ferry to North Sydney on Cape Breton Island.

The day hadn't started and he was already an hour behind schedule.

He zapped himself up and into his jeans, thrusting one arm into a shirtsleeve. He gathered up his underwear and stuffed it into a pocket with his free hand while he jammed his feet into shoes.

Pulling the shirt on, he loped up the hill to the Big House and inside. Naturally, the front door wasn't locked because he hadn't gone home last night. The only reason he ever bothered to lock up in this peaceful backwater was nervous Mainlander guests; Newfies knew better. Mainlanders always asked for a front door key if they were coming home late and verged on hysterical if he told them the door was left unlocked. "Burglars . . . rapists . . . sne ak thieves . . ." The litany was the same and it wasn't worth arguing about, so he'd had a few duplicate copies of the front door key made in case they were needed by the nervous.

He rushed into the kitchen, mind working frantically to think of what he could prepare for breakfast in an hour less than he'd planned. Cleo's nightmare had upset him. He was going to have to sleep with her every night to protect her. He was learning the warming signs of bad dreams and now he knew how to stop them from taking possession of her. There was no reason for her to be torn apart emotionally.

He'd have to insist that she move back into the tiny room she'd occupied when Angela was in residence. Nah, that room was tatty. Why not move her into his apartment even before they got married? She loved the cottage but it wasn't worth the risk of those nightmares. He'd promised to keep her safe, and he intended to keep his promise.

Partridgeberry muffins. Scrambled eggs. Moose sausage. That would be quick, even though it wasn't very gourmet, unlike the breakfast quiche with sides of hash browns he'd planned that took forever to prepare. He'd add hash browns because they weren't much work, and tell his guests it was a hearty Newfoundland pre-ferry meal.

He went on autopilot as he threw the muffins together while planning the rest of his work: peel potatoes, set the table, start the hash browns cooking, throw the sausage in a pan. Get the sausages out of the freezer first so they could thaw.

Everything mentally scheduled, he popped the muffins into the preheated oven and dashed into his apartment. In the twenty minutes they took to bake, he'd grab a shower, wash his hair and dress in a presentable manner. That was the trouble with this job. Not only did the rooms and the food have to look good, he had to look good too. People didn't want a scruffy hobo as their host, and especially not as their cook.

Thank God it's mid-August, he thought as he slipped into the shower. Two-thirds of the way through the tourist season, only six more weeks to go. He enjoyed his work, but would have enjoyed it more if it were a month shorter.

Dressed to charm the clientele in tight jeans and a blue shirt that matched his eyes, Max came back into the kitchen just as the oven timer went off. Pleased that he was right on track, he grabbed a hot pad and pulled the muffins out.

Each muffin was a flat little glob in the bottom of its cup. Not one had risen.

Max stared at the pan, dumbfounded. Then he fished out one glob, swearing when he burned his fingers. The poor muffin was as hard as a rock; it couldn't even be broken in half. He never had a muffin disaster. Was his baking powder out of date? Or ... it was impossible, it was incomprehensible, it was incredible ... had he forgotten to add the baking powder?

He stared at the counter where he'd mixed the batter. The tin of baking powder was not there; he hadn't even taken it out of the cupboard.

Holy shit! He was completely losing it. Mooning over his girlfriend like some seventeen-year-old puppy and he'd blown breakfast.

What was he going to do? Guests always expected a bread product and he hadn't a slice in the house. His bread delivery was every other day and this wasn't the day. Why hadn't he listened to Maria when she'd said, "Keep loaf in freezer, for eemergency." He'd been offended and snubbed her royally for the idea; he never had emergencies.

Except for today, you chucklehead, he scolded himself. Well, he wasn't going to apologize to Maria; she'd gloat for days. But maybe next time he'd listen to her when she had a suggestion.

Enough recriminations. What was he going to do? He glanced at the clock. He was now an hour and a half behind schedule. No time to bake more muffins, it would have to be pancakes; they were quick and easy. He'd skip the hash browns so he could concentrate on getting the pancakes to the table piping hot—always a challenge—and he'd double up on the sausages and give the guests some of the very expensive mixed Newfoundland berries syrup that he made himself and reserved for special occasions. He threw the thawed batch of sausages into a frying pan and pulled more out of the freezer.

By the time the first sleepy guests stumbled into the dining room, he had the table set, juice poured, pancake batter resting, griddle heating and sausages sizzling merrily.

Luckily he'd prepared the early departures' bills yesterday afternoon. He poured the first batch of pancakes onto the griddle, plastered a smile on his face and walked out to greet his guests.

They were delighted with their breakfast. He'd send them on their way, happy and full, and then turn his attention to the regular eight-thirty breakfast victims.

Except that his credit card hook-up refused to accept one couple's card and the special phone number to override such circumstances was busy. The couple fidgeted, murmuring about missing the ferry.

"Go get your luggage," he told them in desperation. "Sometimes it takes a few minutes to get this thing to work."

Just as the last suitcase was loaded into the rental car, the credit card was accepted. It was now ten minutes to the next feeding, and no time to make more muffins. So that batch would get pancakes and expensive syrup too.

It dawned on him as he stood, flipper in hand, that Maria had not shown up. Whatever her faults, she was always prompt when it came to meal service, and she was now half an hour late. He glanced at the phone answering machine, and realized in dismay that it was blinking.

Apprehensive and resigned to the worst, he played the message. "Allo, Boss, ees Maria. I seeck, damn eet. Up all night weef *estómago*. Better check mayonnaise you going to use today on sandweech. Maybe ees not good. I try last night on ham an' rye. Now I seeck as dog."

Swell. Absolutely perfect. Not only was he going to lose Maria's help for the rest of the day, he'd have to make a new batch of mayonnaise, a chore he hated. But he didn't dare take a chance on using the old stuff. If it had made Maria sick, it would make the guests sick and the last thing he needed was five people doubled up, clutching their *estómagos,* and fighting each other for the bathrooms.

And he'd promised a picnic lunch of sandwiches and potato salad . . . damn, that took mayonnaise too . . . for Rooms Three and Four who were heading off to explore the Bonavista Peninsula.

Could the day get any worse? He thought not, until just before twelve when Cleo slunk in, a morose expression on her kitten face, just as he was at the crisis point of the mayonnaise: adding oil to the egg yolk, vinegar and mustard mixture.

"Hi," she said sulkily, managing to package in one monosyllable a variety of complaints all based around her main grievance, that he'd left so abruptly that morning and he hadn't been down to see her after breakfast as usual. She'd repressed her memories of the nightmare but its aftereffects had left her needing comfort and security, something he hadn't been around to give her.

When he responded with a brief nod, she walked to him. "What are you doing?"

"Making mayonnaise."

She noticed the broken shells on the counter. "With raw eggs? Yuck! Don't you know that raw eggs are an open invitation to salmonella?"

"The eggs are irradiated; there's no bacteria in them." When she opened her mouth to argue, he added, "Shut up, please, Cleo. I'm having a crisis."

Offended, she stalked to the kitchen table and plopped herself down in a chair to sit staring at his back. Sure, she knew better than to interrupt him when he was in the middle of some desperate cooking endeavor, but right now she hadn't cared because her sense of injustice was so great. He'd stayed the night with her, used her all-too-willing body in any way he'd wanted, and then bolted up and rushed away without even a goodbye kiss.

She'd awakened just enough to be conscious of his mad

scramble out of her bed, and she was quite sure he hadn't kissed her. That hurt her feelings. Not remembering the nightmare and the comforting cuddle that had followed, she thought that all through the night they'd slept quietly together. Then he'd left her without a word of farewell, not even a comforting pat on the bottom. Now she was virtually invisible and he was ignoring her and he'd told her to shut up, adding insult to her list of grievances.

She knew she was being overly sensitive but she was in a wretched state. A look at the calendar told her she only had eight more days at Last Man Ashore B and B. Her heart told her it was going to hurt a lot if she had to leave without a word from him about love or commitment and the rest of that stupid stuff that women were supposed to crave, and she did, damn it.

She'd tried hard to make her affair with Max into a summer fling but she'd failed miserably. She needed some sign of affection, some sweet words to take home with her. Then maybe they could write to each other, and when she came back for a Christmas visit they could work on a more solid and lasting relationship than being just bedmates. In the last couple of days, she'd begun to think of a permanent arrangement and had even scribbled "Mrs. Max Avalon" on a scrap of paper, which she'd hastily crumpled up and thrown in the wastebasket, berating herself for acting like a lovesick teenager. She didn't understand what was going on in her head, and she couldn't control it.

She glared at his insensitive figure.

Max was aware of her glare and her anger, but he couldn't do anything about it until . . . ah, it was happening. The oil droplets and the egg yolks were beginning to cling to each other like lovers, and in a minute he would have mayonnaise.

Then he could talk. Well, he could talk after he'd made the sandwiches, added the mayonnaise to the potatoes he'd cooked earlier, seasoned the potato salad, and packed it all up with a dozen brownies for the picnic lunches.

Then he could kick back and relax. After he'd changed three

beds and put out fresh towels for new guests, set the tables and done as much pre-dinner prep as he could, since he wouldn't have Maria to help with any of it. Should he scrap the potatoes *au gratin* in favor of roasting them with the rump of beef? Then what would he have to go with the salmon, his other entrée? Potatoes with a meaty taste. Yuck, as Cleo would say.

The mixture turned obediently into mayonnaise and he grinned in triumph. Then, thinking about side dishes, he gave Cleo an appraising look. She was a little cranky, but that was okay. If she was cranky, she wouldn't be brooding about her latest nightmare.

He had a chunk of first-rate cheese in the fridge and a package of his dried homemade noodles. Was she up to making her special macaroni and cheese? It would go great with both salmon and roast beef. "Hi," he said cautiously.

Cleo sniffed and stuck her nose in the air.

Now what? Damn, women were touchy. Max poured the mayonnaise over the potatoes, reserving enough for sandwiches, added salt and pepper and dill, and mixed it up. With that done, he figured he had enough time for a kiss and a chat about macaroni and cheese, as long as he didn't get carried away and forget the time. He started towards her, then stopped uncertainly at the look on her face. "What's the matter?"

Cleo knew he was working very hard but she couldn't stop herself from being angry. "I don't like being ignored."

"The mayonnaise . . ."

"It isn't just the mayonnaise."

"What is it, then?" he said, genuinely puzzled. He certainly hadn't ignored her last night; he'd done a number of things that should have earned her heartfelt gratitude for days to come. Maybe for weeks, he'd been that good. And besides, he'd comforted her after her experience with the nightmare and soothed her back to sleep. And he was going to ask her to marry him, as soon as he could work it into the schedule.

Cleo looked at him sullenly, relishing her hurt feelings. He was up, down, grabbing her whenever he wanted her, ignoring her the rest of the time, rattling her sensitive soul. It was his attitude, damn it, but she couldn't say that, even if she could manage to put it into words. Men never understood such a comment. Even sensitive Charlie would have been baffled, and would have looked at her uncomprehendingly out of innocent brown eyes. She took refuge in evasion, knowing she was weakening her case for a genuine grudge. "You didn't come down for coffee this morning."

"Oh, that." He was relieved. All he had to do was explain the situation and she'd understand and forgive him for his lapses. Wait a minute, he thought. What lapses? He'd had the day from hell so far and it was barely noon. Why couldn't she understand and cut him a little slack? His own temper flared and he growled, "I was busy."

"I see." She rose, her nose stuck so high in the air it made her neck hurt. "Well, I'm sure you're still busy so I'll get out of your way." She marched toward the door.

Max lunged and pulled her into his arms. "You're never in my way." He kissed her, hot and hard, yanking her close to his body, which responded in a predictable way. Damn, he'd like to scoop her up, carry her off to bed and love away her anger.

Cleo moaned against his mouth, "If you're too busy . . ."

"Never too busy for you." Then he realized that was a lie; he really was too busy. He had sandwiches to make and two picnic hampers to pack. "Uhhh, that is . . ."

"I knew it," she snapped, and thrust herself away from him.

"Damn it, Cleo, I've got a business to run here and I'm doing it single-handed because Maria is sick."

That should have slowed her down, and for a moment it did. But her angst over leaving and over what she perceived as Max's total lack of commitment had gotten a firm hold, and would not be deterred. If he were a true friend, if he even loved her a little bit, he'd make time for her needs. She recognized the complete unreasonableness of that thought, and didn't care. It was showdown time and her mouth had a mind of its own. For that matter, her mind was totally out of control. She snarled childishly, "I don't give a hoot in hell about your stupid business."

She had gone too far, and she knew it.

Max looked at her, wounded to his soul. He was proud of his B and B and he loved all that he'd accomplished with it. Sometimes he even liked his guests. Why couldn't this unreasonable female see reason? All he was trying to do was what he had to do. If she couldn't accept that, how were they to be together? His dream of a cozy winter by the fire was flickering, just like the fire. He tried again. "Cleo, if you can wait till after I get these picnics packed, then we can talk."

Cleo broke. "Forget it. I'm tired of waiting. I'm going home."

He kissed the idea of macaroni and cheese goodbye, and bid an unhappy hello to potatoes au gratin, a pain in the butt to make, especially if he had to do it alone. "Hokay. Go back to the cottage, curl up with a book and I'll be down as soon as I can."

"I'm not going back to the cottage. That's not home. I'm going back to Minneapolis and don't ask me why."

His fantasy of love and marriage crumbling into ashes, he blurted, "Why are you going back to Minneapolis?"

"Damn it, I told you not to ask me that."

"Why not?"

If she had a baseball bat she'd slug him with it. "You know why."

"What am I, a mind reader? How am I supposed to know what goes on in a crazy woman's head?" Behind his back the bowl of mayonnaise and the plate of salmon filling quivered impatiently. Visions of indignant guests demanding their picnics flooded his mind. How had he gotten involved in this stupid, time-wasting exercise in futility? Why was this argument his fault?

"I'm not crazy. You know as well as I do that this relationship—if you can call it that—is going nowhere."

Max prayed for patience. Why had she suddenly decided that

this was the time to talk about relationships? Couldn't she sense how he felt and what he had planned for her? He certainly couldn't propose now while she was so upset and he was so deluged with work. He tried again. "Well, let's look at it rationally. Where do you want it to go?"

She sank down on one of his kitchen chairs and dropped her head into her hands. "I don't know."

"You don't know, but I'm supposed to guess? And that's not crazy?" He shook his head sadly and unfortunate, half-joking, words slipped out of his mouth. "Demented, loony, total nut case."

Cleo sobbed. He'd put his finger squarely on her greatest fear.

"Ah, damn it, don't cry, for God's sake; I can't stand it. Please, Cleo . . ." He flung himself on his knees beside her and pulled her into his arms.

She fought him fiercely.

"I love it when you struggle. Makes me crazy with lust."

That was definitely the wrong thing to say.

"So we're both crazy." She put her hands on his chest and pushed, and he nearly fell over backwards.

"The perfect pair. Both fruitcakes." He grabbed her chin with one hand and held it tightly while he kissed her hard, then coaxingly until her mouth opened to him.

This was going wrong and it was going to end up in bed, she knew, in a wild, hot clash of bodies. But not a meeting of minds or hearts. This situation was hopeless. Well, the hell with it. She still had eight days left before she left Newfoundland. If terrific sex was the only thing she was going to get out of this so-called relationship, why not enjoy it? Minnesota was going to seem mighty cold and lonely when she got back. And there'd be nothing to look forward to but winter, and nothing but memories to keep her warm.

She let herself relax against him, responded to his kisses and his hands on her body. Do your damnedest, Avalon. I'm all yours. Eight days and then my little broken heart and I are out of here, b'y.

But she was in for a surprise.

He pulled back and looked at her suspiciously. "What are you up to now?"

"Huh?"

"One minute you're yelling at me, the next minute you're crying your eyes out, the next minute you're all hot in my arms, practically begging me to take you. Are you trying to confuse me?"

"This may come as a shock to you, Maxwell, but you are already confused."

He wasn't confused, damn it. He was in love with her, and if she could just wait until the end of the tourist season, he'd tell her so in a proper way, with flowers and champagne and a proposal. Right now they were having great sex and a lot of fun tormenting each other, and she made him happy enough that he could deal with the madness of the end of the season rush, when it seemed like everyone in the world wanted a little Newfoundland holiday. The money he made now would take him comfortably into winter, when he and his woman could kick back and enjoy each other's company, in and out of bed, while the cold winds howled and fierce storms blew up from the ocean.

He was edgy from overwork, like a greyhound chasing a mechanical rabbit, and it made him furious that she was upsetting his carefully planned program. Why didn't she understand how he felt, and why couldn't she wait for him to tell her? The sandwiches were waiting, after all. Guests waited. Why was she so impatient? His control snapped. "Get lost, Cleo. I've got work to do. Come back when you've got your head on straight."

She stared at him with huge hurt eyes, then turned with dignity and stalked out. She made it all the way to the cottage before collapsing in tears. The worst part was that she didn't know what she wanted, except that it was more than she was getting. Maybe more than she would ever get, more than he had to give. If that was the case, it was definitely time to go home. If her heart was going to be broken she might as well get it over with, and move on to something marginally less terrible. God, her life was a mess.

The awful truth had finally dawned on her. She was in love with Max Avalon and that was a dead-end street. He wasn't interested in that kind of relationship. She'd been fooled by his kindness and the way he'd cared for her when she'd had the nightmares.

Had that turned him off? Did he really think she was a nut case? Maybe she was.

Why should he be interested in a relationship, anyway? What did she have to offer? Bad dreams and tears. Hot sex. She'd acted like a slut with him and he probably thought that was what she was, and was looking forward to seeing the back of her.

Get lost, Cleo, he'd said.

What was she going to do? She knew the answer to that. Run for her life. Get out of here while she still had her pride, if not her heart, intact.

Back in the kitchen, feeling guilty as hell for upsetting Cleo and mad as hell at himself for feeling that way, Max dangled between making potato salad and running after her. Ah, to hell to that, he had too much to do. He'd catch up with her after dinner and they'd have a good long talk. Maybe he'd go ahead and propose to her tonight after they'd made love. Get things settled between them. Why wait any longer? Flowers and a ring and a wonderful dinner were a great idea, but he wanted certainty in his life and she obviously needed it.

Mind made up to a plan of action, he plowed ahead with the day's work and even managed to hum a bit.

Chapter Twenty-seven

Heavy the sorrow that bows the head
When love is alive and hope is dead!

H.M.S. Pinafore, Gilbert and Sullivan

Cleo didn't come back for dinner, and Max didn't come down to the cottage later that afternoon, or that night. Fixing dinner by himself for six guests after his terrible day had worn him out. He didn't even have the strength left to put fresh peanut butter into the mousetraps, for all the good that would do. He had a sneaking suspicion he was dealing with more than one mouse now, and if the health inspector showed up or a guest caught sight of one of the furry little bastards, he'd be ruined. But tonight he no longer cared.

He'd go to Cleo, pour his woes into her pretty ears and let her commiserate with him. She'd be abjectly sorry for being so unreasonable, and he'd let her pet him and cuddle him as an apology for her thoughtlessness. He ached all over; maybe she'd give him a back rub or scrub his back while he relaxed in a hot tub. Little wifely comforts, and he was already looking forward to them.

He staggered into his apartment, meaning to change into fresh clothes before he went to her. He sat down on the bed. Maybe I'll rest my feet for a few minutes first, he thought. He collapsed into bed and sank into exhausted sleep.

Cleo waited, alternating between fury and despair. He'd had his last chance, she thought bitterly. If he'd come and begged her forgiveness, offered one word of love or comfort, showed any sign of tender feelings, they might have made it through this crisis.

He didn't show up.

Upset, frustrated and angry to the point of total unreasonableness, Cleo packed her suitcases. She waited until it was as dark as it got in Newfoundland in summer to smuggle them into the rental car, in case he was keeping an eye on her and might try to change her mind. She'd had it. This was the end. The finish. Get out while the gettin' is good, and to hell with Max Avalon and Last Man Ashore Cove.

She heated up in the microwave all the leftovers in her fridge. Scraps of the yummy meatloaf he'd brought down for a cozy dinner two nights ago. A smidgen of his homemade leek soup. Two of his brownies, groaning with nuts. She piled it all together on a plate, even the soup, and choked it down, weeping. Then she scoured the kitchen until it shone. She even mopped the ugly floor. Picked up the books and card games and magazines and put them away. Eradicated all traces of her presence there.

Very early the next morning Cleo slid out of the bed where she'd lain sleepless all night, and into her clothes. She stripped the bed and piled the linen neatly on a chair, tossing her dirty towels on top.

She cast a last despairing look around the cottage, then went outside, pulling the door shut behind her. She got in the car, started it, and headed for Gander and the airport.

Max had had an exasperating morning. The toddler in Number Five had dropped her teddy bear in the toilet and flushed it. The little girl's parents hadn't informed Max of the catastrophe until they were checking out. "Oh, by the way, I think there's something wrong with the toilet in our room," the father said casually and skedaddled.

After he'd got that straightened out, he'd had a confrontation with Maria, who'd flatly refused to come in to help with dinner that evening. "Ees my night off," she said pugnaciously, arms folded across her chest, feet planted far apart.

"Is not your night off. Is Tuesday your night off."

"Ees Tuesday today."

"Is not. Is Monday." Damn, he was really going to have to learn Spanish one of these days. If Cleo could do it, he could too. *"Es Lunes,"* he ventured.

Suspicious, Maria said, "You sure?"

Of course I'm sure, you chucklehead, he thought, but wisely did not say. "The calendar, Maria, *mi amiga.* Look at *el calendario."*

She looked. "Oh, *madre de Dios,* you right. *Arrepentido.* I back at six, hokay, Boss?" and she swanned out before Max could ask her to stop by the Qwikee-Mart on her way back to pick up some whipping cream.

Hell, he'd have to go himself if he were going to serve bake-apple cobbler for dessert tonight. He'd get Cleo to ride along with him to the store and torture her with wicked suggestions about what he would do with the leftover whipped cream.

Thinking of her indignant, shocked, delighted gasps cheered him up considerably and he loped down the path to Squashberry Cottage, whistling a little tune, yesterday's *contretemps* forgotten, secure in his love and his plans for the future.

But she wasn't there. The cottage was empty.

Max stared stupidly at the ugly, shining linoleum floor, the tidy pile of linen on the chair, the empty, spotless refrigerator, its door gaping open like his mouth.

She'd meant what she'd said last night about leaving.

He'd thought she'd just been threatening him to gain his attention. He sank down on a kitchen chair. She's gone. She can't be gone. Where had she gone? He sprang up again. Gander, of course, to catch a plane. He glanced wildly at his wrist, looking for his watch, and remembered he hadn't put it back on after the toilet incident.

He tore out of the cottage and up the path to the Big House, desperate for his car keys. Head her off at the pass, he thought. The grandfather clock on the landing chimed two o'clock as he burst through the door. He stopped dead. He hadn't heard a car go by from the cottage all day. She must have left at first light. She had hours of head start on him, it would take hours to get to the airport, he'd never catch her.

She was on a plane, starting the long trek back to Minneapolis. He'd lost her.

Dazed, he wandered into the kitchen and sank down onto a chair, head in his hands. On the floor below him was a mousetrap, complete with mouse. When the trap had sprung, it had ricocheted half away across the floor from its perch by the refrigerator.

He picked it up. It held a very small mouse, just a baby, skinny and lightly furred, with a large pink nose and ears that it hadn't had time to grow into. Its neck was broken.

Damn. He hadn't meant to wage war on babies.

He sprang up and rushed to the pantry to check the other trap. It too held a broken-necked baby mouse, one enormous eye open, staring up at him pitifully.

He carried the trap from the pantry, placed it tenderly on the counter by the other one and stood looking at them.

He became conscious of movement behind him, and turned to see Ms Mouse crouched by the refrigerator, paws folded across her breast, looking at him with the saddest expression he'd ever seen on a mouse's face.

Tears rolled down his cheeks, for the mice, for Cleo and for himself.

Chapter Twenty-eight

Love is a plaintive song,
Sung by a suffering maid,
Telling a tale of wrong,
Telling of hope betrayed . . .

Patience, Gilbert and Sullivan

*L*ife without Max. It meant dreaming about him at night, thinking about him all the time, sleepwalking through most of her day, except for the times she spent with her classes. The teenagers, some sharp, some bored, all of them aggravating in one way or another, reminded her of Angela, who was all those things in one skinny body. Hey, Angie, she thought; I hope you're staying out of trouble. She even spared a few moments of sympathy for Angie's mother, the Bitch Goddess, and the Evil Stepfather.

She cried a lot these days. One afternoon a friend, an older teacher, found her between class periods, tears running down her cheeks, sitting in the darkened cafeteria. "You need help, Cleo," she said. "I've been watching you, and I think you're depressed."

That's God's honest truth, Cleo thought, and went back to the psychiatrist who'd seen her after Charlie's death. He was about fifty years old, with graying hair and a comforting smile, his office full of books, pictures of his family and his dog. A philodendron grew up the bookcase and meandered across the top of the office door.

"How have you been?" he said.

Once she got started talking it all poured out. The nightmares of death and entombment were back, and she'd given way again to slutty behavior. Then she got to the tale of Last Man Ashore Cove and Max Avalon.

"Hmm," said her doctor. "Why did you leave him?"

"I don't know," Cleo said, and burst into tears.

He handed her a tissue. "Have you phoned him? Written to him?"

"No."

"Why not?"

"I don't know," she sobbed.

"Wouldn't it be a good idea to make contact with him? Perhaps he was hurt, too."

She thought about that. Max, hurt? Angry, probably, but hurt? Cranky, independent, care-for-nobody Max, hurt? She hadn't wanted that to happen. She wanted only good feelings to remain from her trip to new-fun-land.

"Think about it, Cleo. You'll decide what's the right thing to do."

Psychiatrists, she thought, as she left the office. They don't tell you what to do; they listen, offer support and a couple of suggestions, and leave it up to you to sort out your life. He hadn't even offered her pills this time. He didn't think she was clinically depressed, he said; he thought that she'd had a lot to deal with over the last few years, and on the whole, she was coping reasonably well. She just needed to figure out her relationship with Max and she'd be okay.

Buoyed by that opinion, feeling a sudden lifting of her spirits, she went to the Galleria and bought herself a pretty purse and a jacket and jeans to go with it. She hadn't bought much in the way of new clothes since Charlie had died, and the purchase lifted her spirits amazingly. She was taking her first, tentative steps into a new life.

She didn't try to contact Max, but she was doing a lot of thinking about it. After all, what had he done that was so wrong? Blown up at her once, teased her, and he always growled when he was under pressure, but he'd also been a wonderful lover, and funny and tender, and sympathetic. Like everything else these days, memories of his kindness made her tearful, but the desperate, depressed weeping had left her and so had the nightmares.

Something had changed in her head and she had Max and the psychiatrist to thank for it. Perhaps she'd be able to rebuild her life, after all.

She had a few days respite, feeling that her emotional burdens had lifted, and then she began to worry about Max. Had she really hurt him when she left? Was that why he hadn't called or written? Maybe he'd given her up as a lost cause. Gloom and apprehension began to invade her mind once again.

One day she walked into the Washburn Branch of the Minneapolis Public Library looking for something to read. She couldn't read romances any more; the sex scenes made her too edgy, reminding her of Max's passionate lovemaking. Most fiction bored her; her mind always wandered away from the book and back to Last Man Ashore Cove. Serious novels, with their endless stories of dreary, dysfunctional lives, brought her back to the edge of depression, They made her wonder uncomfortably whether her life was dysfunctional, too. It certainly was dreary.

Why didn't people write happy books to cheer up their readers? She'd had plenty of experience with sickness, death and despair and damned if she wanted to read about it.

So she started reading mysteries. They moved along fast enough for her limited attention span, they were distracting, and they didn't have any hot sex in them, most of them, anyway. She returned unread the ones that did. If she wasn't getting any loving, she didn't want to read about it.

She stood in front of the New Books shelf and froze when she read the title on a mystery on display: *Death at Last Man Ashore Cove.* She snatched up the book and stared at the cover. The author's name was Maxwell Coffeyn. Hadn't Max said his middle name was Coffeyn?

Cleo flipped the book over and stared at the picture of the handsome, smiling, dark-haired author, eyes bright and piercing even though their ice-blue color couldn't be discerned in the black and white photo. A pang shot through her, straight through the heart and into the soul. Oh, God, she thought, it's him.

Maxwell Coffeyn's new thriller, said the blurb on the back cover, and below it were reviewers' enthusiastic comments on another book, *The Sauce for Gander Murders.*

Cleo snatched the tome to her breast and dashed to the reference desk. She said to the friendly little blonde librarian, "Got any more by this author?"

"Let me check . . ." In a minute she was on her feet, darting into the tall shelves.

She came back, offering a book. "This is his first. That's his second you've got in your hand. He's really good; I've read both his books."

Cleo rushed to the circulation desk and checked out the mysteries. She drove off with them pulsating quietly beside her on the passenger seat. Home, she put them on the kitchen table, back covers up, while she made tea and contemplated Max's dual, identical portraits. Then she took her teacup and the books into her living room and curled up.

It was distracting, reading the first mystery, because the author's picture on the back cover burned her hands and she had to keep turning the book over to look at it. Then she got involved in the story.

It was two in the morning when she read the last page of *The Sauce for Gander Murders*. He was as good at writing mysteries as he was at sex and cooking, and that was some good, b'y. After she put the book down she began to weep quietly. Who was she kidding? She was as much in love with him as she'd been four months ago; her entire body ached with need for him. Why had she left him?

Why didn't she go back? The idea, stunning in its simplicity, hit her like a lightning bolt, and it was all she could do not to pull her suitcases out of the closet and start packing. She had her head together now, and she was ready for a full and free discussion of her relationship with Max Avalon. She might tell him that she loved him. She might even apologize for running away.

She went to the kitchen table and began writing her letter of resignation to her principal. Sorry to leave in the middle of the school year . . . urgent family business . . . Words poured out of her pen onto the paper.

She turned the letter in the next morning. When her principal came to look for her in the middle of her third hour class, he murmured sympathetically, "Are you sure you need to take the entire rest of the school year off, Cleo? Maybe you could come back in a month or two. We could get a substitute until then . . ."

She shook her head and looked tragic and mysterious. The principal knew of her past history of depression and didn't argue with her.

Once she'd decided to resign, the rest came easy. A notice on the school bulletin board found a fellow teacher to sub-let her flat. Two sessions on the Internet booked her plane tickets and car rental. She bought two huge suitcases and packed the best of her clothing, make-up, jewelry and shoes. She threw what was left into the basement storage closet, locked it against her new tenant and shut her car in the garage.

The twelve-hour plane trip left her trembling and apprehensive, and the fact that the only food served on the flights was pretzels and a nasty, unsalted, low-cal munchy mix didn't help her jitters. She was too wiped out to grab a butter-dripping bagel at Tim Horton's in the Halifax airport between planes. Horrible, scary thoughts bounced around in her skull. She'd given up everything for this mad dash to Newfoundland. How could she have been so reckless?

Suppose she'd just been a summer romance to Max? Suppose he had another woman warming his bed? Suppose he wouldn't forgive her for leaving? Max was stubborn and unpredictable; who knew what his reaction would be when he saw her?

She picked up the rental car in Gander, and in a sudden fit of nerves booked a hotel room in town. It was late, pitch black, very cold, and the roads were icy. No reason to appear in the middle of the night bedraggled and forlorn, or slide off the road into one of the formidable snow banks she'd glimpsed from the plane and die like a mouse in a trap. Or a moose in a trap. She skipped dinner and went to bed, exhausted.

She awoke very early in the morning, freaked out with hunger and the renewed realization that she'd left her job, her home, her life, all to run after a man she hadn't heard from in months. Probably he'd forgotten all about her.

What the hell would she do if he had forgotten her?

She skipped breakfast, checked out, and began the long drive to meet her destiny.

Chapter Twenty-nine

None shall part us from each other,
One in life and death are we:
All in all to one another—
I to thee, and thou to me!

Iolanthe, Gilbert and Sullivan

Newfoundland's early winter night was settling in by the time that she reached Last Man Ashore Cove. The lane down to the B and B from the main road was narrower than ever, bordered with huge snow banks and studded with chunks of ice. It's worse than Minnesota, she thought, but the enormous drifts made her feel curiously welcome. She'd left snow at home in Minneapolis and come home to it in Last Man Ashore Cove.

Over there was where the patch of partridgeberries had been last summer, and to her right was Max's garden, and dead in front of her was the B and B. A cowardly impulse made her drop off the car at the Big House and sneak down the familiar lane to Squashberry Cottage. A few frozen minutes on its porch would settle her nerves. God, it was cold here. Almost as cold as Minnesota.

The light was on in the cottage, and the door was unlocked. She stepped inside and heard a familiar voice cursing in the kitchen, the curses punctuated by hammer blows. She crept to the door and peered in.

Max Avalon was on his knees laying a new oak floor over the ugly linoleum, just as she'd suggested last summer, and swearing like a television comic when the planks wouldn't line up straight. He was every bit as gorgeous and cranky as he'd been last summer. Her heart hammered against her rib case with each blow he struck. "Bang, bang, Maxwell's silver hammer," in Angie's voice rang crazily in her head.

She stepped into the doorway, offering herself like a cupcake on a plate.

Max looked up in mid-swing. The hammer fell from his nerveless fingers, barely missing the hand that held the plank being nailed.

They stared at each other, speechless.

"Are you an apparition?" he croaked at last.

"No. Are you a mystery writer?"

The familiar scowl appeared on his face. "How the hell do you know about that?"

"I'm a teacher; I can read. We have libraries in Minneapolis and I like to read mysteries. I can put two and two together, Mr. *Death in Last Man Ashore Cove.* Why did you keep it a secret?"

"It wasn't a secret. In the summer I'm a B and B owner, in the winter I write mysteries. You didn't stick around long enough for the mystery part."

"I'm here now," Cleo said softly.

"So you are." He rose slowly to his feet and started toward her.

She'd forgotten how big he was and how menacing he could be. She held her ground bravely when he loomed over her, and braced herself for the worst. What could he do to her that was worse than what she'd experienced since she'd left him?

"Vixen," he growled. "Why did you leave? Why didn't you write to me?"

"Why didn't you write to me?"

He drew back and looked at her in exasperation. "Because I didn't have your address, you chucklehead. When you rented the cottage, you signed the register just Minneapolis, Minnesota, not a proper address with a street name and number. How many people are there in Minneapolis?"

"About three hundred thousand."

"So I should send a letter addressed to Ms Cleo English, somewhere in Minneapolis, Minnesota, address and postal code totally unknown?"

"I'm sorry. I never thought of that," she said humbly.

"I couldn't even find your damned address on the damned Internet. I was going to come looking for you if I hadn't heard from you by April Fool's Day. Come to your town and start knocking on doors." He wrapped his arms around her and yanked her to him. "Three hundred thousand doors to knock on, but damned if I wasn't going to find you."

His shoulders were shaking and Cleo had a sudden suspicion. "Why, Max, are you crying?"

He rubbed his wet cheek against hers. "Guys don't cry."

"It's okay. At least I know that you're a human being."

He drew back. "You think I'm not a human being? I'll show you just how human I am." He swept her up in his arms, carried her into the bedroom and dumped her on the bare mattress of the stripped bed.

Here it comes, thought Cleo. Hot sex, and I haven't had a chance to wash my face or take a pee. She wriggled with lust, willing him to have his wicked way with her.

But he surprised her again. He flung himself down beside her, gathered her tenderly into his arms, and scattered kisses on her face. "Sweet Mother of God, Cleo, I nearly died when you left me like that. I thought I'd never see you again."

"Me too." She gave him back kiss for kiss.

"Let's make love," he whispered in her ear.

So now he was asking first? He could wait, she thought, until she'd had a shower and combed her hair. Maybe put on a sexy little nightgown; she'd packed several. On the other hand . . . his hand was pulling up her skirt and pulling down her panties.

Then he put her down on her back, rested all of his weight upon her and took her mouth in a manner that brooked no opposition.

And the next minute he was sliding into her, and it was better than it had ever been. Darling, wonderful Max, she thought as he sent her into blissful oblivion.

He surprised her for a third time. "Marry me," he growled into her ear.

"Huh?"

"You heard."

"I heard, but I didn't believe it."

Max lifted his head and stared down at her. "I said, marry me, you little witch, and don't think of saying no. I'm going to lock you in this bedroom until you say yes."

"Will you lock yourself in the bedroom with me?"

"If that's what it takes." He began to move in her again.

Many dazed moments later, she whispered, "I'm at your mercy. I quit my job, I sub-let my flat, I packed my sexiest panties to bring with me to Last Man Ashore Cove."

"You won't need the panties."

Cleo laughed, a long crazy laugh filled with pure joy.

After a moment he began to laugh with her. "May I assume that's a yes?"

"Never assume."

"Smart ass woman. Just my type."

"Good, because I'm here, jobless, homeless, all my bridges burned."

"We'll build new bridges."

"Maybe one between the Big House and my cottage? To help you get over the snow banks when you come to me at night?"

"It's not your cottage any more. I'm going to need it next season for rental."

"I'll pay you rent."

"The hell you will. You think I'm going to take money from my woman? Besides, you don't have a job. You won't have any money to pay rent."

"Maybe I can offer you a service in exchange." She moved her hips suggestively against his.

"Damn right you'll offer your services. You'll help me with the B and B in the summer. Cooking, cleaning, sucking up to the clientele, all that stuff that I do. You can be the bossy manager, and I'll be the temperamental chef. We'll do it together. And by together I mean married, b'y."

"What will we do in the winter?"

"You'll help me drink wine, and eat my good cooking, and think up ways to kill people in my books. At night we'll sit by the fire and I'll write and you can knit little thingies."

"What sort of little thingies?"

"Baby booties, I hope."

Her eyes widened. "You mean . . ."

"Yeah. I want another kid or three that I won't lose at a couple of years old. Kids I can raise and fight with and love."

"Suppose I don't want . . ."

"You want. You know you do."

He was right. She did.

He kissed her into submission, then rolled off of her. "You've gotten even skinnier. God, woman, do you ever eat? Come on, I have the urge to cook a feast and I've got a couple of cases of fine Italian Pinot Grigio and Australian Shiraz cellared to get me through till April. We can get tight and eat and tell each other jokes in front of a roaring fire. Make popcorn in the microwave, like normal people do. Are you hungry, Cleo?"

Her stomach growled in response. "I'm starved. I haven't eaten since I left Minneapolis. There wasn't anything open between Gander and here, not even a gift shop where I could get a candy bar."

"Nah, nothing's open; there's no tourists. Just us Newfies holed up together for the winter, cozy as mice behind a refrigerator."

"Nice metaphor."

"Yeah. Write it down; I can use it in my new book."

"What's your new book about?"

"The usual, murder and mayhem. But this one's going to be different: it's going to feature lots of hot sex, now that I've got my inspiration back."

"I promise to be very inspiring." She sat up on the bed and put her hand on his bare thigh as he was pulling up his jeans. She smirked when he twitched at the contact.

He looked down at her. "Did I remember to tell you I love you?"

She wrinkled her forehead in thought. "I don't think so. Did I remember to tell you the same thing?"

"You did not. Who's going to be the first one to say it?"

"Ha, I win. You already did."

"Then it's your turn, vixen."

She sat up on the bed, turned to face him, and stared him straight in the eye. "I love you, Maxwell Coffeyn Avalon. Right now, next year, and forever."

He held out a hand. "Works for me," he said. "Come on up to the Big House. I've got something to show you."

They crunched through the hard snow, hands clasped together, stopping now and then to share a kiss and admire the endless stars of a Newfoundland winter sky. He retrieved her suitcase from the car, and they went into the house, through the Victorian parlor, through the kitchen, scene of many triumphs, to his apartment. "Here we are," he said, leading the way into the living room.

On a table next to the fireplace was a large wire cage, and inside was a fat gray mouse. She was sitting on her haunches, nibbling a ball of peanut butter and seeds.

Cleo stared. "Is it ... could it be ... Ms Mouse?"

"Her name is Ethel. I killed all her babies. I had to do something to relieve my conscience after that, so I caught her in a live trap and put her in a cage so she wouldn't have any more kids. Holding all those little mouse funerals was getting me down."

"Mouse funerals?"

"You didn't think I would put their bodies in the garbage, did you? I buried them under the rose bushes and said a few words over each one. Rest in peace, enjoy mouse heaven, that sort of stuff. Then to make sure I wouldn't get any new little visitors I got Lucy. Say hello to her." He pointed to the chair by the fire.

A large red tabby cat with glittering yellow eyes was sitting there, watching them placidly, her front paws curled under her chest. Her purr could be heard across the room.

"Lucy does kitchen patrol every morning. I don't ask her what she finds on her rounds and she doesn't tell me. But I don't have any more mice."

"You've worked it out very well."

"Yeah, master of compromise, finder of solutions, that's me. The only thing I couldn't work out was you. Didn't know where to find you, didn't know what to do with you if I did find you, didn't know what I'd do without you for the rest of my life."

He moved forward and took her in his arms. "I know what to do now. Will you stay with me and join my harem? Lucy, Ethel and Cleo. And in the summer, Maria and Angela. Surrounded by females; what a sweet deal for any guy."

She grinned. "Okay, but I want top billing."

"Right, you're on, but just remember that I'm the boss."

Cleo put her arms around his neck. "Hokay, Boss," she said.

Chapter Thirty

We'll rant and we'll roar, like true Newfoundlanders;
We'll rant and we'll roar, on deck and below.
Until we see bottom inside of two sunkers,
Then straight through the channel to Toslow we'll go.

"Ryans and the Pitmans"
H. W. LeMessurier

They had a glorious winter together with plenty of delicious food, wine, sex, good talk, and many laughs. Cleo was introduced to the concept of kitchen parties, gatherings of friends to share food, some of it raised in roadside gardens and now gracefully shared. Max cooked his famous Jiggs' Dinner, Mrs. Puddester's musical son brought his fiddle, and Cleo danced her first-ever jig with Grandpa Puddester, who was eighty-five if he was a day and as spritely as a young elf.

On Christmas Day Max cooked a traditional turkey dinner, and all their friends came for a jolly day of fun. Those who'd had too much fun to make it home safely were accommodated overnight in rooms at the Big House and fed a sumptuous breakfast the next morning.

On the day after Christmas, with their friends present, Cleo was inducted as a Newfoundlander at a screeching-in ceremony, and she discovered that the local screech was, indeed, potent. It had been distilled by Wild Ernie in his homemade still in Gros Morne National Park, and he'd brought it along with a dead cod for the backside kissing part of the ceremony.

In January she made Max get rid of his old computer and buy a new one, then spent hours inputting his reservations file, menus and recipes. She spent even more hours trying to teach him how the programs to retrieve the files worked. He wouldn't give up his handwritten recipe box, though, since he had an innate distrust of a mainlander's loodle-laddle like an electronic box of tricks that had once eaten his first two chapters.

In February he finished his third book and sent it off to his agent, after Cleo ran her professional teacher's eye over his grammar, spelling and sentence structure. He had to admit her input made for a better manuscript, and his agent confirmed that. In fact, he said, "Max! You've learned to speak English!"

In March Max starred as Bunthorne in the Three Peninsulas Very Light Opera Company's production of Gilbert and Sullivan's *Patience,* and Cleo had a great time painting scenery and singing in the chorus of Rapturous Maidens. They played the show from Twillingate to Dildo to Carbonear and even over to Quidi Vidi, but had to cancel the performance in St. Anthony because a blizzard on the Northern Peninsula dumped fourteen feet of snow there. Cleo regretted the loss of the opportunity to have another meal of fried cod at the Harbour End.

Angie came up for a visit during school spring break, and they all went into St. John's for a visit to the Newfoundland Museum and dinner at Tim Horton's.

In between singing and visitors and writing bouts, Max cooked wonderful meals, testing recipes for next year's tourist trade, using lots of cream, eggs and butter. He still wouldn't tell Cleo where he got the butter, but allowed her to share his stash for her breakfast pancakes on Sundays. She gained weight, much to his pleasure and her alarm. When her panties got too tight around the hips she talked him into perfecting lower calorie meals, arguing that some visitors might prefer lighter fare. She started a daily exercise program just in case the low cal meals didn't work.

Adding up all the good times they were having together, Cleo decided this love story was going to be a keeper. After the screeching-in and before *Patience,* she indicated subtly that she was ready to consider a formal offer of marriage. So one evening he trotted out the champagne, the filet mignon, the lemon crème brulée, the ring that he'd had Sylvia make (this time with a diamond in it), and proposed in front of a blazing fire, with Lucy and Ethel watching solemnly. They plighted their troth and set the wedding date for mid-June.

The only problem with that was Cleo was pregnant. She wasn't surprised because they'd run out of condoms late one February night, and the roads were too bad to drive into St. John's for a new supply. If they waited until June, she said, she'd look weird in a wedding dress, like a balloon with ruffles. So they moved the date up to the first Saturday in April, keeping their fingers crossed that the weather would cooperate.

It didn't, it rained buckets, as Mrs. Hoh would say, but nobody cared. The ceremony and the reception were in the Big House and guests squeezed into and socialized in every nook and corner. Max couldn't keep them out of the kitchen; there was a Newfoundland jam session going on there at one point, but he didn't worry about it because Mrs. Puddester was catering, so the kitchen was her problem. Despite the distractions, the food was a smashing success, and Mrs. Puddester, for once, felt no need to make excuses.

Hans Argetsinger of the Edelweiss Café made the wedding cake, a three-tiered affair of chocolate layers, strawberry filling, and chocolate frosting, and no cabbage. He discovered in himself a previously unknown talent for cake decoration when he created a flow of colorful fondant spring flowers cascading down the sides of his creation. After hearing the cries of admiration from the wedding guests, he made a mental note to add wedding cakes to his restaurant's portfolio of goodies on offer.

For their wedding trip they went to Nova Scotia by way of Minneapolis so that Cleo could retrieve her remaining possessions, sell her car and cancel her lease. Next they went to Owatonna where Cleo received her former in-laws' tearful blessing of her marriage. They saved for last the visit to Charlie's grave. Max leaned against a nearby tree humming quietly to himself, waiting while she sat by the tombstone saying her last farewell and thinking over their time together, sometimes laughing, sometimes smiling wistfully, sometimes choking back sobs.

At last she rose, put her hand on the stone and said, "Goodbye, sweet Charlie. I'll carry you in my heart forever." She meant it; he would always be a part of her.

Then Cleo turned, extended her hand to Max and they skedaddled for home.

To New-fun-land.

Epilogue

I'll tell you a tale about Newfoundland dear,
We haven't got money or riches to spare.
But we can be thankful of one small affair
Thank God we're surrounded by water.
The sea oh the sea the wonderful sea,
Long may she roam between people and me.
And everyone here should get down on one knee
Thank God we're surrounded by water.

"Thank God We're Surrounded by Water"
Tom Cahill

The baby was a boy. They named him Charlie.

AUTHOR'S NOTES AND ACKNOWLEDGMENTS

If you go to Newfoundland, and I hope you do because it's a beautiful place full of pleasant people, there are a few things you should know:

1) You won't find butter. The dairy industry was never strong on the Rock, and a margarine company that was started in 1925 (called the Newfoundland Butter Company–no Truth in Advertising laws in those days) quickly cornered the spread market. Margarine manufacture was banned in Canada from 1886 to 1948 (it was undercutting the sale of butter), and its continued legal status in Newfoundland was a negotiation point when Confederation was being arranged. Term 46 of the Newfoundland Act prohibited the sale of margarine to the rest of Canada, but allowed it to be manufactured and sold in Newfoundland. So margarine has an iconic status in the Province.

2) Newfoundland was an independent country until Confederation with Canada was approved in 1949 by the thin margin of 52 to 48 per cent. Whether or not the voters' decision was correct is still a much-debated question, and some dissenters still fly the pre-Confederation of pink, white and green as a protest. One Newfoundlander told us that the Province should have become part of the United States long ago, and he meant it.

A nineteenth century song expressed the anti-Confederation viewpoint:

With our face turned to Britain
Our back to the Gulf,
Come near at your peril, Canadian wolf!

3) A town like Little Last Man Ashore Cove is an outport, a small isolated coastal community, one of the earliest European settlements in Canada. After Confederation, the government forced

resettlement of residents from some outports to inland communities, so that services could be provided more cheaply. Critics have called this"cultural genocide" of outport society.

4) The cod industry supported rural Newfoundlanders for 500 years, and the moratorium on fishing for cod imposed by the Canadian government in 1992 cost thousands of jobs and seriously damaged communities dependent on the fishing industry, which was all of the outports. Initially planned to last only two years, the ban continues to this day and the numbers of the Northern cod have not rebounded. Dave Stone wrote and the folk group McGinty recorded "Don't Go Out in Our Waters" about the moratorium:

Don't go out in our waters till 1994,
Just tie up the trawlers and longliners on the shore.
It's only for the next two years so pay heed to the freeze;
We have to boost the Northern stocks 'cause fish don't grow
on trees.

5) There is another variant on the "mother-in-law entrance" story. This one says that after Confederation, Newfoundland was bound by the Canadian law that required two entrances to each dwelling place. The defiant residents of the Rock built the damned doors, but nowhere in the damned law did it say they had to provide steps up to them.

6) Newfoundlanders have a decided accent, reminiscent of an English provincial accent of earlier times, hardly surprising because of their isolation from the time of settlement up to the twentieth century. Ferrylanders sound so Irish you'd think they were just off the boat from the Auld Sod. We never met anyone who talked like Mrs. Hoh, but I imagine she exists. The expressions she uses are accurate, according to *The Dictionary of Newfoundland English* (edited by Story, Kirwin and Widdowsin, University of Toronto Press, 1999, 2nd edition).

7) Newfoundland folk music is tuneful, salty, down to earth,

and a lot of fun. I've included some sample verses as epigraphs, and recommend that those of you who are interested seek out recordings by Great Big Sea, McGinty, and Shanneyganock, to name just three excellent bands of the Province.

What I've written about Newfoundland in this book is as correct as I could make it, and is based on experiences and conversations my husband Mike and I had while on the Rock. Newfoundlanders are kind and friendly, and I feel sure they will take note of my good intentions in representing the Province, and forgive me if I have erred.

Thanks to the usual crowd for help with *The Woman Who Loved Newfoundland*: to Mike for a wonderful trip that was the germ of this book, to Judith Palmateer for editing and all-around assistance, and to Chris Fayers for e-publishing, and to Sherry Ladig for encouraging words.

Love to my family, Mike, Michael, John, Anita, Carla and Aaran.

And last and never least, thanks to the resident lapwarmers, Teddycat and Bailee Burmese.

To the memory of Twm Sion and MacDougall, the world's best kitties.

www.ScottishIslandNovels.com